ZOMBIE REVOLUTION

D.D. Charles

Wayward Cat Publishing

CHAPTER ONE

In his book, *Zombie Revolution: A Guide to the Stabilization of Zombies in Recovery*, Dr. Arnold Krenske claimed that zombies in recovery would occasionally crave brains; but Cole didn't believe it–until *she* moved in across the street. Cole could understand that zombies would crave foods like brownies and potato chips, because there was history there. They may be undead, but zombies still had minds and those minds remembered potato chips, sometimes with fierce determination.

Dr. Krenske assured the zombie community that his pills would keep them sane and alert; and with that promise of normalcy came the unfortunate truth that, though their minds would remember food, their stomachs could no longer adequately digest it. But brains? Why would Cole, if he took his pills daily as prescribed by Dr. Krenske, crave the human brain–something he'd never seen, smelled, or certainly tasted?

But now Cole understood.

The first time he saw her, standing in the driveway of the vacant house across the street, her dark hair slightly lifted in ringlets off her shoulders by the wind, her pinkish eyes glowing in the moonlight, Cole knew what it was to want to crush a skull with his bare hands and slurp out its juicy brain. No brain had ever appealed to him so much—no brain had ever appealed to him at all! But now his zombie sense was exposed, irrevocably heightened, and he knew that he would want her for the rest of his unending, undead life.

Z

Cole sat in the zombie corner of the noisy lunchroom at Darkspur Night High School and stared across the room at the vamps, where the new girl from across the street sat next to Darlene Chriss, better known as the white vamp. Next to Darlene's fair hair, washed-out brows, and deathly pale, bony frame, the new girl was dark, mysterious, and luscious.

Her name was Livia, but Cole wouldn't tell Alan that, no matter how many times he asked. As far as the zombies were concerned, Cole didn't know anything about the girl. He didn't know that she smiled just a bit crooked and had really soft skin on her cold hands. He definitely didn't know what she sounded like when she laughed.

Cole couldn't know these things because vamps don't talk to zombies. And that was the one thing he absolutely would never let on that he knew: Livia Duvessa talked to him like he was not a zombie. She'd moved in on Saturday and came right over to introduce herself. She and her mom sat in his living room with his mom, and talked for an hour, while Cole sat in the kitchen at the bar listening, occasionally walking through to go up and down the stairs to and from his room for no real purpose. On his fifth pass through the room, his mom took his somewhat unconscious hint and introduced him. Livia held out her hand and he took it in his and was surprised at its coldness; he'd never touched a vampire before. He did his best to appear uninterested, but her smile was tattooed on his dead brain.

As he sat staring across the lunchroom mindlessly he could still hear his mother's voice trying to welcome the first family of vampires to their predominantly zombie hood. "With enough sun screen and a good pair of Ray-Bans, and an umbrella of course, your Livia can even go out in daylight here."

While the regulars, the magick, and the two Franks ate lunch, the zombies huddled in their corner, avoiding occasional angry stares from the vamps. Zombies didn't like vamps any more than vamps liked zombies. Unfortunately, most of the high school population favored the vamps.

Cole Bertrand could think of many reasons why this was unfair. For one thing, the zombies looked normal. Their skin was gray, sure, and some of them wore repair patches where it rotted and threatened to fall off; and their eye color was dulled. But the vamps were ghostly pale with eyes just a shade too pink. Their bodies were rendered thin and wiry from the virus, unlike zombies who retained their original proportions—a frustrating circumstance for the overweight zombie who found that undead fat cells had to be surgically removed while the vamp virus apparently dissolved them for nourishment.

Vamps were delicate, beautiful creatures. Normal people liked that sort of thing. The regulars and magick loved being recognized by the vamps. They followed them around and hung on everything they said and did.

But not the zombies. And not the Franks, either. The Franks were too confused most of the time and spent their nights in special classes. And the zombies, well, to put it bluntly, they were too smart to lust after shallow vamps. Zombies had brains; it was part of the zombie virus. They got real smart after being infected, and that overload of brain activity was the thing, Dr. Krenske found, that caused them to zone out, drool, and go on rampages for fresh brains. Sure, being dead didn't help. But the Zom-be-Gon pill made them almost normal again, except for their smarts and their lack of rosy cheek color.

The vamps, wiry and sleek, ruled the school. They walked the halls three and four abreast and everybody got out of their way, even zombies. If they wanted a regular's answers on a test, the regular gave them the answers. If they wanted his book report, they got it. If they told a joke about zombies and brains, everybody laughed—even zombies. If they stuck a note on your back that said, "zombie in recovery," you just left it there for a while so they could have their fun. And if they wanted a regular to punch a zombie, the regular did it—regulars would do anything to get noticed by vamps. And zombies took it. The punches didn't hurt. The jokes didn't hurt. And zombies were too smart, and too polite, to retaliate against the sniveling wannabe regulars. They were only doing what they could to survive in Darkspur, after all. Nothing ever changed. The vamps were cool and the zombies weren't and there was nothing Cole could do about it.

Suddenly Cole realized he was staring at her and Livia turned to look at him, her dark eyes stark against her pale skin; he jumped in his seat.

"Are you off your meds or something?" Winston said.

"Just a little jumpy, that's all."

Cole realized that Winston, Rachel, Isabella, and several others had joined him and Alan at the table while he was out of it. Was it Livia? Or did he need a higher dosage of Zom-be-Gon?

"I have an extra pill, if you need it."

"You have Zom-be-Gon at school?" Stu Martin said.

Cole smiled. "Winston is obsessive compulsive. He's got pills everywhere, just in case."

"What if I were to forget to take my dose in the morning?" Winston said, looking over his thick-framed glasses at Cole. "I'd need a back-up, right?"

"But Winston," Rachel said, smiling. "You would never forget your pill. You're the most organized zombie in the world."

"Well, you may be willing to bet on that," Winston said. "But I'm not."

He dug into the plastic pocket protector in his shirt pocket, pulled out a small, flat pill box and shook it.

"My back-up plan."

"How can you not know her name?" Alan said, frowning. "She lives right across the street."

"She's still a vamp. Have some zombie pride, man. Stop worrying about Slade's blood clique."

"This isn't idle curiosity. We have to know the enemy by name. We can't let them get an edge over us."

"Oh, please," Stu said. "She's a female. You're interested in every female."

"I'm not a vamp lover," Alan said with a whine.

"But you're a chick lover."

"But not vamps."

"What's the difference?" Rachel said.

Alan's face darted from one zombie to the next as he seethed with embarrassment. Finally they all laughed at him. Winston nudged him.

"You have to admit you're obsessed with girls."

"I can't help it."

"Isn't the new vamp in your Lit class?" Stu said.

Cole glared at him. "I don't remember her name, okay?"

A tingling sensation filled his face as his skin tried to blush. He couldn't let the others, especially Alan, know of his new-found obsession with Livia Duvessa.

Alan Patterson, while claiming the title of biggest zombie whiner of the year, was also the most stringent vamp hater in the group. Every day Alan had a new scheme–leer at any vamp who wandered too near, mumble the word brains at them, or growl as you pass their lockers–and he tried to start up growling workshops to help them release their inner zombies. Alan had issues. Whining and complaining were not the traits of a self-actualized recovering zombie any more than hate was. But Cole knew, as most of his friends did, that Alan's vamp hatred was driven by jealousy. There wasn't a regular or magick girl in school who gave him a second look, once a vamp smiled at her. And any time any girl noticed a zombie, a vamp was sure to discover her and change her mind.

"We should do something about lunch," Cole said.

"Not again." Brock Hanson said, falling into his usual chair across from Cole.

"It's not fair we have to sit here and wait while the regulars eat."

"I like sitting here," Rachel said. "It's good to spend quality time with you all."

She smiled at Cole and he tried to smile back. Rachel's straight blonde hair was thinning, more every year, and the big Skin Like New patch on her round face could only be re-glued so many times before it would fall off for good, exposing the decayed flesh beneath. He remembered when they first met, how she tried to cover her rotting skin with thick, beige make-up and then hugged everyone as they were introduced, leaving their faces and collars smeared with it.

"You're allowed in the library or the gym, you know."

Stu said.

"We should get an extra class."

"Don't even go there." Brock said. "It's bad enough you made them let the regulars in."

"I didn't do it all by myself."

"You started it. Just mind your own business."

Alan suddenly reached his hands out across the table and leaned low over it. He whispered.

"Look at the magick."

They all turned to look at the corner near the cafeteria line.

"No, don't look."

"You told us to look, man," Stu said. "What are they doing?"

Rachel laughed loud and snorted, setting off giggling and laughter through the zombie corner.

The magick had lit candles on their three round tables and were standing in a large circle around them, swaying back and forth, holding hands.

"Quiet, quiet," Isabella said. "What are they chanting?"

"Very entertaining lately," Winston said.

"It's Cole," Stu said. "Every time he writes something about them in the school paper, they get weirder."

"They're trying to prove they really have powers." Brock said.

A high-pitched scream rang out and one of the regular girls darted into the cafeteria from the main hall, frantic and panting. Nurse Frommer huffed in after her.

"I need help," she called, wheezing, to the zombie corner. "Bill's off his meds again."

The regulars panicked and jumped from their seats screaming. The magick broke ranks, their ritual cut short, and dashed toward the kitchen, toppling one of their tables. The alarm sounded and Principal Lute's deep voice boomed over the loudspeakers with an echo.

"Do not panic. Please stay seated."

Chairs crashed to the floor as Brock, Alan, and Cole leapt up and ran toward Nurse Frommer, dodging students.

"Where is he?" Brock shouted over the din. Amid the chaos, a loud growl reverberated in the hallway and Cole pushed past Nurse Frommer and out of the cafeteria. Bill Teeter lumbered slowly toward him. The fluorescent lighting of the hall did nothing for the zombie gray, but Cole winced at the sight of Bill's face, now a sickening pale green.

He and Brock ran toward him; Brock tackled Bill to the floor.

"Take it easy," Cole said, sitting on Bill's legs.

"Just shut up and hold him. Stupid zombie."

"He can't help it." Cole said.

"He's a whacko," Alan said, sitting on the cold, tiled floor behind Bill's head and grabbing his face to hold it still.

"Have you got him?" Nurse Frommer said. She knelt down beside Bill on his left side. "Are you sure?"

"Hurry," Brock said. "We can't hold him all day."

Nurse Frommer took the hypodermic from her zombie kit, held it up and flicked it twice before jabbing Bill in the neck with it while Alan held Bill's jittery face away from her hands.

"All right, all right," she said breathlessly, standing up and shuddering. "Taken care of. Thank you boys." She gave Cole a trembling smile.

"Just be quicker about it next time," Brock said, still sitting on Bill's chest.

"This is dangerous business, Brock Hanson. Don't lecture me about it. One bite and I'm—"

"You're what? A monster? Like us?"

8

"I didn't mean that."

"Leave her alone." Cole said. "It's okay."

"Yeah, we understand," Alan said, standing.

Bill's body twitched a few times and he let out a loud moan. Brock climbed off him and pulled him to his feet.

"Idiot. When's the last time you took your pill?"

He moaned again.

"I'm tired of holding you down."

"Seriously, dude." Alan said. "One of these days you're going to eat somebody's brains out and we'll all suffer for it."

Bill shook his head and rolled his dull eyes around. "Man," he said. "What happened?"

"Your pill, idiot." Brock said and punched him in the chest. "Take your god-damned pill every morning."

"That's quite enough," Nurse Frommer said. "Bill, come with me for a few moments of observation in the clinic."

Cole watched them walk away, petite Mrs. Frommer in her nurse's cap, beside the big oaf Bill the Zombie, and was suddenly aware that a crowd of kids had gathered outside the doors of the cafeteria. He turned and saw Livia, her brow furrowed and her pouty lips slightly apart with a question. Cole sucked in a breath at the sight of her. She looked up at him and a tiny smile touched her mouth and lit up her eyes.

Suddenly, the voice of Mrs. Hemple, head cafeteria lady, and anger management candidate, bellowed from the cafeteria.

"Who lit candles in the lunch room?"

As he collected his backpack from the disarrayed cafeteria, the bell rang and Cole sought Livia out on his way to art class. His pulse quickened somewhat, considering how dead he was, when he saw her enter Mrs. Haggerty's art room. Haggerty pulled Livia up to the

9

front of the class and forced her to introduce herself. Cole's stomach twisted into knots with anxiety for her as she stuttered, her eyes darting nervously to the floor. One tiny ringlet of hair dangled over her forehead.

"Thank you, Miss Duvessa," Haggerty said and hacked out her cigarette cough.

She went on to lecture on perspective while the class drew a street scene on their art pads. Cole tried to draw, but his eyes were constantly diverted one row over and two seats up, to Livia's desk where she drew on a borrowed sheet. Her pale slender hand glided easily and quickly with the pencil, a street he didn't recognize erupting on the ecru paper.

"Mr. Bertrand," Haggerty's dry voice broke the rhythm of her lecture. "Draw, please."

Livia turned to look at him; he knew he'd blush if his skin was able. He caught Darlene Chriss, in front of Livia, glaring back at him protectively. And Rachel, one more seat up, shaking her head at him with pity.

The rest of the school session, Cole charted her class schedule; he watched her out of the corner of his eye and followed her, pretending to forget where he was going. At two-thirty a.m., after his final class, Cole walked to his car and saw Livia standing near the bike rack in the dark. He shivered against the new fall chill and wondered if vampires got colder than zombies, since they started out so cold.

He glanced at her and pretended he didn't see her smile at him—her eyes hidden in the shadow of the building. Once in his car he sat and waited for Brock, watching her. He tried to convince himself she was no different than the other vamps. She just seemed different because she was from down south. Maybe things were different down south. Maybe because it was hotter they smiled at zombies more often. Cole knew that made no

10

sense at all.

He watched as Darlene and Kevin Oder met her and they all walked to Darlene's car. She looked over at his car several times and he pretended not to see her. But he knew she could see better than he could in the dark. Why was she always looking at him? Just because her mom brought her over to meet his mom and just because she lived across the street, didn't mean they had to be friends or anything.

Brock rocked the car as he slid his muscular frame into the passenger seat.

"Man, I'm tired. I think I need a boost in my dosage."

Cole turned to him and smirked. "You're joking, right?" Brock was the largest, loudest zombie in school.

Brock smiled. "Yeah. I'm joking. But I am tired. I had to pull a regular off the roof after lunch."

"What for?" Cole turned the key and the engine of his car hummed.

Brock shook his head and rolled his eyes. "He didn't know we got Bill medicated right away. Didn't want his brains eaten out, I guess."

Cole snickered. "Why didn't they get a Frank to do it?"

"You saying I'm not strong enough to climb up on the roof?"

"You're strong enough. But the Franks are stronger."

"And stupider. You never know what you're going to get with a Frank. I might have ended up having to pull the two of them down."

"I guess."

"Why did you support that school board decision, anyway?" Brock said.

Cole shrugged as he pulled his car out of the school parking lot and headed to Brock's house.

"Everyone should be allowed to go to night school if

he wants."

He knew he sounded agitated, but he was getting tired of defending the rights of the regulars. It should be obvious, he thought, to everyone.

"Who wants to get up at six a.m. and go to regular school? And they don't bother us that much," Cole said. "Not any more than the magick, anyway."

"Did you learn anything more about them?"

Cole shook his head. "No. A lot of talk, but nothing concrete."

"But you still think they're in on some kind of conspiracy."

"I never said that."

Brock smiled. "A grudging admission; I'm not impressed. Giving up on your conspiracy theory so easily?"

"I never said it was a conspiracy. Why would the magick create or spread the viruses?"

"Don't ask me. You're the one with the crazy ideas. But when you think about it, their being here doesn't make sense. They can't really do any magic."

"We don't know that for sure yet."

"And besides, people smarter than us would have figured it out by now."

"But it could be something...something like a virus."

"There you go; that's the old familiar Cole. The magick are some kind of alien species; they've been here all along. Hiding. Biding their time. Waiting."

"Waiting for what? This? For vamps and zombies and Franks and night school?"

Brock laughed. "I don't know. It's your theory."

"That is not my theory." He couldn't help but laugh at himself. "I haven't found any evidence that they're anything more than goofy religious types. Their spells look like positive thinking run amok."

Brock shook his head. "Then why do they call themselves magick?"

"Why do regulars go around pretending to be vamps?"

Brock opened his mouth and closed it again; he turned to look out the window into the early morning darkness.

Finally, he said, "I'm glad you're finally resigning yourself to the idea that the magick are just here by happenstance."

Cole shook his head. "That doesn't mean that there isn't something going on."

Brock chuckled at him, but Cole's thoughts stuck with the idea. Maybe he'd been looking in the wrong place. Maybe it wasn't the magick he should be researching.

"And what about the vamp virus?"

Cole pulled up alongside the curb at Brock's house in Crane Park and put the car in park.

"I haven't found out anything. I'd have to have access to medical records."

Brock turned to him with a sly smile. "If the vamp virus is spread only by biting and sucking blood, where'd the first vamp come from?"

"You could ask the same about zombies."

Brock reached up and pulled at his own hair. "I was just joking. You are way too grim. Lighten up."

Cole watched Brock as he trudged his way up the driveway, his hair sticking out oddly on top of his head. He had to smile. Brock was right about one thing. Without him, Cole would be downright depressing.

Driving Park Avenue, through Noche de Sangre toward home, Cole wondered why he never liked to think about that particular question. Brock liked to pose it at parties as some sort of chicken-or-the-egg conundrum, but it was a serious problem. How exactly had the vamp virus started? Cole had lately had to give up the theory that vamps had truly existed as a separate species some time before they began to appear in literature and mythology. If that were true, why were they hidden until now? If they had a secret society, where were the remnants of that society now? Where was the vamp government? Vamp leadership, at least? Vamp societal moors? And why weren't vamps anything like the stories?

But more importantly, how could the virus spread, if not through the vampire bite? Over and over again the media repeated that the virus could be caught, not transferred only through a bite. But nobody seemed to know exactly how.

The streets shined damp under the street lamps as he drove and he rolled his window down, stuck out his hand and felt the wetness in the air. Cold rain. He shivered and rolled it up again.

Darkspur was the only home Cole had ever known, but he knew it was the most beautiful place in the world. A tiny city of a few thousand people, nestled against the Colorado River in the Rockies. Dr. Arnold Krenske founded Darkspur when he built his enormous Welsh Corporation complex more than thirty years ago. It was almost as if, Cole thought, he knew the world was going to change and this was the place to be when the zombie and vamp viruses spread. True enough, Darkspur was where it all began, and was home to the largest vamp and zombie populations in the world.

As he passed River Rapids Park, where the vamps hung out, Cole saw Darlene Chriss' car in the small lot at the edge of the park. His heart quickened, dead as it was. Now Darkspur had an even better attraction—Livia Duvessa. He scolded himself.

"What are you going to do, Cole?" He said aloud. "Go hang out with the vamps just to be near her?" And after a pause in which he fumed, he mumbled. "Get over it, already."

After a last, quick glance at the dark pavilion in the park, Cole turned back to the street to see a dark figure pass in front of his headlights. He jammed his foot against the brake and the car skidded to a stop. Rick Slade stood in the road in front of the car, glaring at him with glowing, blood-red eyes and a sneer, posed like an action hero in a movie, his long black coat pulled behind him on one side. It started to rain, and Cole knew he was in trouble.

CHAPTER TWO

In his chapter on the perils of the recovering teen zombie, Dr. Krenske outlined the seven most common problems facing teen zombies including: never-ending acne, being caught in puberty, and the tendency to zone out during chick flicks; but he failed to mention Rick Slade and other vamps who considered themselves bad asses, in the horror genre sense.

Rick stood in the spattering rain, the headlights spotlighting him, with his legs spread apart; he twisted at the waist for action-hero effect, and made a rolling motion with the index finger of his right hand. Cole sat and watched him do it again, daring himself to smile. Finally, Cole threw up his hands from the 'I don't have a clue what the hell you're doing' class of expressions and Rick called out, "Roll down your window, stupid."

Right. Cole was the stupid one. He pressed the button and his window slid down. Droplets of rain tickled his shoulder.

"Get out," Slade said.

"What for?"

"Because I said so."

"Are you my mom?"

"Just get out."

"I'm not getting out."

"You afraid of a little rain, zombie?"

"I don't like it much. How about you?"

Slade shook his head, bothered, and walked to Cole's side of the car.

"What do you want?" He said.

"You stopped me, genius. What do *you* want?"

"You're driving through my neighborhood."

"Zombies can't drive on your streets? You're kidding, right?"

"This is vamp territory."

"Ah, shut it man. You think you're in *West Side Story* or something?"

"*West Side Story*? What's that?"

"Classic film. Sharks and Jets. Dancing and finger snapping."

Slade stared down at him blankly.

"Chemenko made us watch it in English Lit last year, remember? It's a Shakespeare thing."

Still blank.

"So you slept through it. Suffice it to say, you don't get to tell me where to drive."

"Well, maybe I do get to tell you what chicks to look at."

"Uh, no, you don't."

"Maybe I do."

"Look, Slade, I—"

"I'm telling you, zombie boy, stop looking at us, especially that new girl. Leave her alone."

"I don't know what you're talking about."

Cole smiled inwardly. He could see it all over Slade's face. Cole had ruined a perfect scene. He should have

18

stepped out of the car, they should be standing in the rain so Slade could pose; it should be an Old West face off, of a sort. Instead, Slade stood in the rain talking into a car.

"Just stay away from her, recovering moron."

"I'm the moron," Cole said absently.

"I just said so. Why don't you zombies recover already. You gonna recover all your life? You're not even real zombies. Why don't you just do it. Let it go, eat brains. You know you want to."

"Are you finished?"

Slade had the door opened and was pulling Cole out by the collar of his shirt before Cole realized he'd pushed some kind of attack button in him. As he was being dragged out into the street he wondered if 'are you finished' was something maybe Slade's dad said just before punching him—or maybe Slade's mom used to say that and she ended up killing herself over something Slade always said in reply, like shut the hell up.

Slade pushed him and let go of his collar sending him to the road, sprawled and scraped.

"What the hell's wrong with you?" Cole said.

"I'm not getting through, wanna be."

Cole sat amazed as Slade actually made quotation marks in the air as he said, wanna be.

"You and your zombie buddies better get back where you belong." Slade stood over Cole and tilted his head menacingly to one side.

"Where do you think we belong?"

Slade stared at him for a few seconds.

"You all better just leave us alone."

Cole got up and wiped his hands off on his jeans. Vamps were gathering around his car and watching. He saw Livia standing with Darlene.

"We do leave you alone, Slade. We don't want anything to do with you and your kind."

"Well you're not doing a good enough job. You keep Alan away from us. And stop gawking at us at lunch."

"Unlike vamps, zombies don't worship people who push them around. I'm not the leader of the zombie pack. I don't tell them what to do."

"Maybe you better start."

Cole rolled his eyes. "This is stupid." He walked to his car and as he reached for the door, Slade grabbed him by the collar again.

"I'm not finished with you."

"Leave him alone."

Slade glared hard at Cole after Livia spoke. He sneered.

"Seems you've got a fan," Slade said. "You gonna let a little vamp girl defend you?"

"What do you want, Slade?" Cole said. "Are you just looking for someone to beat up?"

"I'll tell you what I want. I want you zombies gone."

"We're not going anywhere. Get used to it."

"How about I kick your ass every day, then?"

"How about I have you arrested?"

Slade pushed Cole into his car door.

"Recovering wuss. Be a zombie or die, already."

"You don't like that we're not fully zombies?" Cole said, though he figured he ought to get in his car and leave.

"That's right," Slade said.

"Why do you have a problem with it?"

Slade sneered again. "If you were a full-fledged zombie, I could whack your head off with a hatchet and nobody would care."

"Oh," Cole said and got in his car. Well, at least he had a reason.

He smiled as best as he could and drove away.

Z

Livia walked back to the pavilion with Darlene and the others, and pulled herself up onto the end of one of the picnic tables. She ran her fingers through her damp hair and shivered. Darlene tossed her a blood box and she poked the tiny straw through the foil and sipped. Her legs dangled over the end of the table and she kicked nervously in the air while the other vamps gathered. In the darkness, they reminded her of ghouls: hovering, waiting.

Rick Slade pushed through the others and walked straight to Livia.

"Don't ever tell me what to do, especially in front of zombies."

"Why not?" She knew her voice sounded braver than she was.

"Don't question me."

Livia looked around at the group but none of the vamps she'd befriended would look at her. The tall blonde, Elena Worthington, always protective of Rick, glared at her with shiny red eyes, and Ciara Wister, dark and brooding, pouted at her with a dull-eyed gaze. Livia turned back to Rick.

"I don't care for bullies," she said.

"I'm not a bully."

"You were pushing him around."

"So. It's fun. It's what I do."

"I think that's the definition of bully."

"What makes you so smart?" He said.

Livia shrugged and sipped; she did her best to steady her trembling hand.

"Vamps pick on zombies. And zombies stay out of our way."

"Why?"

"Do you like them or something?"

"What's not to like?"

"Uh." He chuckled. "They're zombies."

"You said they weren't zombies."

Rick looked this way and that, confusion on his face.

"Don't try to confuse me," he said.

Livia noticed Darlene smile just a bit, though her eyes were on the cement at her feet. She turned back to Rick. He was still staring at her—his blue irises rimmed in pink, his polished face marred by the sneer of his lips.

"So, what's not to like?" She said again. "If they're not really zombies."

"Vamps don't hang with zombies."

Livia shook her head and blinked. "If you say so."

"I do say so and you better not forget it."

Several more vamps stepped under the pavilion and distracted Rick. Ciara Wister's brother Liam, and older vamps that weren't at school, took in the group in with smug sneers. A tall girl Livia recognized smiled at her and walked forward. She had a bulky bag over her shoulder and from the top peeked a tiny, trembling Chihuahua.

"I'm Wanda Quaid." She said. "You live over on Buckley Street, right?"

Livia nodded. Wanda's pale square face was dominated by thick dark brows and ruby red lips.

"You'll be moving soon enough," Rick said. "Once your parents realize you're in zombie territory."

"This is my brother, Todd." Wanda said.

Todd smiled with difficulty, sipped at his blood box and turned away. He was nearly a foot shorter than his sister and looked like the vamp virus had sucked his chest inward; his slouch didn't help. He reminded Livia of a cat, crouched in pain.

"He's not very friendly," Wanda said. "Just turned."

"He'll be fine. Won't you Todd?" Rick said with a

smile at the kid.

Todd's eyes widened and he seemed to grow taller with Rick's attention.

"You come out with us this morning for a little fun."

"He can't." Wanda said. "We have to get home."

Todd glared at his sister. "I can go," he said. His voice was raspy like sandpaper.

"Good."

Rick reached out and took the blood box from Todd and threw it across the pavilion toward the trash can. It bounced off the edge and landed on the ground, spitting synthetic blood.

"My dad says they've almost rounded up all the ferals." Wanda said with a brief pitying glance at her brother.

"They'll never catch them all," Rick said. "There will always be ferals and always more turning."

Wanda looked back to Livia and smiled. "Some people think so. Where are you from? Much trouble with ferals there?"

"Florida. Lots."

"Ferals are a good thing," Rick said. "If we stopped turning regulars into vamps, we'd die out."

"So what?" Wanda said.

"Can we not start this argument again?" Darlene said, her white brows creased with concern. "Can we at least get to know Livia before we—"

"Yeah, let's get to know Livia," Rick said turning on her with a deep frown. "What do you think of the ferals?"

Livia's hands trembled when Rick glared at her.

"How would we die out?" She said. "We're undead."

"Answer the question."

"Leave her alone," Darlene said.

"Do you think ferals should be arrested?" He said, moving closer to Livia.

"It's a violation of personal rights—"

"Just answer the question."

"I don't think we should let ferals attack people, if that's what you mean."

"But don't you see," Stephan Hack said, pushing off his seat and coming to sit down at Livia's picnic table. "If we just die out, we'll be a, uh...what's the word? A minority again."

"But if it's a virus—"

"Aw, come on." Stephan said, his wide mouth curved in a smile. "You don't buy into that, uh, what's the word?"

"Contagious," Todd Quaid whispered hoarsely.

"That's it. Contagious. You don't buy into that, do you?"

"You're saying regulars can't catch vampirism without being bitten?"

"How did you get it?"

"Well, I was bitten, but..."

"How did we all get it?"

Stephan jumped up and turned around, his arms outstretched, until he came full circle to look again at Livia, his green eyes teasing her.

"We were all bitten."

"Then why do they say it can be caught, like a cold?"

"They don't want to scare everybody, I guess." Darlene said. "They don't want them to know that the ferals are that big of a problem."

"But the people should know, so they can protect themselves."

"Protect themselves?" Rick said. "The ferals are giving them eternal life."

"And," Stephan said, sitting on the bench again, looking up at Livia. "If we don't let the ferals turn more vamps, they'll start making those laws again."

24

"What laws?"

"Laws against vampires and stuff. They'll try to get rid of us."

"That's right," Rick said. "You don't think regulars would chop you up and set you on fire if they got the chance?"

"The burnings will return," Stephan said with a nod, awe in his voice. "We'll be back to where we were thirty years ago, hiding, having to eat rats."

"What burnings?" Livia said. "What are you talking about?"

Stephan said, "When all this started, they hunted us down like monsters."

Livia shook her head. She never heard of pogroms against vampires. She never heard of any time of hiding or feeding on rats.

"Are you saying," she said, "that we increased our population on purpose? Are you saying the ferals are just...vamps like us?"

"That can't be proven." Rick said.

"So you think it's okay to let the ferals go around killing people and turning some into vampires? They do kill people, you know."

A low growl rose up across the pavilion and the rain eased up leaving them staring at Livia in silent darkness.

"Even calling them ferals is wrong," Rick said, finally. "They're just doing what vamps are supposed to do."

"Is that what you'd like to do? You want to kill people?"

"Turning isn't killing? It's the opposite, really."

"But they do sometimes kill."

"Well," Stephan said. "Accidents happen."

"It's no use with her," Rick said. "She hates her own kind—"

"Come on," Darlene said. "Can we drop it?"

"I don't hate my kind. We have a virus that makes us want blood, but we don't have to bite people. Why should we allow ferals to do it?"

Several of the others popped open their umbrellas and walked away.

Livia stared at Rick and he sneered at her and shook his head.

"You started it," Darlene said. "Not her."

"It's not like she's the only one who says it." Jenny Salts said. They all turned to her, shrinking and small at the edge of the group.

"I don't have to listen to it." Rick said.

"But you asked," Livia said. "If you don't want to know what I think, don't ask me."

Rick popped open his umbrella and most of the others followed. They walked out into the sprinkling rain and across the park. Todd stood for a moment, agitated, then turned toward the pack. Rick waited for him, smiled broadly at Wanda and put an arm around Todd's shoulders.

"Hungry?" Rick asked him.

Livia turned to Wanda as car doors slammed and car engines came to life. She was still watching as Rick's black Jaguar vanished into the dark morning, concern on her face.

"Don't worry about them," Darlene said. "They'll get over it in a day or two and you can try again."

"Try what?"

"You know," Wanda said. "To get in."

"In what?"

"The bloodline of course," Jenny said. "Lone vamps are bad news."

"I don't care."

"You will," Jenny said. "You need them. We all need them."

"You can't be shunned by the bloodline," Darlene said. "They have to like you or..."

"Or what?"

"At best, they'll run you out of town."

"And at worst?"

"You're dead." Jenny said with a slight smile at her pale lips.

Livia laughed, but she looked back and forth between them and they were dead serious.

"They'd actually kill me?"

"In a manner of speaking," Darlene said with a shrug. "You'll never be seen again, anyway."

"Vamps killing their own?" Livia shook her head. "I think I liked it better in Florida."

CHAPTER THREE

Todd Quaid beamed with pride as he rode shotgun in Rick Slade's black Jag along the curving, hilly roads in the still, cold darkness of the morning. Stephan Hack glared at him from the back seat, but Todd only smiled back at him. Wet streets glistened and rain spattered the windshield as Rick drove them through mid-town Darkspur, along Forks Creek Road, and up a curving, tree-lined avenue for several miles.

Todd had only just started reading his sister's worn copy of *The Vampire Dilemma* by Dr. Arnold Krenske. But what did that Krenske guy know about it, anyway? He kept going on about morals and rules and people's rights; but what about the vampires' rights?

Todd had heard the rumors that Rick Slade led a group of ferals and figured Rick could probably help him sort out this whole vampire thing—tell him if his blood cravings were cool or not, and what he should do about them. What could Dr. Krenske know about a shy dork suddenly thrust into the coolest clique in school? Nada. Zip. But Rick Slade? He knew it all.

He turned to catch a brief glimpse of Rick's sharp profile and decided he wouldn't bother reading the rest of the book. Rick Slade was all the book he needed.

"The Welsh corporate mansion," Rick said as they passed it and headed into the woods.

"Are we allowed to be here?"

Rick laughed, slicing off the edge of Todd's self-esteem.

"I am. And you are as long as you're with me."

They rode the tree-lined dirt road a few miles until a small clearing appeared lit up by a fire, silhouetting bodies. When he got out of the car, Todd heard music and voices.

"Welcome to party HQ." Rick said with a deathly white smile.

He put a hand out to stop Todd from following Stephan.

"What do you think?" He said, motioning toward the fire.

Todd looked at the small gathering of vamps and regulars huddled around the blaze. He recognized the vamps, and one of the regular girls was Tina West, from school. The two regular girls she was with, he didn't know.

"She's a magick, isn't she?" Todd said. "The one in the white shirt."

Tina's hair was pulled into a band and fell down her back like a long, dark knife. She was dancing in circles and laughing.

"Is she drunk?"

Rick winked at him. "Maybe. Have you ever been drunk?"

Todd shook his head without thinking, his eyes locked on Tina West.

"Hungry?" Rick said, his voice like the hum of his car

engine.

Todd licked his lips. "You got a blood box?"

Rick laughed quietly. "We don't drink synthetics."

Todd's attention was pulled away from Tina. "You don't?"

Rick shook his head slowly. "We drink the real thing."

Again, Todd's gaze fell lustily over Tina, her neck beckoning. An urge, like a knot being pulled from his gut, rose up in him, almost forcing him toward her. He fought it; Rick couldn't know how weak he was.

"How drunk is she?" He said.

"Pretty wasted. Why don't you ask her to take a little walk with you?"

Todd shrugged and lowered his eyes to the ground.

"She wouldn't go with me."

"Come on, Todd. You're a vamp. Don't you know you've got the power of seduction? All you got to do is look deep in her eyes, and talk real low like this and she'll do whatever you want."

"My mom says that's not true. She says we don't have any seduction powers, any more than we can turn to bats."

"What does your mom know? Look at me. You telling me I don't have the power of seduction?"

"You're Rick Slade. I'm Todd Quaid. We're miles apart."

"No, we're not, my man. We're brothers. Vamps. Our names even rhyme and all."

That much was true.

"You just need to learn to use your powers."

Todd looked again at Tina West and she turned to smile at him. Tiny droplets of rain on her face danced in the firelight. His cold blood pulsed through him in a sudden rush, sending tingles all over his body.

"So, you think she'll come with me?"

"I know she will."

"And I can bite her?"

Rick nodded with a sly grin.

"But she's a magick. What happens when a vamp bites another immortal?"

"We'll find out. And think of it this way, my man. You turn her, and you can have her."

"Have her?"

"I'll give her to you."

Todd followed Rick to the group of vamps and regulars by the fire, careful to notice the looks of respect they gave him for arriving with Rick Slade. The fire popped and sizzled; bits of ash rose up in the cool wind and smoke filled his nose. He stood beside her, his body electrified by her nearness.

"Hi," he said turning to look up at her.

She smiled at him again and his eyes roamed from her deep red lips, along her jaw line to her neck. She was tall. That place at the curve of her throat where his mouth longed to feed was the perfect height for him.

Todd shoved his hands into his pants pockets and stared hard into Tina's eyes

"You want to go for a walk?" He hoped his voice came out smooth, like Rick's, but he couldn't help noticing the slight look of pity on her face.

"Sure," she said. "Let's go."

Amazed at his enormous power, Todd looked back at Rick. If he'd been physically able to wink, he would have. He followed Tina along a path into the woods until the other voices and music faded into the distance. The early morning chill made him feel deader than usual, but Tina didn't seem to mind as she chatted constantly over the wind. What was she going on about? She talked and talked and all he could think of was sucking the blood straight out of her neck. But should he? Was this all just

32

some kind of joke? Was Rick setting him up? If he sucked the life out of Tina West would Rick have him arrested as a feral?

"But I told them I wasn't afraid." She was saying. "You all drink synthetics, after all. I mean, everybody knows that the whole feral thing is about wild vamps, right? I mean, we could spot them pretty easy. I've seen pictures. They look really bad. Messed up. You know what I mean? So they think they're all brave and all coming out here, but not me. It doesn't take bravery to hang out with the vamps. Not you guys, anyway."

She wouldn't shut up.

"So maybe we can hang out some at school, you know? We could, like, be friends, or something."

"You'd like that?" He said.

"Well, sure, who wouldn't? I mean, well, everybody knows how cool you guys are and everything. And well..."

Todd stopped walking and nodded at her.

"And you want to hang out with us."

"Well, sure who doesn't?"

"Why did you come out here with me?"

She finally shut up and stared at him, her eyes wide and her mouth slightly open. Then she started yapping again.

"Oh, well, it's not so bad as it looks. I mean, I like you and all. I mean. I've seen you around school. I remember you from before you were turned. Well, yeah, I guess you were sort of nerdy then and yeah, I guess I wouldn't be caught dead talking to you then. But now, well, you're a vamp now and sure–"

"Why did you come out here with me?"

"Well, okay, but don't take this the wrong way but Evie, she's the tall one back there, you know the redhead. She's my sister's friend and well, she dared me to be alone with one of you guys. So, well, you asked. But I'm not saying—"

With a surge of rage and power unlike anything he'd
ever felt, Todd lunged at her and had his teeth sunk deep
into her neck before she could stop her yakking. Her jaw
jerked up and down against his head as she tried to
continue her stupid, senseless chatter; then she gurgled
and spat and let out a loud hiss of air. He held her
convulsing body against his and sucked her dry, finally
falling to the ground above her corpse, warm blood
dripping from his chin and coursing through his body. He
felt strong, energized, free. He felt really cool. And full.

"Holy crap, noob, what the hell did you do?"

Todd turned, still kneeling over Tina, to see Rick and
Stephan Hack staring at him. The other two regular girls
came up behind them and let out piercing screams. They
turned to flee but the vamps grabbed them. The sky
erupted and a cold sleet fell like icy darts all around.

CHAPTER FOUR

ole found himself standing aside the window in his upstairs bedroom staring out at the rain. They often came out in the rain. He'd never cared before. A small car with darkly tinted windows pulled into Livia's driveway. Livia got out of the passenger side and waved as the car reversed and pulled away.

She stood in the driveway for several minutes staring up into the darkened sky, rain beating against her face, her hair soaking it in. Suddenly she turned and stared hard at Cole's window before walking up the walk and into her house.

Headlights lit up the road and his mother's car pulled into the garage.

"Cole," she called up the stairs a minute later. "I'm home."

He left his room and went down to see her.

"How was school?" She asked, standing at the stove pouring spaghetti sauce from a can into a pot.

Cole shrugged.

"Don't be a zombie," she said. "Talk to me. Is

everything okay? You look wet. Did you forget your umbrella? How did Livia get along with the vamps?"

"How would I know?"

"You have eyes."

He shrugged again. "She did okay I guess. She was at River Rapids Park after school with Darlene Chriss."

"That's good. Did you talk to her? Is that why you're wet?"

"Where were you when I got home?"

"School board meeting. I should have brought you. You'd have found it very interesting. Mrs. Welderheim was there again. That woman can talk, can't she?"

She put a lid on the pot, wiped her hands with a kitchen towel, walked over to the bar and rested her elbows on it, across from where Cole sat on a stool.

"The new curriculum isn't exactly what the vamps were hoping for." She smiled. "You remember they wanted more vamp related topics?"

Cole nodded.

"Now they're complaining about it."

"What about it?"

"Mostly Vlad the Impaler, from what I gather. Mrs. Welderheim nearly had a fit. I think she spit on Mr. Drakes, or at least his briefcase."

"What did they expect?"

She smiled. "Who knew? They're not very smart, are they? Now they want the curriculum rewritten to add positive portrayals of vamps; and they want Vlad out. Was he all that bad? I confess, I don't know as much history as you do."

"But he's historical."

"I'm not the one you should be talking to about it. I don't really care one way or the other."

"But it's censorship," Cole said with a frown.

"Is it really? Was it censorship before, when they

36

didn't mention Vlad?"

Cole frowned deeper, creasing his brow.

"And it's history." She said. "You know? Boring wars and presidents. Nobody likes those classes. And anyway, there's too much history to teach all of it. So what if they leave out Vlad?"

"I don't know what to say about before, but this is clearly censorship. To call for more vamp related topics, but only positive portrayals. Definitely, Mom. You have to admit, that's censorship."

She sighed. "I don't know. Maybe. You're not going to start a fuss about it are you?"

"A fuss?"

"You don't like that word?"

Cole laughed. "I have other things to do."

"Start with your homework."

Cole lifted himself off the stool and headed back upstairs.

"And be in bed by ten-thirty this morning, you hear."

He changed out of his wet clothes and sat at his computer. It wasn't the magick he should look at, he decided. It was history. When did it start? How far back did he have to go? Before he knew it, the sun had risen high in the sky. He must have unconsciously got up and closed his curtains. He sat, staring at the monitor, and rubbed his eyes.

He heard a light rap on the door; his mother pushed it open and peered in.

"Cole," she said, exasperated. "It's noon, why aren't you in bed?"

"Sorry, mom," he said. "I'm really into this... assignment."

"You can finish before school tonight, can't you?"

"I'll go to bed soon," he promised. "Mom?"

She poked her head back into the room.

"Can I ask you something?"

Her face brightened with a smile and she danced into his room and took a seat on his bed. Cole turned in his desk chair and looked at her.

"How old were you when the vamps started showing up?"

"Oh," her faced shadowed with disappointment. "I was nine or ten."

"Were you scared?"

She tilted her head and made a face. "Scared?" She shook her head. "I don't remember being scared. I remember my parents telling me not to be. There wasn't anything to fear, they said."

"But, well, I guess that's what I'm asking. I've been searching through the news archives and I thought there was an outbreak or something. I thought the vamps would have been going around biting. But I can't find anything like that."

"I don't remember anything like it."

"What do you remember?"

His mom shrugged like it wasn't important. "They just started showing up. They said it was a virus, but there was the blood substitute. So nobody needed to be afraid."

"How did they get the vamps to drink the substitute? I mean, isn't it in their nature to bite?"

She shook her head again. "It wasn't like the movies. That's what my parents said and as I grew up I realized they were right. The vamp virus, just like the zombie one, they aren't like in the movies."

"So, the vamps didn't just show up and start attacking? There weren't any kinds of trials and witch hunts and then later they came up with the blood substitute?"

"Not that I recall. My parents told me about the substitute at the same time they told me about the

38

vampires."

Cole looked back to his computer monitor. That was all he could find out, too.

"It's almost like," his mother said. "Well, I mean, as I got older and got used to the idea, it just always seemed like they had the substitute ready. Seems like I heard that they had invented it before and now they had a use for it. Something like that."

"Isn't that kind of strange?"

"Not really. That Dr. Krenske, well, he was just a kid back then. He was one of those prodigies."

"Dr. Krenske?"

"Yes, your favorite author. It doesn't surprise me that he would have some wacky inventions just lying around waiting for a use."

Cole sighed. "Thanks, Mom."

"Is that all you wanted to talk to me about?"

He was already engrossed in Google, but he heard her close the door quietly behind her as she left. An hour later he was sure there was something strange going on. He could hardly wait to tell Brock. Cole fell into bed still clothed and could hear himself snore before he was asleep.

Z

"I don't know about the magick," he told Brock that evening on their way to school. "But there is something going on."

"So, your dream has come true. A conspiracy."

Cole laughed. "Maybe."

Brock slapped his hands on his thighs. "And Cole Bertrand will be the one to bust it up."

"Do you want to hear about it or not?"

"Okay, okay. What is it?"

"The Welsh Corporation invented the blood

substitute two years before the outbreak of vamps."

Brock sat watching Cole, his mouth still open, but the smile gone. After several seconds he turned to the windshield and the road ahead.

"Is that it? That's the conspiracy?"

"Yep."

"I'm not seeing conspiracy written on it. Were they trying to replace human blood with a substitute to turn us into robots or something?"

"I doubt it."

"Well, were they going to use the blood to create a new race of super humans?"

"No."

Brock shook his head slowly. "So, are you going to look into the magick some more?"

"You don't get it, Brock. Ask me who created the Welsh Corporation. Go on, ask."

"I know who created the Welsh Corporation. It's common knowledge."

"And who is it?"

"For Christ's sake, you know you want to say it yourself."

"Dr. Arnold Krenske."

A loud sigh escaped Brock as he seemed to deflate in the passenger seat. "And so what?"

"So what? So what?"

"That's what I said. So what."

"So, two years before the first vamps showed up, Dr. Krenske had what they needed. And three years before the first large group of zombies showed up, there were five incidents of zombies near the Welsh laboratories, in their woods. The zombies had to be macheted."

"So?"

"Put the pieces together. Dr. Krenske knew. He knew something was going on. He created the blood substitute and the zombie vaccine. If there's anything going on with the magick, Dr. Krenske will know about it."

"Oh, let me guess. You're going to try to meet him."

"Yes, yes. Now you're getting it."

Brock turned to look at him as Cole pulled his car into a parking space in front of Darkspur Night High School and shut off the engine.

"Man. You've been obsessed with Krenske since you were eight-years old. This is all about him. It's all about you wanting to meet Krenske."

Cole shook his head in silence.

"You've got that book in your backpack, don't you?" Brock said. "It's in there, like always."

"So what? It's an important book. Every zombie should read it."

"We're living it, man. Did your mom buy you one of those what's happening to my body books, too? Did you have to read that to know how to be a man?"

"As a matter of fact, my mom did get me that book and it was very helpful."

"Come on, dude. We don't have to read what some regular scientist thinks. "

"A regular *genius* scientist."

"Whatever. What could a regular really know about being a zombie?"

"You're saying he doesn't know anything?"

"He knows a hell of a lot, man. He created the blood box drinks, in all sorts of cool bloody flavors for the vamps. And he invented a formula that keeps zombiism at bay, strangely enough after finding zombies in his back yard." Brock rolled his eyes. "But that doesn't mean he can tell you what it's like to be a zombie."

"You really can't have an opinion without reading the book."

"You're supposed to be trying to find out why the

magick are changing us into zombies and vamps, not finding reasons to meet your super hero."

Cole shook his head. Now that Brock was there, his discovery of the day before didn't seem quite so conspiratorial.

"Maybe you're right."

"I am right. But hey, don't let it stop you. You should go interview Krenske. Heck, maybe he started the viruses."

"Now who's thinking irrationally? Dr. Krenske's the greatest mind of this generation. You think he's stupid enough to start up a zombie, vampire society?"

"Well, you just go ask him. Get your interview."

"Nah." Cole grabbed his back pack from the back seat and opened his door. "Zombies may be smart, but that's not enough for Krenske to grant an interview with a high school kid."

Alan walked in front of the car and held up his right hand in the Vulcan manner. Cole shuddered. So unzombie-cool.

"That reminds me," he said. "This morning–" The bell rang. "I'll have to tell you later. But see if you can keep Alan away from the vamps tonight."

"It'd be easier to cure the virus."

Z

Cole was in American Lit before her and when she walked in, he couldn't help but look up. She smiled at him.

"Hi."

His mouth fell slightly open and he turned away.

That morning in history class, before Mrs. Peppermill could begin her lecture, Cole raised his hand and asked her, "Is it true that some of the parents want you to stop teaching about Vlad the Impaler?"

Mrs. Peppermill pushed her glasses further up on her nose and looked down at Cole with a smirk.

"There won't be any change in this class yet," she said with her squeaky voice.

"But what about the complaints?" Slade said from his seat in the back corner. "You can't keep teaching it until it's settled."

"On the contrary, Mr. Slade. We don't make changes to our curriculum based on complaints."

"I would hope not," Cole said, glancing behind him at Rick. "You can't censor history just because a few vamps don't like it."

"Vlad the Impaler is not vamp history," Slade said.

"But he is part of world history."

"He's a misrepartation of vampirism, Mrs. Peppermill, and shouldn't be part of our class."

"I think you mean, misrepresentation, Mr. Slade."

"What are you afraid of?" Cole said, turning in his seat to glare at Rick. "Can't stand looking in the mirror? Oh, wait..."

Laughter spread through the class.

"That's enough," Mrs. Peppermill said. "Vlad the Impaler was inserted into our world history curriculum in an effort to broaden your knowledge of the origins and legends of vampirism."

"But it's not right to say that Vlad the Impaler was even a vampire."

"That is up to the student to judge, Mr. Slade, after careful study and thought."

"Maybe vamps have a problem with deep thought, Mrs. Peppermill," Cole said.

Again, laughter echoed in the room.

"Not another word, Mr. Bertrand. Mr. Slade, Vlad the Impaler is a part of the cultural history of vampirism, whether you like it or not."

"Why can't we learn about good vamps?"

"When you can name one, maybe we'll learn about him," Cole said.

"Cole Bertrand." Mrs. Peppermill stood looking down at him. "Would you like to visit Principal Lute's office?"

Cole frowned. "No ma'am."

"Then I should expect not to hear a word from you for the rest of the class."

Cole glanced back at Slade and saw that he was fuming. His eyes glowed red and his cheeks seemed to pulsate. He remembered the morning before in the rain. The problem with being smart, Dr. Krenske should have warned, is learning when to keep your big mouth shut.

When the bell rang, Cole darted out of class ahead of everyone else and stormed to his car. He sat on the hood, with his feet on the front bumper, waiting for Brock. He tried to understand why he was so angry with Rick Slade. Sure, nobody liked to be glared at by a vamp. All the experts swore the vamps could control their bloodlust these days, with proper synthetic supplementing. But Cole still harbored the unspoken notion that vamps had anger issues that could lead to uncontrolled fits of aggression against non-vamps. But as often as Mr. Hood, the gym teacher, repeated that vamps were semi-cured, Cole heard some rumor about them getting bent out of shape and attacking regulars, magick, even the Franks and zombies, as hard as that was to fathom.

But was that it? Was he afraid of Slade? No, it couldn't be that. But one thing he knew for sure was that he disliked Rick more and more every day. He looked for Brock, only to see Livia leaving the school with Slade and Darlene. He leered at them both with a deep frown.

"What the hell?" Brock came at him from nowhere and Cole flinched.

"I didn't see you come out."

"Were you growling?"

"Was I?"

"You were totally growling. Are you off your meds?"

"No." He said, but thought carefully to make sure he took his pill that morning.

Brock looked at him curiously. "Mr. Hood says that zombies can still growl, even on meds, but only if they're having, you know, like deep emotions or something."

"I don't know what you're talking about," Cole said and got off his car. "Deep emotions. Let's just get out of here." He didn't look back to see Livia and regretted it.

Z

Todd climbed into the passenger seat of Wanda's old four-door after school, still energized from the morning before. He knew he looked different; all the regular girls and even some of the vamps eyed him seductively all night at school. He felt transformed. He walked taller. He was sure his clothes looked better. Where before he was a nerd with too-short hair and tight pants, today he was a cool vamp. He'd gelled his hair up so it stuck out all over. He decided he would get an earring, if Rick okayed it. Even Rick said he was cool now. Everybody thought he was cool. Everybody.

But when he turned to Wanda, she only glared at him. Well, she was his sister. Sisters didn't count.

"This is what he does," Wanda said, her voice steely, like anger would burst out of her at any second. She started the car and shook her head as she drove them home.

"He takes you when you're newly turned and gives you a taste of real blood, before you've learned to control the craving."

Todd turned to look out the window. He didn't have

to listen to her anymore.

"Didn't you read *The Vampire Dilemma*? This is just the thing it warns us about."

"What does Krenske know?"

"He knows that turning people into vampires is immoral."

"That's just his opinion."

"Are you happy to be a vamp? Are you glad you have to drink blood out of a box? Is this what you wanted for your life?"

He turned to her and smiled. "I'm a better vamp than I was a regular. Why shouldn't other people have the same chance."

"Will you ask them? Before you bite them, are you going to get their permission? The feral that bit you didn't ask first, did he?"

The memory of Ciara Wister, lunging at him in the dark, flashed in his mind. And for several seconds, Todd relived the morning before, the cold air, the rain, Tina's warm pulsating neck nourishing him. He shuddered with delight.

Wanda saw the look on his face and turned back to the road. "I'm going to have to tell mom and dad. They'll make you stop hanging out with Rick Slade. But if you tell me you won't see him again, I'll give you a chance to do the right thing."

He smiled. "Whatever you say, Sis."

CHAPTER FIVE

When Cole opened the front door and walked into his living room, the aroma of baking cookies filled his nose.

"Can you smell them?" His mother called out from the kitchen.

He paused to force a casual smile on his face before entering the kitchen where his mother was putting cookies on a plastic plate. She was smiling up at him hopefully.

"They smell good," he said.

"Would you like to try one? One little bite?"

Cole shook his head. He felt sorry for his mother and tried hard not to let it show. Why couldn't she understand that he was dead? He couldn't eat cookies. He could barely taste them and they would just hang around in his rotted out stomach and intestines for days until they'd finally figure their way out at some inopportune time. But his mother seemed to hold out hope that Dr. Krenske's magic pill would actually make him alive again.

"Not even a tiny taste?"

"They don't taste like they smell, anymore," he said. "To me."

She frowned just a bit.

"It's no big deal mom. It's not like I want to taste them and I can't. I have no desire for food."

"But it smells good?"

"Like smelling a rose," he said, smiling, trying to make it all right.

She looked at her plate of cookies and then her eyebrows rose and she gasped a tiny bit.

"Do you think it's okay to take these to Mrs. Duvessa and Livia? I mean..."

"Mrs. Duvessa isn't turned."

"Good," she said. "Come on. We're heading over right now."

"I don't have to go...do I?"

"Of course you do," she said. "Come on. Right now."

She had that tone of voice that told him there was no point in arguing and he wondered if she'd planned for him to go all along. He tried to come up with an excuse, but he knew it was no use. He wanted to go. He wanted to see Livia again. Cole followed his mom across the street in the dark and let her ring the bell. Mrs. Duvessa opened the door and beamed at them both, welcoming them into her living room and calling up the stairs.

"Livia, look who's here and they brought cookies."

Cole grimaced. He could only hope Livia would know the cookies were his mother's idea; and Mrs. Duvessa seemed to be as clueless as his own mother about the undead. The house smelled like peppermint and cinnamon. Three seascapes were hung over the fireplace and the mantel was covered with family photos—no two frames were the same size or shape. Cole found himself drawn to them, until Livia padded lightly down the staircase. He saw her feet first, in pink shoes, and watched her emerge. She smiled at him before saying hello.

They all sat in their front room on plastic-covered furniture, squeaking and sliding into comfortable positions. Livia took a seat in an easy chair by the fireplace where Cole couldn't look at her long without his mom noticing. A copy of Dr. Krenske's *The Vampire Dilemma* sat on the end table by her seat. He glanced up at her briefly with admiration. Though clearly Krenske intended the book for vamps, even *he* said, in the forward, that he couldn't expect many to actually read it. The lust for blood, as he explained throughout, dulls the intellect and the thirst for knowledge.

"It was kind of you to come visit," Mrs. Duvessa said. She was a short, plump, woman, and she sat on the edge of her chair across from them with her knees together primly. "You know, no one else in the neighborhood has so much as waved hello. I told Livia it looked like it would be as difficult for me here as it was back home."

"Don't be too hard on them," his mom said. "It doesn't have anything to do with us, really. People are just busier nowadays and less friendly. But I thought we ought to try to get these two kids together. Maybe they could share a ride to school."

Cole's eyes widened and he stared at his mom in a panic.

"Oh, well." Mrs. Duvessa stammered over her words. "I don't know."

"It's not that Cole doesn't have friends," his mom continued. "But he doesn't have enough girls in his life, if you know what I mean."

A groan escaped Cole and he could see Livia smirk and turn to the fire.

"Oh, I don't think that would do at all," Mrs. Duvessa said, taking a cookie from the plate on the table and biting into it. "I don't mean to be too blunt, but, well,

49

Cole—" and here she turned to him with a nod and then back to his mother—"is, after all, I mean, it's not like an insult to say so, it's a plain fact. He's a zombie."

His mother cocked her head to one side and her brow furrowed. Cole tried desperately not to roll his eyes. He knew what the woman was going to say as soon as she'd muttered, 'I don't know.' But then, he'd lived most of his life lately at the night school and no matter how much he tried to make his mom understand vamps and zombies, she was just not getting the undead.

"Yes, Cole is a zombie," his mom smiled. "That much is true."

"And Livia is a vampire," Mrs. Duvessa said.

Cole now turned completely to Livia and saw her eyes widen, staring down at her hands.

"Yes," his mom said with a perky smile back on her face.

"Well, I don't think it's appropriate for zombies and vampires to...shall we say..."

"Date?"

"Exactly, yes."

"Oh, well," his mother was still not getting it. "I wasn't suggesting they date. I was just saying they could be friends. Not dating." Her words began to trail off and Cole knew she was working things out in her mind. "Are you saying that you don't believe in inter-undead dating?"

"Well, no, of course not."

"But...why not? I mean, they're both undead."

"But Livia is a vampire. Vampires, well, they stick with their own kind. And even though I'm not a vampire myself, I believe it is right that they should."

His mom opened her mouth, still smiling, and closed it again. She finally got it.

"I see. Well, as I said, I only thought they could be friends."

50

"I'm not sure that would send the right message," Mrs. Duvessa said.

Cole saw Livia close her eyes and shake her head almost imperceptibly. His mom changed the subject to the gardenia bushes the Duvessa's planted the other morning and after the excruciatingly silent moments between he and Livia, she finally stood to leave.

"Can you believe the nerve of that woman?" His mother said as she stomped back across the street. "The nerve."

"A lot of people think that way," Cole said.

Craig, his stepfather, was home when they got there and Cole sat in the kitchen listening as his mother related the story, with great enthusiasm, to him.

"Have you ever heard of such a thing?"

"Sure," Craig said. "We have parents like that at work. Vamps though. The Zombies don't seem to feel the same."

"Well, who do these vamps think they are?"

"So, you're all for Cole dating a vampire? Maybe even...you know?" Craig said with a teasing smile.

His mom put her hands on her hips and said, "What two consenting undead people do together is their own business."

Z

The next Friday, in home room, the loudspeaker crackled and Mr. Lute's voice echoed through the halls.

"The Vamp Pride Club will be hosting the school for dessert today in the cafeteria, after lunch. Be sure to stay and enjoy their special dessert. Uh. Thank you."

The bell rang for first class and Cole walked as slowly as he could down the hall. He told himself he was just taking it easy. No hurry to class. No reason to get there before the bell, anyway. He moved to the left side of the hallway and at the next set of lockers, he saw Livia pulling a book out of hers. She turned to him and smiled.

"Hi," she said.

Cole looked to the floor.

"It's all right, you know," she said as he moved slowly past her. "You can say hi."

He turned back to look at her. "Hi."

Then he looked around to see if anyone noticed.

"Hey," she called to him.

He turned around.

"The vamps invited me to help them with their dessert thing at lunch."

Someone rushing past bumped into Cole, knocking him back a bit.

"Is that good?"

She shrugged. "Well, I didn't think they'd want me in their pride club or whatever."

"Why not?"

"I don't know. You have to have certain ideas about vampirism to get in, you know?"

Cole shook his head. "Don't you just have to be proud to be a vamp and super popular, or something?"

This time Livia looked around at the thinning crowd rushing past them. She shook her head. "It's a little more than that. Some of them can be a little extreme."

"But you're going to help them out today?"

"Yeah, well," she sighed. "It's nice to be wanted. You know."

Cole gave a brief nod and held up his hand. "See ya." He turned and walked away, mentally kicking himself. What was that whole hand waving thing? What a dork.

At lunchtime, Cole went through the line to get a bag of Fritos to smell, though his sense was declining, as was expected, according to Dr. Krenske. He could still smell Fritos and chocolate and peppermint. But he had to admit, the only reason he went through the line was to look behind the dumpy cafeteria lady and see if he could see Livia in the kitchen. He did. Her brow was furrowed and she stood with her hands on her hips watching Rick and a few other vamps turning little bowls upside down onto plates. She was shaking her head.

"Move along, dude. I'm hungry."

Cole turned to see one of the regular kids looking up at him, both hands on his tray, trying to slide it along the bar. The kid trembled when Cole looked at him.

"Sorry," he said. "I can go around."

"Don't bother," Cole said. Leaving his Fritos on the bar, he walked around the line at the register and crossed the noisy cafeteria to the red section where the zombies were sitting.

"What's wrong with you?" Brock said.

"Nothing."

"Something's wrong with you. You're mad all the time."

"I am not."

"Are so."

"Ever since I asked you about that new girl," Alan said.

Suddenly the whole table was silent and they all stared at Cole. He caught Rachel's pained expression and felt a tinge of regret.

"What?" He said.

Alan smiled. "You like her."

"I do not."

Vamps started filing into the room carrying white plates full of something greenish brown.

"What the hell is that?"

They set plates down in front of the regulars and magick and Cole noticed several of them turning to the zombie corner and smiling or laughing.

"What did they make?"

"It looked like a gelatin mold," Cole said and they all turned to him again. "When I was in line, I saw them."

"What were you in line for? I thought you didn't like inhaling."

"I like Fritos sometimes."

"But you didn't get any," Brock said.

"He just wanted to see her back in the kitchen."

"I did not."

Three vamps sauntered up to their table. One carried a tray lined with plates. The other two took the plates off the tray. They smiled a bit, so far as vamps do, and set the plates in front of Cole and his friends.

"Oh, man," Alan said before the vamps turned and left to get more desserts.

Cole looked down at his plate. On it sat what looked like a small greenish-brown brain. Slimy and shiny.

"Very funny," Rachel said.

"It is not funny," Alan said.

"Well, it's a little bit funny." Brock said.

"They went out and bought a gazillion brain molds?" Stu said.

Rachel let out a snort of laughter.

"It's not funny," Cole said. "To serve us food at all isn't funny and they know it."

"It's just another one of their jokes, Cole. No big deal." Stu said.

Cole pushed his chair away from the table and stood.

"Aren't you tired of it?" He said.

He stood staring at them before turning to walk out of the cafeteria. When he realized his friends and the rest of the zombies were following, he felt a surge of pride. As he neared the door he saw Livia coming out of the kitchen. She looked at him with a hopeful smile, but he glared at her. That time, he heard the growl himself—

54

something of a low, vibrating rumble escaping his throat. Even as he told himself he was overreacting, he growled.

After school, Cole paced back and forth in front of his car as he waited for Brock to make his trek from the phys ed building to the front of the school. He seethed. The brain joke had him out of sorts all day. The other zombies were beginning to agree with him that it was sick and shouldn't be tolerated. It was bad enough the vamps were the popular kids, always pushing everyone else aside in the halls and telling everyone else what to do all the time. If they thought they could get away with ridiculing the zombies, they were mistaken. Cole was sure there would be payback, he just didn't know what kind.

"Cole?"

He jumped and turned to see Livia standing on the grass, her books cradled in her arms.

"What do you want?" He knew his voice was much harsher than he intended it to be, but he was angry and decided he liked it.

"I heard some talk that you and the zombies are mad."

"So?"

"It was just a joke."

"The vamps may have you convinced that they're just having a bit of fun, but I've known them longer."

"You're saying it wasn't a joke?" She raised her eyebrows at him and smiled.

"I'm saying it was just another attempt to manipulate us, to keep *us* down and them up."

"It was just some Jello brains."

"And that's funny to you? How would you like it if I hung a dead bat in your locker?"

"That wouldn't be funny; but we didn't give you real brains."

"A rubber one, then. Is that funny?"

She looked to the ground. "Maybe."

"It's not funny."

She shrugged. "I didn't think they meant any harm."

"They want to control everyone. They want to rule the world."

"Oh, come on, that's a bit much don't you think?"

"Why am I even talking to you about this? You're one of them."

"I'm not one of them."

"You're a vamp aren't you?"

She turned and stomped off toward Darlene's car. Cole saw Darlene turn to him and he thought he saw her frowning in the dark. Finally Brock showed up and they could leave.

"What do you think brains taste like?" Brock said once Cole pulled the car out of the parking lot.

"What?"

"Don't bite my head off. I'm just asking."

"Not lime Jello, that's for sure."

"Salty, you think?"

Cole nodded.

"When we go full zombie," Brock said. "You suppose we even get to taste the brains we eat?"

CHAPTER SIX

"Come on, let's get out of here," Alan said, after rolling his window down. "Why did you want to meet here of all places?"

Cole lifted his body from his own hood and walked over to Alan's running car with Brock following behind him.

"Where else can we meet?"

"River Rapids Park."

"The vamps are always there."

"We have our spot at the playground."

"The playground," Cole sneered. "They sit under the pavilion and make us hang out at the playground like four-year olds."

"Somewhere else then," Alan said. "Come on let's go, this place is creepy."

"It's a grave yard, dude, and you're a zombie."

Alan sighed deeply, turned the key in the steering column, silencing his car, and opened his door.

"Hanging out in the cemetery is just another reason for them to down us, man."

"What's the big deal," Brock said. "Some of us were even buried here. It's like a little piece of home."

"But they'll say we're out here looking for brains or something."

"What do we care what they say about us?" Cole said.

"What do you want anyway?"

"Wait for the others and we'll start."

"Is this like a meeting or something?" Alan said.

"Yep."

Cole led them to the gazebo in the middle Wakefield cemetery where they sat on benches in the cold darkness. The office by the road was dark, but far across the several acres of tombstones, rising up like claws from the earth, the little white chapel was dimly lit for nighttime mourners.

Cole shivered absentmindedly.

"I told you this place is creepy. The church doesn't help." Alan said.

Two cars pulled into the parking lot and their lights shut off; doors slammed. Cole saw Winston, Rachel and Bill Teeter walking across the graves, several other zombies followed.

"Man this place is creepy, ain't it?" Bill said.

"I thought you'd like it," Rachel said.

"You guys hear about the West sisters?" Bill said. "It was just on the radio."

Cole shook his head. "What about them? Do we know them?"

"Tina West," Rachel said. "She was one of the magick. She's missing. They're both missing, along with another girl."

"So?" Brock said.

"Slade probably buried them somewhere." Cole said.

"Ha ha. Very funny," Rachel said. "He only buries vamps."

"Why do you guys believe this stuff." Brock said.

"You don't?" Alan said. "I've heard it straight from vamps. If you don't follow the rules of his little blood gang, you get buried alive."

Brock shook his head. "It's all just part of the aura. He wants you to believe it."

"It could be true." Cole said. "But why would he bury magick girls?"

"I'm not saying Slade had anything to do with it," Bill said, perturbed. "I'm just saying there are three girls missing since Tuesday morning. That's all. So why are we here?"

"Yeah, what do you want?" Kyle, a newly undead corpse said, shuffling his feet and looking around nervously.

"I want to talk about the vamps and what we're going to do about them."

"They need to be taught a lesson," Rachel said.

"What can we do?"

"We have to show them that we won't put up with their stupid jokes anymore. We have to show them that we aren't going to be second-class anymore. We're just as cool as they are."

"Cooler," Rachel said and several zombies turned to look at her. "We are. What have they got? Huh? They're cool looking that's all. The regs think they're all mysterious and all. They brood and pout and walk around like they're on the verge of some emotional outburst."

"Why do the regs think that's so cool?" Alan said.

"Who knows? But we've got the brains. We're smarter than they are."

"Yeah, smart ought to be cool." Bill said.

"But it's not," Kyle said. "Smart isn't cool. And we can't change that. It's the same with the regs. I mean, look at 'em. The girls are either all over the big jocks who can hardly write a coherent sentence or the scrawny, overemotional vamps; and the guys either like the stupid brainless cheerleaders or the scrawny vamp girls. We can't change them."

"Why not?"

"Because it's the way it is. It's, you know, high school."

"Well, I don't care. I say we do something about it."

"Like what?"

"Just a joke. Like their little brain dessert joke. Nothing major."

Cole watched as the others turned; he followed their gaze to see the moonlight glance off the edge of a hatchet blade. A large figure approached and an audible sigh of relief swept through the group.

"Mr. Roginaldi," Cole said, surprised.

The cemetery caretaker lowered his hatchet and smiled. "You zombies scared me. Thought you were...you know."

"Sorry, sir," Rachel said.

"It's been a long time since any of you's dug yourselves up from the dead. Better safe than sorry, eh?" He held up his weapon and patted it.

"No problem," Kyle said. "We're all vaccinated."

"I could tell. It's all in the eyes."

Z

Two evenings later, Livia rode to school with Darlene and followed her up the front steps.

"I'm just saying," Darlene was talking at the same time she was nodding at kids she passed in the main hall. "People are talking. You spend too much energy on trying to talk to Cole Zombie. It looks bad."

"I can talk to whoever I want," Livia said.

"Sure you can."

They rounded the corner to the vamp locker section and found themselves behind another group of vamps, including Rick Slade. Once they approached the lockers, they stopped undead in their tracks and a low, seething mumble began to surge through the group. Rick turned on Livia and Darlene as they approached. He glared at Livia.

"Did you know about this?"

"About what?" Darlene said.

The group spread out and Livia noticed they were looking up. From the ceiling hung a dozen crosses, fashioned out of popsicle sticks and twigs. Rick stalked to his locker and had to try his combination several times before the lock released, he yanked the door open and inside were several thin paper crosses. He turned back to the group of vamps who stood glaring at each other. Then his eyes settled on Livia as she pulled her books from her locker.

"You knew about this." He said.

Livia shook her head. "I didn't know anything."

Rick slammed his locker shut.

"They're going to pay for this," he said. "You tell your zombie boyfriend he's a dead man."

"Well," Livia said.

Rick stormed to her and put his face inches from hers. "Well what?"

"He's already dead," Livia said.

Instead of laughter, or at the very least a sigh of giggles, a deep-throated growl wafted around her. Rick continued to eye her with fury.

"Maybe you want to die, too?"

Livia tried desperately not to smile.

"You think this is funny?"

She shook her head.

"Leave her alone," Darlene said. "She's right. The

zombies are dead. What are you going to do?"

Still staring intently into Livia's eyes, Rick smiled fiendishly.

"Whack their heads off and burn them, what do you think?"

Livia shook her head.

"This is just a joke." Her voice quavered. "Just like the brains. Can't you take a bit of your own medicine?"

"This isn't a joke. It's a threat."

"No more so than your dessert. I'm sure Principal Lute will understand—"

Rick pushed Livia until she was pressed against the row of lockers.

"We make the jokes around here. Nobody else."

"Leave her alone," Darlene said.

"Stay out of this." Rick said and turned on Livia, pressing her shoulders hard against the metal doors, forcing one of the locks into her back.

"Maybe we need to show Principal Lute just how much of a threat it is."

He turned to the others.

"Get a chair from one of the classrooms. Anybody got a knife?"

"What are you going to do?" Livia said.

Rick glared at her. "Whatever we do, you won't say a word about it. But you can tell your zombie boyfriend to watch out."

He gave her another shove into the lockers and she turned and hurried down the hallway. Darlene and some of the other girls followed.

"Are you all right?" Darlene asked once they were around the corner.

Livia nodded. "He's just pissed, right? I mean, he doesn't mean anything he says, does he? He wouldn't cut off a zombie's head, would he?"

62

"I don't think so," Darlene said.

"Sure he would," Jenny Salts said, shifting her stack of books in her arms. "Don't you know who he is?"

"Hush, Jenny," Darlene said.

"What?" Livia said. "What do you know?"

"It's just rumors." Darlene said.

"Tell me."

Ciara Wister stopped walking and smiled at Livia. Darlene, Jenny and Livia stopped to look back at her.

"He's the leader of a group of ferals. He's turning regulars and killing off a few zombies while he's at it."

"He can't just kill zombies," Livia said. "The law states that as long as the zombie is in recovery he can't be killed. Only if he goes vague and starts attacking–"

"What would a feral care about the law?" Ciara said, still smiling. "All he really cares about is blood. Blood. And turning more regs into vamps." She turned and walked down the hall toward the classrooms.

"Do you believe her?" Livia asked Darlene.

Darlene hesitated before saying, "No."

"Do you think it's possible?"

"Anything's possible."

Z

"Mr. Lute, I promise you, when we hung the crosses, they weren't sharp. We never would hang daggers from the ceiling."

Cole pleaded with the principal in his office, sitting in a large padded chair in front of his desk. Brock sat next to him in a similar chair, designated the secondary instigator. Alan, Winston, Bill, and Kyle stood behind them. Only Rachel had escaped the wrath of Principal Lute and none of them was going to offer her up.

Lute's round face was grayed; he wore a Skin Like New patch over the bridge of his nose, and black thick-

63

rimmed glasses perched atop his balding head. Cole tried not to stare, but the patch on his nose was the wrong shade of gray. Lute was an old, tired zombie, but clearly still strong despite his short stature.

"So you want me to believe that someone came along afterward and sharpened them?"

"Sure," Brock said. "Isn't it obvious the vamps did it?"

"No, I'm afraid that's not obvious at all. You admitted to hanging the crosses–"

"Yes, we hung the crosses, but they weren't sharp."

"But they ended up sharp and that's where we are. I'm afraid you're in quite a bit of trouble."

Cole fumed. "If I can get proof that they weren't sharp when we hung them, will you believe us?"

"Well naturally I would believe you if you had proof. But you don't have any."

"But I might be able to get some. A witness, say–one of the vamps who saw them first."

"Until you do, you're all on detention after school."

Cole heard Alan let out a whining moan.

"For how long?"

"Five days," he said.

"Five days?" Alan said.

"That's without proof of the daggers. If you can get proof that you just hung crosses, only three days."

"But why? If we have proof," Cole said. "It was just a joke."

"Just a joke that insulted at least one Christian student who happened upon the scene."

"There's a Christian at our school?" Brock said.

"At least one. And you've insulted him rather harshly."

"Come on, Mr. Lute," Cole said. "It was just a harm-less joke."

64

"It was clearly a threat, Mr. Bertrand, even had the crosses not been sharpened into daggers."

"But everybody knows that crosses don't bother vampires. That's just movie stuff."

"It's part of our culture. Whether anyone believes it to be effective or not, it's still a threat."

Cole sighed. "But you thought it was funny, didn't you?"

Principal Lute stared at Cole across his desk. "You know I can't have an opinion on it, Cole. I appreciate your intentions."

"And you didn't do anything to the vamps after the brain thing." Alan said.

"Because I can appreciate a joke. But the involvement of a religious symbol—"

"That's freedom of speech," Cole said. "There's no protection of their symbol."

"If it were an art project, perhaps I would agree, Mr. Bertrand. But you used them to tease the vamps. And so far, I have no reason to believe that you zombies didn't sharpen the crosses into daggers."

"No reason? Our word, as zombies, isn't good enough?"

"And Rick Slade's word that he saw you hanging them early this evening."

"Well, that's a lie. We hung them after school yesterday morning." Brock said.

Principal Lute rested his elbows on his desk and sighed heavily, removed his glasses from his head and put them on.

"This interview is over. You will all report to detention in the cafeteria after school starting tomorrow morning."

Grumbling, the zombies filed out of Principal Lute's office and stood in the hallway.

"I can't believe a zombie would believe Rick Slade over other zombies." Winston said.

"He's principal, first," Cole said. "He can't play favorites."

"I just can't believe this," Brock said. "Man, when the vamps hear about it, we're toast. Toast, man."

Cole shrugged. "I think I'll bring my laptop. I can do some more research on our history project."

"Leave it to you to enjoy detention," Brock said, shaking his head sadly. "What about that witness?"

"Yeah," Kyle said. "Who did you have in mind?"

"Livia?" Alan said with a sneer. "Let me talk to her."

"Leave her alone," Cole said. "You'll get her into trouble with Rick. He doesn't like any of his little tribe talking to us. I'll talk to her."

"Why do you get to do it?" Alan said.

"Hello. She lives across the street from me."

Brock nudged Cole as they trudged through the empty halls to their classes.

"Do you think Jesus was a zombie?"

Cole turned to him, astonished. "He did rise from the dead."

"Maybe he was the first zombie."

Cole shook his head. "I still think true zombiism is a new phenomenon."

"You don't know that. But," Brock twisted his face with disappointment. "None of those disciple guys wrote anything about him eating out their brains or anything."

"That's true."

"Still. Maybe some things are just too hard to put on paper. You know what I mean?"

Cole laughed, slapped Brock on the back and left for class.

Z

Cole waited, watching from his window, until Darlene dropped Livia at her house across the street and then he walked over in the dark. She answered his knock with surprise and came out onto her driveway to talk to him. She stood in front of him, her hands in her back pockets, bouncing up and down on her heels. He could see her ghostly pale face lit in the street lamp and he almost, without thinking, reached out to pull a ringlet of hair from her forehead. He stopped himself just in time with his hand upraised. With a goofy smile, he turned it into a brief wave and scolded himself. That was the second time he'd waved at her; his zombie senses were abuzz with dejection.

"Sorry to bother you and all," he said, recovering by pulling his raised hand over his hair.

"Don't be." Her pouty lips broke into a smile and he felt a rush of warmth all over. "I heard you and your friends got detention."

Suddenly Cole went cold again. "I bet Slade is thrilled."

"I don't think he likes you."

"No kidding. Slade hates zombies more than most vamps do. Anyway, I'm sorry about the other day. With the brains and all."

"I'm sorry, too. I didn't realize it would make the zombies mad."

"And I'm sorry I said you were one of them. Well, you are a vamp and all. But, you know what I mean."

"You want to walk down to the playground?"

He stammered for a second, in shock. "Sure."

They walked along the sidewalk, moonlight casting shadows. Mr. Grayson walked his dog on the other side of the street and waved as they passed.

"You're not really like the other vamps around here." He said.

"It was a lot different back home. The vamps didn't get along much with the zombies, but there weren't that many of you guys. Only two that I knew about, until the big outbreak. It wasn't like here at all."

"Well, this is Darkspur; this is where it all started."

"Yeah, I was excited to move here. My dad got a job at Welsh; he's a chemist, you know?" Her voice was filled with pride. "They offered him the job before I was a vamp and he wouldn't take it."

"Why not?"

"He thought it was too dangerous here for a regular. But once I was turned, he figured it couldn't be as bad as Florida."

"Your mom's a regular."

"True, but she was an ER nurse back home. She said she could handle Darkspur."

"Is she working at the hospital?"

"No. She doesn't work anymore. What do your parents do?"

"My mom teaches at our school."

"She does?"

"Yeah, she teaches the two Franks. Special ed."

"That's cool, I guess. What are the Franks, anyway? My dad says they're zombies."

Cole shook his head. "Nobody knows really. We call them Franks because, well—"

"They look like Frankenstein's monsters. That's why my dad says they're zombies. He said that the people at work whisper about weird experiments."

She stopped walking and turned abruptly. "I probably shouldn't have said that."

"Experiments? You mean, the Welsh Corporation created the Franks?"

"I don't know. Really. I just overheard my dad talking. I could've gotten it all wrong. What about your dad? What does he do?"

Cole's first instinct was to lie, which he found strange. He batted the idea from his mind and took in some of the cool night air. "My dad's dead."

"But...?"

"Craig is my stepfather."

"Oh, I'm sorry. I didn't mean to bring up bad..."

"It's okay."

But of course, it was not. They started walking again and Cole's arm brushed against hers. He was overwhelmed, briefly, with the desire to crush her head between his hands. He could almost hear her skull crack and a low groan nearly escaped him.

"When did it happen?" She said.

"Three years ago." His voice was constricted; he struggled to force the image of her juicy brain from his mind.

"How?"

She turned to him as they walked and looked at him in surprise. He tried to force the pained expression from his face.

"I'm sorry," she said. "You don't have to tell me. I'm being nosy."

"It's okay. He—" Cole thought about it for a few seconds. He'd never actually said it out loud, had he? "He was infected and we didn't know. My mom," He hesitated again. "She caught him attacking me. He bit me. And she hacked his head off with one of the butcher knives in the kitchen."

He heard her gasp and suddenly her hand was on his arm and they'd stopped walking again.

"I'm so sorry; that must have been awful."

Cole looked down at her and smiled. "It was kind of gross. But, she had to do it. She saved my life."

"And she got you the vaccine?"

"We got it at the hospital."

"That's just awful. To have to kill your own husband. Oh..."

"I'm sorry. I shouldn't have told you."

"No, it's okay. I've seen and heard my share of awful stuff, too."

"You said there was a big outbreak where you lived?"

She nodded. "My mom was called into work and she made me go with her. She didn't think I should stay alone."

"She was right."

"My mom was amazing. I didn't see much, but I did see her covered in blood. She saved a lot of people from going full zombie. But it was mayhem in the ER. After, well...she told me she had to kill a lot of people, er...zombies."

"Why doesn't she work here in Darkspur?"

She shook her head. "She can't work anymore. It did something to her."

"What?"

"Scared the crap out of her, I think. She freaked out a little bit. She nailed all the doors and windows shut and started stockpiling weapons. My dad thought she needed to get away from there."

"So he brought her here? To Darkspur, where it all began? With the largest population of zombies and vamps in the world?"

Livia chuckled. "Well, she's better now. But Darkspur is also known for its civility. In places like Florida, where the viruses are just getting started, it's like anarchy sometimes."

They turned and started walking again, past houses lit inside and voices in the back yards, barbequing, swimming, enjoying the darkness before it was time to sleep for the day.

70

"So, in Florida, the vamps don't get along with regulars?" He said.

"Not at all. And they're not so, I don't know."

"Rude? Snobbish?"

"Popular, is what I was going for." She chuckled.

"Really? You must have been popular."

"Maybe a little. But after I was turned, it all changed. My friends didn't want me around anymore. The vamps stayed clustered in their little group and I had to join them, or be shunned completely. There's a lot more fear of vamps back home."

"So you were turned by a feral? I mean, as opposed to catching the virus?"

She shrugged. "I don't really know. I was on a date and..."

"You don't have to tell me about it."

"I guess I feel foolish. I thought he wanted to make out. But he bit me."

"I thought you said you didn't know how it happened."

She looked up at him quizzically. "Oh, no. I didn't know he was a feral. Maybe they all were. Who knows? I mean, Dr. Krenske defines a feral as an outcast vamp who doesn't live by the rules or associate with civil vamps."

"In *The Vampire Dilemma*."

"You've read it?"

"Sure I have."

"But it's for vamps, really."

"And people who want to know about them."

She smiled. "Anyway, I learned that, back home, you couldn't tell the difference between ferals and plain old vamps. And I guess that's why they were shunned. Here, everybody thinks the vamps are cool. And the ferals are just a bad strain, like Krenske says. You get me?"

Cole nodded. "Well, then, this is better for you, right? Here, you can be popular again."

She stopped walking just as they reached the playground at the end of the street and turned to him, her face lit in the light of the street lamp. She peered at him somberly and shook her head.

"I don't think I want to be popular anymore. I just want to fit somewhere. You know?"

"Most kids would die to hang out with the vamps here."

She laughed a little. "Maybe it's Rick. Who can resist him?"

"I hope you're joking."

"He's like an idiot one minute, and a vicious dog the next. I'm not sure why he's so popular with the vamps. He's really, really good looking. Do you think that's it?"

Suddenly Cole felt pressure in his chest. It was odd enough that he was standing on Buckley street talking to a vamp. Odder still that she was so incredibly beautiful. But here she was also talking crap about Rick Slade. It was like a dream come true, except for the constant urge to crack her head open and slurp out her brains.

"I'd rather not say," he said.

She looked at him and smiled. "That's very diplomatic."

"You know, now that I think about it. You seem to be more intelligent than the others."

"Well, I don't think the virus affects our brains, like the zombie virus does."

"So, the vamps here were, how shall we say, not so bright to begin with?"

"They might not seem smart to you, but you've got that zombie brain thing."

Cole smiled and nodded slowly. "I forgot."

"You forgot you were more intelligent than everyone

else."

"You know, we're not all that smart. Dr. Krenske says we can focus better, study better, learn more. We don't have the bloodlust thing going on. The vamps just got it in their heads we were smarter, but I think it's just because they're so..."

"So what?"

"Popular."

She smiled at him.

"Popular equals less intelligent?"

"Sure, I mean, look at the dynamics of any regular school. It's not so much that the cool kids are stupid, as it is that the super smart kids are geeks and nerds. They're not into sports and cheerleaders. They're into science and debate and chess."

"Wait a minute, Cole. Are you saying being infected with the zombie virus turns you into a geek?"

He laughed. "I guess that's what I'm saying."

"Come on, geek," she said. "Let's swing."

Cole could feel his mouth stretched unnaturally into a wide grin but he couldn't pull it back no matter how he tried. He sat on the swing next to Livia's and backed up, let go and rushed forward into the wind.

"This is the girliest thing I've ever done."

"Oh, come on, you must have swung when you were little."

"I swung when it wasn't girlie. Now it's girlie."

"Cole, I think using the word girlie is girlie."

They laughed together and suddenly Cole remembered why he'd gone to her house. If he asked her about the crosses and she confirmed what he knew must be true, he couldn't tell Principal Lute. He couldn't ask her to go to Lute and he couldn't have her called to see him. Slade would find out and make her life hell with the vamps. As he listened to her laughing, he decided he'd take five days after school detention.

CHAPTER SEVEN

In his book, *The Vampire Dilemma,* Dr. Arnold Krenske did his best to explain the seduction of the vampire. Years of cultural influence, he argued, had conditioned the general public to prefer a particular physique when it came to romance: the muscular ectomorph. Or better stated: the underwear model.

Something about the vampire virus thinned the body into a svelte line, amped up the eye color and edged it with a touch of burgundy, strengthened the bone structure in the face, and lengthened the muscles forming a graceful silhouette with a deadly edge, like that of a cheetah. All this, Krenske surmised, gave the vampire an allure like no other creature.

But a lean, poised appearance could not mask the basic problem facing the vampire: the rage of bloodlust. While Krenske touted his synthetic blood as a workable substitute, and indeed, insisted on the morality of the choice, he hinted in chapter six, "Taming the Beast," that once satisfied by the allure of true blood, the vampire may be an emotional wreck unless he repeatedly succumbed to his constant, nagging desire to feed.

The next night at school, spurred on by the sympathy they received from the regulars over the cross incident, the vamps were in rare form. They leered at zombies, spouted verbal threats, hissed as they passed them in the halls, and made howling noises at lunch.

"Howling?" Brock said as he sat in the zombie corner of the cafeteria.

They turned to look over at the vamp corner and caught sight of something hairy walking toward their table.

"Werewolf," Brock whispered.

He was carrying a cafeteria tray loaded with food, with Rachel and Winston following him to the zombie table. Average height, muscular, dressed in jeans and a gray t-shirt. No jacket. Covered head to toe in thick, brown fur. The regulars and magick all leaned back in their chairs at once, as if trying to get as far from the wolf man as possible as he passed them.

"This is Trevor," Rachel said, as if werewolves were an everyday occurrence.

Trevor smiled nervously and took a seat, letting his food-laden tray slide across the table.

"Mrs. Roddenberry gave him to us," Rachel said.

"Gave him to you?" Cole said.

"To take around, you know. Get him acquainted. It's his first day and he's the only one, you know."

Cole looked across the table at Brock and Brock looked back at Cole.

"Now try to tell me there isn't something seriously wicked going on," Brock said. "Werewolves?"

"I'm not a werewolf," Trevor said.

"He's not a werewolf," Winston said.

Rachel nodded in agreement.

"Dude," Brock said, "What the hell are you, then?"

"I have congenital generalized hypertrichosis terminalis."

Brock snorted with laughter and then pulled his face
into a concerned pinch. "You what?"

The werewolf sighed, annoyed. "You can call it
CGHT. I have an extra bit of DNA that causes me to be
hairy all over. Okay? I'm not a werewolf. I don't howl at
the moon."

Another round of howls emanated from the vamp
table in the opposite corner and the wolfman rolled his
eyes.

"Dude," Brock said to Cole. "Do you know what this
means?"

"A conspiracy?"

"No, man. It means that this school is turning into a
freak school. They're unloading all the freaks here."

"What's next?" Alan said. "Demons? Orcs? Cats with
wings?

"I'm not a freak. Not anymore than you are. It's in
my DNA."

"Isn't that what a freak is?" Winston said.

"That's enough," Cole said. "He's not a freak."

"Were you meaning to imply," Trevor said to Brock.
"That if I were, in fact, a werewolf, I would not be a
freak? But because I simply have a genetic disorder, I am
a freak?"

"No one's saying you're a freak," Cole said.

Trevor looked at him and pointed to Brock. "He is."

"Not anymore." Cole said. "No one is saying you're a
freak. Anymore."

Trevor smiled, baring large white teeth and Cole
thought he caught just a hint of sharp canines.

"I'd like an answer to my question," Trevor said.

Brock shrugged. "Maybe we're all freaks."

"That's more like it," Trevor said. He smiled again

and shoved a handful of tater tots in his mouth, growling as he chewed. With his mouth full of tater mush he said, "At least I'm alive."

"Okay, now you're just being an animal," Rachel said.

Another set of howls filled the room. Cole stood and said, "That's it, I'm saying something to them."

The sound of chairs scraping across the linoleum floor echoed through the room as the zombies stood up. They followed Cole across the room. The regulars grew suddenly silent, along with the two Franks, looking concerned and confused, and the magick who seemed to be whispering chants to themselves. The vamps continued to howl and giggle and make fake scared faces as the zombies approached.

"What's wrong with you?" Cole said to Slade. "Are you an imbecile?"

"What did you call me?" Slade took his arm off the back of Elena Worthington's chair and the front feet of his landed on the floor with a thump.

"I'm asking you," Cole said. "You've been in high school thirty years, now. Don't you think it's time to grow up?"

"What did he call me?" Slade looked around the tables at the vamps.

"Imbecile," Livia said.

Slade's face clouded with anger and he pushed himself out of his seat.

"What is it?" He said. His voice squeaked, bringing out a smattering of laughter around the room. "What does it mean?"

Cole rolled his eyes. "It means, are you stupid?"

Slade struck a pose, his feet spread apart, one forward, one slightly back. He lowered his chin and turned his head to one side and glared at Cole, the red in his eyes deepening. The other vamps stood, except for

Livia, and did their best to pose threateningly. Livia shook her head.

"That's the last time you call a vamp stupid," Slade said.

"Rick Slade, please come to the office," Mrs. Roddenberry's voice squeaked over the intercom and Slade ducked instinctively, looking around at the ceiling.

"Rick Slade," Mrs. Roddenberry repeated, "please come to the office."

Slade grimaced and pointed his finger at Cole. "I'll deal with you later. You guys just keep howling. Make the werewolf feel right at home." He slung his backpack over his shoulder.

"He's not a werewolf. He has congenital generalized hypertrichosis terminalis." Rachel said.

"Yeah, so?" Slade said and walked away.

Cole shook his head wearily, taking a moment to look at the vamps, careful to avoid Livia's face, before turning back to the zombie corner of the room. The rest of the lunch hour passed without howls.

After school, Cole met his friends in the cafeteria for their hour of detention. He set up his laptop while Alan plugged into his mp3 player and Winston opened up his copy of *The Hitchhiker's Guide to the Galaxy* and began to read. Bill and Kyle set up a chess board and Brock leaned back in his chair, his feet stretched out under the table. He tucked his left arm behind the back of his chair and lay his right across the table in front of him. He tapped, tap, tap, tap, at the table with a pencil.

The door burst open and Rick Slade stalked in. Cole rolled his eyes.

"Great. What are you doing here?"

Slade said nothing but stomped over to his corner of the room and plunked himself down heavily into a chair. He sat and stared at Cole for an entire hour. Cole could see him out of the corner of his left eye and pretended not to, but the effect was that he couldn't concentrate at all on his research. He was in the zombie lounge on the Viral Episodes website, trying to post a question about the history of the vamp and zombie outbreaks as it concerned the Welsh Corporation and the magick, but when he hit the post button, he wasn't sure exactly what he'd written. Unnerved, he clicked on his own post and reread it several times, his face struggling to find enough blood for a blush.

Finally, he shook his head, closed the laptop and slammed his hand down on Brock's tapping pencil.

"Enough," he said.

Mrs. Roddenberry entered the room, her fat feet stuffed into red high-heeled shoes. "It's three-thirty, you can go home now," she cheeped.

Cole waited until Slade left before standing.

"Are we going to have to do five days of detention with Slade?"

"Maybe he confessed to sharpening the crosses. Maybe we don't have to do five days." Alan said.

"Dream on, man." Brock said.

Cole and Brock walked through the empty hallways to the front door, and down the front steps into the early morning chill.

"Cole," a loud whisper came from behind him.

He turned to find Livia, carrying her backpack by the strap. A gentle, cold wind lifted her hair from the right side of her pale face.

"Livia," he said, surprised. "What are you still doing here?"

Brock turned sharply to Cole, his eyes wide and his mouth open. Cole knew he was grinning like an moron, but he couldn't stop himself.

"My mom can't get me until three-thirty." She said.

80

"You need a ride? What happened to Darlene?" He'd started bouncing slightly on his toes and Brock's brow furrowed.

"She didn't come to school today."

"Where's Kevin? Doesn't he ride with her?"

Brock nudged him in the arm and Cole shook himself out of what felt like an idiot trance. What had he said? How bad did he look?

"He caught a ride with Stephan Hack." Livia said.

"Why didn't you?" Brock said; his tone was accusatory.

Kyle and Alan came down the front steps to join them. Alan stood next to Livia and looked slightly down at her with a leer. Winston and Bill joined them, dropping their backpacks to the ground and squirming into their jackets.

"What're you doing?" Winston said. "Planning something? Park? Or bowling alley?"

"Nah, it'll be dawn soon."

"Oh, ho," Winston suddenly realized Livia was standing with them. "Hello," he said.

"Livia, this is Winston, Bill, Kyle and Alan. You know Brock?"

"We haven't met, no," she said and smiled around at the group. She shifted her weight several times and Cole sensed she was nervous. She seemed so small and thin with the zombies standing around her that way.

"See you guys tomorrow," Cole said. And he waited for them to take the hint and leave. But they all stood there looking at him like zombies.

"Don't you have to get home?" He said.

"No, not really," Alan said and turned again to Livia as if he were ready to pounce.

"Did you see Slade leave?" Brock asked Livia.

She nodded.

"Do you know anything about his detention?" Cole said.

"They did a locker search in the vamp hall and found a knife in his locker."

"So, students are allowed to have weapons in case of a zombie outbreak or a feral attack."

"This was a little pocket knife," she said. "Wouldn't do anybody any good on one of you guys."

"So he got detention?"

"Something about that doesn't make sense," Brock said.

"Don't think too hard on it. Maybe it's some evidence against him."

"Against him for what?" Livia said.

"Sharpening the crosses."

She said nothing.

"Do you know anything about it?" Brock said.

"Who me? No."

"But when you saw the crosses, they weren't sharp, were they?" Brock said.

"I don't think so," she said.

"Well, why don't you go tell Mr. Lute." Winston said.

"She's not going to do that," Cole said.

"Why not?"

"Yeah, why not?" Livia said. "Is that why you're in trouble?"

"No," Cole said. "We'd still get detention even if they weren't sharpened."

"But less detention." Brock said. "And everyone would know we didn't sharpen the crosses."

"I'm pretty sure they weren't sharp when I saw them."

"They weren't," Brock said. "Because we didn't hang sharpened crosses."

"Rick sharpened them then?" Livia said.

82

"Of course he did." Cole said. "And I'm sure Mr. Lute believes he did. But he can't do anything about it without some evidence."

"That must be why they got him for the pocket knife," Alan said.

"Well, I can go tell—"

"No, you can't." Cole said.

"Why not?" Brock said, angry now.

"It'll get her in trouble with Slade."

"So what?" Brock said. "He's nothing but a poser."

Cole shook his head.

"He wouldn't know I told," Livia said.

"He'll know. He'll find out." Cole said. "Don't worry about it. It's just detention. It's no big deal."

"For you, maybe." Brock mumbled.

Headlights hit them and they turned to see Mrs. Duvessa waving in her SUV with a worried smile. The window slid down and she called out, "Let's get you out of here, Livia. Come on now. Quickly."

"Well, I have to go now. Thanks for waiting with me. It was nice meeting you all."

Alan grunted and Winston nodded.

"Next time, you know, I can take you home, if you want." Cole said.

Brock nudged him again, gave him a wild-eyed stare, and stalked off to Cole's car shaking his head. Cole found him sulking in the front passenger seat when he got in and started up the engine.

"I'm as frozen as a corpse. Where's the heat?" He said.

"Sorry." Cole reached for the control and turned the heat up as far as it would go. "It'll take it a while to warm up."

"It's blowing cold air on me," Brock complained.

"Make up your mind." Cole said. "On or off."

"What were you doing?" Brock said once they were on their way to his neighborhood. "She's a vamp. We should have groaned at her and faked being full zombie or teased her about the dark circles under her eyes or made bat noises—"

"What are you, twelve?"

"Anything. We're zombies, she's a vamp. And we're standing around talking to her like she's—"

"She's just like us."

"She is not like us. Not at all. For one thing, man, she's a vamp. She's a snob. She hangs around with Rick Slade, who by the way, will make our lives hell if he finds out we're making friends with his vamps."

"Are you afraid of Slade?"

"It's not about being afraid, which I'm not. It's about having to listen to them hiss and laugh and tease and make really stupid jokes. I just want them to leave us alone. And she knows! She knows Slade sharpened the crosses."

"She doesn't know."

"I saw the look on her face, man. She knows. And she offered to tell Lute and you told her not to. I can't believe you told her not to."

"Slade may be stupid, but he's mean. He's not just mean to us, he's mean to them, too. I told you what he did to me the other night."

"He didn't hit you or anything; you said so."

"He might have."

"Might have." Brock shook his head, tired. "All your talk about zombie pride and trying to get Alan in line and now you're drooling all over some trampy vamp."

Cole put on the breaks and Brock fell forward into his seatbelt.

"What did you call her?"

"She's just a vamp, man."

"That doesn't make her a tramp."

"It rhymes, that's all."

"I know it rhymes. You made it up when we were in sixth grade. Sixth grade, Brock. Don't you see–?" He stopped and looked in the rearview mirror at approaching headlights. He pressed on the gas and headed for Brock's street.

"See what?"

"You gotta help me with the research. I have too much homework and my mom and Craig gave me a chore list a mile long and I don't have the energy for it all."

"See what?"

"See that we're stuck here. We're stuck at seventeen for the rest of our lives. Longer. I want to find out the truth. If it's the magick, I want to know. Maybe we can do something about it."

Cole pulled his car into Brock's driveway. Brock put his hand on the door handle and turned to Cole.

"I was just joking, really. About the magick. I don't really think there's some kind of world domination conspiracy. It just is what it is."

"Why did they have the blood already...before the vamps starting showing up?"

"The Welsh Corporation invented it."

"Why?"

"Who knows? Who cares?"

"I care."

"It won't change anything. You'll still be stuck at seventeen forever."

"Maybe."

After a pause, Brock said, "Do you think after you're, like, fifty, your mom can still make you do chores?"

Cole stared at him.

"I mean, 'cause you're still sort of...seventeen?"

Cole said nothing and Brock got out of the car, passed in front of his headlights and disappeared.

Brock said little to Cole throughout the next week, even over the weekend he was conveniently out of town. Monday and Tuesday detention went the same as the week before, with Slade coming into the room, pausing for an evil pose, and sitting in the vamp corner staring menacingly at Cole for an hour.

Every morning Cole took Brock home, but Brock didn't say much even then. During the excruciating trips Cole did his best not to think of Livia Duvessa, knowing that Brock assumed that was exactly what he was thinking about. Instead, he thought about Brock's question—about being seventeen forever, and watching his mother and Craig grow old. One day, they would die and he'd still be seventeen. Would he always feel like seventeen? Or would he start to feel old and tired? Could he, he wondered, stop taking his pills, go full zombie and hope someone would whack his head off before he hurt anyone? Then it would be over. Or would he be too chicken and instead be forced to live forever alone, wandering the earth undead, never-ending, all by himself, with nobody else? Well, with Brock.

On Tuesday morning, the zombies waited in the cafeteria at three-thirty and watched Slade leave.

Alan sighed. "I really hate that guy."

"What are we afraid of?" Winston said.

"Who says we're afraid of him?" Brock said.

"Then why are we sitting here waiting for him to leave the school before we go outside?"

Cole shrugged. "It's not fear."

"Exactly," Alan said. "It's just hatred. I'm sick of watching him and his posse leering at us."

"Whatever," Winston said.

"Nobody's stopping you from leaving," Brock said.

Winston shook his head slowly with a smirk. "Well, is it safe? Can we go now?"

"Oh, all right," Cole said, pushing his chair back and standing. "Let's go."

"I'm riding home with Alan tonight," Brock said as they walked down the front steps of the school and across the lawn.

Cole looked at Alan who didn't look back.

"What for?"

"He lives closer to me," Brock said.

"Are you mad or something?" Cole said.

"Nah, man. I'm just riding home with Alan today, that's all."

Cole stood in the damp grass in the dark morning air and watched as Brock got into the back seat of Alan's car. Bill got in the front passenger seat and Alan opened the driver side door and without looking up, got in and started the engine.

"I'd be your ride buddy," Winston said. "But you know I work most days at my mom's shop. Unless you want to hang out there for a while. It's mostly old people; not much to see. But once in a while we get a cute girl in for a new one."

"No thanks."

Winston's mom ran a Skin Like New shop over on Toronto Boulevard. She matched patches for zombies and custom dyed the harder shades of gray. Very boring.

Cole watched Alan's car leave the school parking lot and nodded a good-bye to Winston. He shook his head back and forth obsessively as he walked to his own car and got in. He drove down Fifth Street alone, fuming, trying to figure out what was wrong with Brock all of the sudden. There was an empty sort of pit in his chest and he seemed to remember feeling it before, but he wasn't sure when. It hurt. And it angered him.

Ahead, in the dim light of the street lamps, he saw two figures walking along the sidewalk. He slowed the car and recognized Livia and Kevin Oder. He pulled off the road into the grass along the sidewalk and waited for them to approach his car. Kevin glared at him, his eyes glowing pink in the darkness.

Cole pushed the button and the window on the passenger side slid slowly down.

"Walking?" He said.

Livia leaned on the window frame and smiled in at him.

"Darlene wasn't in school again today and we missed our bus."

"It was your fault," Kevin said from behind her.

"How was it my fault?"

"You didn't know which bus was ours."

"Neither did you." She looked back into the car at Cole. "My mom drove us this morning but she had to go to Glenwood Springs and won't be back for a while."

"Why didn't you wait for me to get out of detention? I can drive you."

Livia shook her head. "We waited for Slade." She glanced sourly at Kevin. "But he wouldn't give us a ride."

"He had to go somewhere important," Kevin said. "He couldn't help it."

"Well, come on. I'll take you home."

"Great," Livia said and opened the door. She slid into the passenger seat and looked out at Kevin. "Get in," she said.

"No thanks. I'll walk."

"Aw, come on," Cole said.

He left the car idling for a minute, waiting. Kevin didn't get in, but he didn't start walking either.

"Look," Cole said. "You can lie down in the back so no one will see you and I'll drop you off wherever you want."

Kevin looked around like a guilty kid with a cookie. "There's a wooded lot at the entrance to Noche de Sangre."

"All right, come on, let's go."

Nervously, Kevin took another look around and waited until no cars were approaching. He ducked down low, pulled the back door open and jumped in, slamming the door behind him with a clanky thud.

Cole looked to Livia with grin and a shake of his head. "Do you want to lie down, too?"

"No thanks.

He pulled the car back onto the road and headed for Noche de Sangre.

"Is Darlene sick?"

"Just sick of school, apparently. Kevin says she doesn't show up sometimes. She's bored. Did you know that most of the vamps were turned thirty years ago, when the whole thing started?"

"My parents told me."

"They've been in high school for thirty years."

"Well," Cole said with a smirk. "You gotta stay until you get it right."

"You should talk," Kevin said from the back seat.

"I've only been in a couple of years extra. I skipped the first year after I was infected."

"Are you going to stay in forever, too?" Livia said.

"Nah, this will probably be my last year. There were lots of classes I wanted to take."

She shook her head. "I just can't see staying in high school and acting like a–" she turned partially toward the back seat. "I mean, just staying in high school that long. Don't they want to move on?"

"What for?" Kevin said. "It's fun."

"Maybe college would be fun." Livia said.

"Nah, you just go to college to get a job and who wants to work, anyway?"

"Who pays the bills?" Livia said.

"The government," Cole said.

"You mean the tax payers."

He glanced at her with a smile.

"Gotta love that FEMA." Kevin said.

"That's only if your parents die, and you don't have enough to live on."

"The magick get it, too, which I find strange." Livia said.

Cole felt another surge of pride for her. Suddenly he was possessed by an overwhelming desire to stop the car and grab her.

"For now." Kevin said. "But since they found those girls..."

"What girls?" Cole said.

"Tina West was one of them." Livia said. "They found them out in the woods. Dead."

"Dead?" Cole said. "But she was one of the magick."

"I guess they're not so immortal, after all," Kevin sang from the floor of the back seat and then laughed.

"They never claimed to be undead, did they? Just magic." Livia said.

Cole shrugged and checked the rearview mirror; he caught sight of Kevin and Kevin ducked back down onto the seat.

"Nobody even asked them to prove they're magic. They were taking advantage of a national crisis, in my opinion."

Cole pulled off the road into the wooded lot fifty yards from the Noche de Sangre welcome sign.

"Are you sure you don't want me to take you farther in?"

"No, here's fine," Kevin said, slipping out the back

door. "Thanks for the ride," he whispered, closed the car door and darted into the trees.

Cole continued on to their neighborhood, driving along Park Avenue.

"There's Darlene's car," Livia said as they drove by River Rapids Park.

"Did you want me to let you off here?"

"No, I'll go home with you."

Cole liked the way that sounded and when he pulled his car into the driveway he said, "My mom's not home yet. You want to come in?"

"Sure," she said. She followed him into the house.

As they went upstairs Cole said, "So, what happened to Tina?"

"Ferals," Livia said.

"They killed her?"

"And her sister and another girl."

"Why didn't we hear about it? Was it on the news?"

"Rick told us at lunch today," she said.

He turned to her once they were in his room and watched her as she looked around. He stopped worrying about Tina West and started wondering if he'd written her name anywhere or drew a heart with an arrow through it and put it on the wall. He wasn't sure why he'd do that sort of thing, but he knew he'd been acting out of character since he'd seen her that day she moved in across the street.

His room looked childish when he saw it from her eyes. His AC/DC and Metallica posters were inane, and his curtains and bedspread for a six-year old. He lifted his shoulders and offered her an apologetic smile.

"Your desk is a mess." She said taking a seat on the edge of his bed.

"I'm in the middle of a project."

"For school?"

He shook his head. "I'm researching the history of the viruses."

"Really? What for?"

"Brock suggested the magick might be responsible."

She laughed. "The magick? You mean, like, it's a spell or something?"

"That would be silly."

"So, what do you think?"

"I never thought there was much to the magick. Brock just likes to get me involved in all these conspiracy theories."

"Sounds a little wacko."

"He's not so bad. He said he was just joking, really. But. Well, come on, I'll show you some articles I found on the early vampires. You might find them interesting."

Cole rifled through the printouts on his desk looking for the news article about the first discovery of vampirism.

"Here it is," he said, handing her the papers. "I thought it was weird that the early attacks by vampires were very isolated. Now the media says most have been turned through contracting the virus accidentally."

"Accidentally?"

Cole sat at his desk across from her. "Exactly." He said. "Everybody has this idea that we can catch vampirism like a cold. But nobody thinks of zombiism that way."

"True."

"What do the vamps think?"

She bit her lip and let her pink-tinged eyes wander the room. "It's sort of something they don't want us to talk about, I think."

"Why not?"

"I don't know. I guess they want people to think you could catch it."

92

"But you have to be bitten, don't you?"

"I'm pretty sure." She nodded. "But we don't really know for certain."

"If it only spreads through the bite, though, then there are a lot more ferals than we think. And that makes me wonder how it all really got started."

"How could you find out?"

He looked at her carefully. "Somebody has to know." He turned to his computer. "I've been posting on this zombie message board," he found himself saying, absent mindedly.

"Oh?"

"Yeah, but so far everybody ignores me. It's like nobody wants to know."

"Maybe they don't."

"But isn't it more frightening not knowing?"

She shook her head. "If you can't just catch vampirism, it would be like random acts of violence. That scares people. So, maybe we don't want confirmation of that."

"But what if it's not random?"

"What do you mean?"

"What if some of the turnings are calculated."

"Calculated. You mean, someone is choosing people to turn?"

He nodded.

She laughed. "And you accuse Brock of involving you in conspiracy theories?"

He smiled and turned back to the computer. Maybe she was right.

When Livia went home, Cole raced back upstairs to log onto the Viral Episodes website. He entered the zombie lounge and started to scroll down to his post on the virus history. It was buried under the newer posts, but he found it—the thirty-second post down. Someone had replied. Cerebellum34. He clicked on the title and read Cerebellum's response: "Have info for you. Can you meet me in Darkspur?"

Cole sat back in his desk chair and stared at the monitor for a while, rereading the brief message. He could almost hear his mother's voice in his head warning him about meeting strangers online. But this was different, wasn't it? There wasn't any conversation. It wasn't like he was in an open chat room. It was the zombie lounge under a heading about history. How sinister could the guy be? Nobody asked him if he was a girl or a guy, or how tall he was, or what he was wearing or anything like that, at all.

So, it seemed to Cole that it was just as risky for the guy as it would be for him, to meet somewhere in Darkspur.

Cole replied that, yes, he could meet somewhere in Darkspur.

CHAPTER EIGHT

Pay attention," Rick said, again.

But Todd was having trouble focusing. The hollow pit in his gut trembled and his canines ached.

"Okay, okay," he said. "I don't leap. I move in slow."

"After the seduction."

"Right, right."

In the street in front of Stephan's house, Todd sat on the hood of Stephan's car. Rick had spent twenty minutes lecturing him on how to seduce and turn a regular, while Stephan paced in front of them in the dark, kicking up tiny rocks off the asphalt. Elena, pale as vanilla ice cream leaned against Rick's Jag admiring her fingernails and Ciara Wister, dark with leering lips, stood motionless, glaring. Her brother Liam and a group of older vamps had wandered down the street whispering; Todd was sure they were laughing at him.

"Then it's one or two long drags, and that's it. You let go."

"Just like that." Todd said.

"Just like that. Nothing to it."

"Then what happens?"

"They pass out, usually."

"Not always," Ciara said.

Rick turned to her and then back to Todd with a smile. "Sometimes they slap you and run off screaming."

"I wasn't screaming," Ciara said. "I was cursing. There's a difference."

"But what if I want more?" Todd said.

Rick's shoulders sagged and he rubbed his palms on his forehead.

"Todd. If you want more, you find another vict—er, willing participant. There are plenty of them around. Even in Darkspur."

Todd nodded slowly. A cold wind hit his face, sending shivers through his chest. He needed to feed now.

"I'll try." He said. "Can we just do it?"

"Are you sure you've got it? One or two long drags. And then you let go."

He nodded. "Got it."

"Where to?" Stephan said. "Mall?"

"I hate the mall," Rick said.

"Yeah, trying to get people to go out by the dumpsters is so lame." Ciara said.

"Where else can we go?"

"What about that park over on Magpie?"

"Nah, there's always a bunch of kids there." Stephan said.

"You got a problem with kids?" Rick said.

"I think we should stick to adults."

"He's right," Elena said.

"We should turn whoever we want."

"Can we just go?" Todd said. He jumped off the

96

hood of Stephan's car and walked to Rick's Jag. "Come on."

Grudgingly, Rick agreed. Todd was forced to give Elena the front passenger seat and sit smashed between Ciara's brother Liam and one of the older vamps in the back seat.

He smiled up at the old guy.

"Todd." He said, trying to hold out his hand for a shake. The man leered at him and bared his fangs.

"Okay," Todd said.

That was the way with the older ones. At first Todd thought it was because he was...well, a nerd. He imagined that as the coolness factor developed in him, the gray guys would loosen up and start treating him like he was one of them. But he realized quickly that these elderly dudes rarely spoke, even to Rick. They just hung around, watching, listening. They freaked Todd out. They'd pose, their heads tilted just a bit to one said, but their eyes would move back and forth to other vamps as they spoke. Secret Service men. That was who they reminded him of. The vamps, he reasoned, had a Secret Service of old dudes.

With Stephan and Ciara following in the other car, Rick drove once around Darkspur until he settled on the small patch of woods outside the hospital where nurses escaped to a splintered picnic table for cigarette breaks.

"Smokers smell awful." Ciara said.

"Don't taste so great either," Stephan said.

"Drink your synthetic, then," Todd said. "But shut up and let the rest of us feed."

Stephan turned to Rick, his mouth open in protest, but Rick was silent, and the old guy said nothing. They huddled in the bushes until two nurses, gabbing and laughing, came into the small clearing hidden from the hospital and sat at the table.

"Remember," Rick said. "Just approach casually and strike up a conversation."

Todd grimaced and moved forward. He rounded the bushes and both nurses turned to him. The male was thin and gaunt, could have been a vamp himself. But the fear in his eyes told Todd he was regular. The woman was lush and plump. Her thick auburn hair pulled back in a bun at the back of her head.

"You scared us," she said, her voice trembling.

Todd said nothing. He felt Rick behind him. Then Stephan moved forward.

The nurses rose.

"That's okay," Rick said. "We didn't mean to bother you. Sit back down."

The nurses stood, staring at them, wide-eyed.

"We—uh—were just on a break. We'll be getting back now."

"No, really, it's okay," Rick said. "Have a seat."

"Oh, forget it," Todd said.

He had the female in his mouth before either could scream. He heard the scuffle as the others took down the male. As he drew the woman's blood he cradled her in his arms as if they'd been dancing and he'd pulled off a romantic dip—one arm around her waist, the other behind her head. The fingers of his left hand gently played at her hair. But her blood was bitter, like ash. He drank his fill and dropped her to the ground; her head bounced off the table's bench.

Turning to the others, Todd wiped a bit of blood from his lips. The old guy was looking at him with a bit of a smile.

"Aren't you hungry?" Todd asked him. But as usual, he said nothing.

"We did it again," Stephan said, dropping the male's wrist and standing.

98

"It's your fault," Rick said, still leaning over the nurse's neck.

"How is it my fault?" Stephan said.

"You should have left him all for me. I could have done it right if you weren't over there sucking on his wrist."

"What difference did that make?"

"I don't know. I felt like it was a race or something."

"You're telling me you killed the guy because you thought we were racing?"

"We both killed him."

They turned to Todd.

"What are you smiling at?" Rick said.

Z

Rick dropped Todd off at his house and he watched as the Jaguar roared down the street. When he turned, Wanda was standing in the yard, her arms crossed at her chest.

"I thought you weren't going to go out with Rick anymore."

"Why would you think that?"

"Have you been smoking?"

Todd laughed and walked past her up to the front porch.

"I mean it, Todd. You need to stop this or I'm–"

"What? You going to tell on me like a three-year old?"

"You're not taking my toys, Todd. You're running with a pack of ferals. Who'd you turn tonight?"

"None of your business."

"I'm telling."

Todd sucked in a breath and let it out slowly.

"Okay," he said and tried to look defeated. "I won't hang out with them when they hunt. But I like Rick. I'm glad he's my friend."

"You promise you won't hunt with them?"

He smiled. "Promise." The taste of blood and cigarettes tingled on his tongue.

Z

Cole waited to hear back from Cerebellum for three hours, long after his mother came home and the sun rose, but there was no response. It wasn't until that evening before school that Cerebellum34 posted again. "Darkspur Mall, bench in front of fancy bra shop. Tomorrow, four a.m. Come alone."

Fancy bra shop? Cole thought for a minute and then remembered the one with the zombie mannequins posing in lingerie in the windows. Rachel had protested the mannequins; they were really just regular girl dummies painted gray. The shop owner then pasted patches on their faces and added a bit of drool with gel glue at the corners of their mouths. Cole and Brock thought they were hilarious; but Rachel wasn't amused.

That morning he was glad that Brock was riding home with Alan, and he didn't mind Livia coming along with him, until she started to sound like his mother.

"You're meeting some strange man?" She said, following him to his car after school.

"In the mall. It's not like I'm meeting him in a dark alley."

"But, you're still meeting him. He has your name and now he'll know what you look like. He could follow you home."

"What for?"

"To rob you, or whack your head off or something."

Cole laughed. "He just wants to give me some information about the history, that's all."

"Come on, Cole. You're a zombie, you're smarter

100

than that."

"You don't believe him, then?"

"I don't know. But I'd be very careful."

"You'll be there to protect me." Cole turned and smiled at her.

"You want me to hide behind one of those fake trees?"

"You could be shopping in the bra shop."

He caught her take a quick look down at her chest and then she shook her head. "I wouldn't want to be seen in there. I'll pick another store. And I'll be watching you. Still, be careful."

Cole smiled inwardly. He got behind the wheel and started the engine. Livia was talking about something: the mall, the cookies she used to get in Florida, a store with red shoes? He wasn't sure. Staring at them from the front steps of the school were the vamps, Slade at the front of the pack, his red eyes glowing. Livia, busy with her seatbelt, didn't see them there as he reversed the car and headed out of the school parking lot.

Just to be sure not to scare Cerebellum away, Cole had Livia go inside the mall first and followed ten minutes later. Darkspur Mall was open all night for the majority population and only closed from ten a.m. until three p.m. so the regulars could have the place to themselves while the night crowd slept. It was warmer inside than the autumn cold outdoors; zombies and vamps slung jackets over their shoulders, shopped and lounged along with the elevator jazz that filled the building. The smells of cinnamon and chocolate-chip cookies hung in the air, but naturally only a few regulars sat in the food court.

As he approached the bra store, Cole saw a man in a dark suit and tie sitting on the bench out front in between two fake ficus trees. He wasn't at all what Cole was expecting. He was clearly a zombie, for one thing. And somehow Cole was expecting Cerebellum to be underfed. As Cole approached, the man smiled, waved, and stood up. A woman joined him, carrying two shopping bags, and together they walked down the mall. Cole took a seat on the bench, looked around nervously, and waited. He caught sight of Livia in the record store opposite the bra shop, thumbing through CDs. He stared at her, knowing she wouldn't look up to catch him. She was trying hard to stay undercover. He smiled. Dark ringlets fell forward over her creamy face as she studied each CD.

"Don't look at me," a gruff voice echoed behind him.

Cole turned to look. "Huh?"

"I said don't look at me."

Cole caught sight of a bum with a long, gray beard, wearing a dumpy, yellow plaid coat, before he turned away. That was more like it, he thought. Malnourished and filthy. The old tramp shuffled around the ficus and took a seat at the other end of the bench. A strange mix of tobacco and camphor floated about him.

"I got what you're looking for," he said.

"Oh, sorry. I thought you were a guy I was supposed to meet. I don't do drugs."

"Shut the hell up," the man growled. He pulled a large manilla envelope from his coat and slid it across the bench at Cole. "Everything you need is in there."

Taking the envelope, Cole said, "How do you know what I need?"

"You asked, didn't you?"

"But I'm not even sure what I'm looking for."

"You'll be sure after you read all that."

Cole turned to look at him.

"Don't look at me," the man said and stood up. "My contact information is in the packet, but only use it if you really need to. I don't want any part of this, anymore."

102

Cerebellum shuffled off behind Cole and he turned to watch him.

"Stop watching me," the man shouted.

Cole turned back around quickly and smiled, nodding at the people staring at him. He opened the envelope and slid out a thick bundle of papers, held together at the top with several large paper clips.

"So what is it?" Livia asked, sitting on the bench.

"Art work?" Cole said and shook his head. The first page was a drawing of a vampire. He sighed. "I think that man was a little crazy."

"No kidding," Livia said.

"And I'm sure he was a vamp. A really old one."

As Cole drove them home, he felt awkward. He couldn't think of anything to say and she didn't seem to have anything to say either. He tried to stop feeling her presence in the passenger seat but all he could think of was touching her. If he let himself think about it long enough, he'd start imagining her brains in his hands and then he knew he'd start growling or something and that would freak her out. So he tried to think of other things. He counted the streetlights on Park Avenue; glanced repeatedly at the moon; felt her breathing a couple of feet away; how odd was that? He thought of Trevor, the wolf kid; what might happen to him in a full moon? He wondered what might be in the packet of papers the old man gave him; remembered the old man was insane. Felt her presence, as if it pulsated across the car to him; he was intensely aware of where her eyes were. She turned and watched the darkness outside pass by as he drove past vamp park. He could feel her. That was enough, he had to start talking.

"You know I heard this thing once."

"Yeah?"

He shook his head. "Never mind."

"No, what?"

"Well, I heard...it's some kind of philosophy thing, you know. It's stupid really."

"Just say it."

Cole rolled his eyes. Why the hell did he start talking? "Okay it goes like this: you speak, when you cease to be at peace with your thoughts."

"That's deep."

"You're teasing."

She smiled at him. "Maybe a little. It's ironic, is what it is."

"Ironic?" Cole realized he was more surprised by her knowing the word ironic than her knowing what he said was ironic. Suddenly, he was struck by the oddest thought. He'd been drooling over Livia, just like a regular vamp lover. Her hair, the dark circles under her eyes, her smudgy looking lips, her thinness and gaunt appearance. He was just like the regulars who followed them around and thought they were the coolest things in school. But now he realized that Livia was different. Livia was smart.

"Sure," she was saying. "You're telling me this great philosophical precept, and it fits you perfectly."

"You're saying I'm not at peace with my thoughts?"

"Were you?"

"No. That's what made me think of that saying."

"And yet, you had to say it out loud."

"I had to say something."

"Why?"

"To stop thinking." He turned to her and smiled.

"Is it the old man? Do you think the information he gave you will help?"

"I doubt it."

"There's probably nothing there, you know."

"I know. But it's curious."

"If it gives you something to do."

104

"What does that mean?"

She shrugged. "I don't know. I'm bored, I guess. Darlene and Jenny told me about some books to read, but they're just trashy vampire romances. I told them I wanted to read something substantive, like, I don't know, Dickens, and they just looked at me like I was stupid."

"Well, sure. They don't know what substantive means."

Livia laughed.

"Anyway, they always want to hang out at the park, but all they do is argue with the other vamps."

"They argue?"

"All the time."

"What about?:"

"They don't agree on things. Vamp things. To me, we're just infected, you know? We share a virus. But to some of them, we're like a special force to be used for good or evil. And they argue about whether we should be used for good or evil. And then there are the few of us who think we shouldn't all think alike and be one way or the other."

"Good or evil?"

"Yeah, some of them think the ferals are a good thing and that more people should be turned. They want a majority vamp population."

Cole slowed the car a bit and turned to look at her. "Are you serious?"

"Sure. Didn't you know?"

"Why would I know?"

"I don't know. I guess I figured it was common knowledge."

"It's not," he said. "What else do they think?"

"Well, just that, mostly. I mean, they say other things, but...just that. Mostly."

"Tell me. What other things?"

"I'm not sure I should be talking about it."

"Do they talk about killing zombies?" Cole wasn't sure where the idea came from but suddenly it was hard in his vision: the vamp population growing, rampages, turning others, and turning on zombies. Maybe the vamps were the ones who started the whole thing. But why zombies? Why would they create a zombie virus in the first place?

"I don't think they mean it. I think. Well, I think they get aggressive is all. When they talk about the pogroms and stuff."

"What pogroms?"

"Maybe there will be something about them in the old man's papers. He said he had history for you, right?"

"So, you're saying that the vamps think that they're a persecuted minority and they want to become a majority, so they can persecute the minority?"

"Well, when you put it like that. No. I mean. No, I don't think that's what's going on. It wasn't like that. Really."

"It is what they've been saying, isn't it?" He could tell by the furrow in her brow and the way she turned from him.

He pulled into his driveway and shut off the engine. They sat for a few seconds in silence.

"I guess some of them are saying things like that." She said quietly and looked down at her hands in her lap. "I guess I never really thought they were that serious. They're just letting off steam. It's not easy being a vamp, you know."

"I read the book."

"Then you know."

"Why didn't you say anything about this before?"

She turned to look at him. "Why?"

"You don't think this is bad?"

"I just said, they're just letting off steam. It's just teenagers talking."

"Thirty some-odd-year-old teenagers."

"So are some of your friends."

"None of them are that old. Rachel and Alan are maybe twenty five; but me and my friends aren't talking about turning people into zombies and taking over the world."

"Now you're talking stupid. That's not what they're saying. They're just spouting off you know. They're frustrated. Teens are always frustrated."

"Look if they're talking about killing zombies, you have to tell someone."

She rolled her eyes, but Cole was sure she was scared. "It's not like that. Really, it's not."

"You better be right." He opened his door and got out, slamming it shut.

"Don't be mad," she said closing the passenger door behind her.

"I'm not mad," he said. "I'm a little freaked, though."

"Come on. They're just talking. It's all talk."

"And you just sit there and listen to it?"

They walked to the back of the car and stood in his driveway.

"I argue with them. And I'm not the only one. There are a few of us who don't think the way they do."

"You should call the police."

"I'm not calling the police on my friends. What would the police do, anyway?"

Cole stared at her in the pre-dawn darkness. Maybe she was right. Once back in his room, he dropped himself in his desk chair and pulled the thick set of papers from the envelope. Some were index cards with writing and drawings scribbled on both sides, coffee-stained and covered with burnt spots. Some were what looked like architectural drawings, schematics, and doodles of rooms with too many doors. Others were drawings of zombies, vampires, and Franks, but not the two Franks Cole knew from school. And still others were yellow legal pages covered completely in tiny scrawling handwriting top to bottom, sides, margins, arrows pointing this way and that to other lines.

Cole tried to read it. "Took tea into the lab," he said, trying to make out one line. "Tasted cough won dog?"

Cole tossed the stack of papers onto the floor beside his desk. Cerebellum34 was insane. Clearly.

CHAPTER NINE

The murders of Tina West, her sister, and another girl erupted all over the news the next evening before Cole left for school. His mother stood in the kitchen at the bar sipping coffee from her mug, staring across the room at the television and shaking her head.

"So close to home," she muttered and sipped again.

"And dead," Craig said. He leaned in to kiss his wife on the cheek and smiled at Cole before heading off for an evening of work.

His mother shook her head again and turned away. "I just don't get it."

"What?" Cole said.

"Well, they're dead. All of them. Some ferals got to them and, well..."

"Sucked them dry."

She turned to him and glared.

"Sorry. But they've killed before."

"Yes, they have, but not like that. Before we've always assumed it was an accident. Groups were turned and one might happen to fade away and die from lack of blood. But all three? And the brutality of it. They say that the girls appeared to have put up quite a fight."

Cole turned to the television. It was odd, he had to admit.

"So what do you think?" He asked.

She shook her head again. "I don't know what to think, really. But it scares me. You make sure to keep an eye on Livia."

"What does Livia have to do with it? She's already turned."

"I know. But something about all this worries me. I can't explain it."

When he arrived at school an hour later, Cole stood in the main hallway staring at the walls. They were covered with brightly colored poster boards, pink, blue, yellow, and green. He stared at the first one he'd seen as he entered school. "Fight descrimmination of Vamps," it read. "Stop teaching about Vlad the Impaller."

"They're all over the school," Brock said, appearing beside him. "They've learned some new words."

"They spelled discrimination wrong," Cole said.

"They didn't get many of the others right either."

Cole walked to his locker, reading the posters along the way. "Oppression? Bashing? Stop the hatred against vamps? What the hell?"

Brock laughed.

"And they want all the vamps at a school board meeting for the vote. In the morning?"

"Amazing isn't it?" Brock said. "They're turning into activists. Like you." He nudged Cole in the arm.

"But they can't do this."

"I'm sure they got permission."

"No, I mean, the school board. They can't have this vote without letting us know. Nobody's prepared. Come on, we need to see Mr. Lute."

Mr. Lute was standing just outside his office door, as if expecting them. When he saw Cole, he put his hands up defensively and shook his balding head.

"They have the right to put up posters," he said, absent-mindedly pressing his Skin Like New patch against his nose with his thumb and forefinger.

"And so do we." Cole said.

"Of course you do."

"But you should have told us about this meeting when you found out, before they put the posters up. They have the advantage."

Mr. Lute frowned. "It's not my job to keep you up on school board meetings. It was posted on the school board website."

"How did the vamps find out?"

Mr. Lute lifted his shoulders and shook his head. "Rick's dad is the mayor, you know."

"You could have called me."

Cole started to continue the protest, but Mr. Lute's cell phone rang and he held up his hand again to end the conversation and disappeared into his office.

"Boys?"

Cole turned to see Mrs. Roddenberry standing timidly behind the office counter, her hair up in one of those old-fashioned buns and her reading glasses hanging from a beaded chain around her neck.

"I thought you could use these." She held up poster boards. "I overheard the vamp plans this morning." She smiled and blushed.

"Thanks, Mrs. Roddenberry," Cole said, taking the posterboard and her markers.

Before first class, Cole and Brock had all the poster board handed out to the zombies, and even a few regulars who agreed to help. And when the bell rang after first period, they all stuck their posters on any blank spot they could find. "Stop censorship," most of them read. And Cole was sure to illicit promises from all the zombies that they would attend the school board meeting the next morning after school.

After art class, Cole walked with Livia to her locker.

"So, what was in the envelope?" She asked.

He shook his head and smirked. "The guy must be crazy."

"I hate to say I told you so."

"Are you going to the school board meeting?"

"If my mom wants to go; she's picking me up today."

They stopped at her locker and she worked her combination. Cole leaned against the locker next to hers and watched the concentration on her face. His insides awoke and churned slightly. He looked away and caught Slade, Stephan Hack, and Todd Quaid across the hallway glaring at him. Todd bared his fangs.

"I'll see you this morning then," he said.

She looked up at him and smiled.

When Cole and Brock showed up at the meeting, the room at the Darkspur School Board facility was filled with parents and students. The vamps had taken their position in the front of the room on the right side. They all sat, posed, some on the backs of their seats with their feet in the seat, some slouched lazily, some with their hands resting on seat backs, or casually on top of their heads.

"Such posers," Cole said.

"Do you think Vlad the Impaler was really a vampire?" Brock said as they made their way through the crowd looking for seats.

"Nah. There weren't any such things as vampires until this weird virus started up. You know that."

"Maybe real vampires, yeah. But do you think he

112

drank people's blood?"

"He wouldn't be the first person in the world to do that."

"So, tell me again why we care if he's in the curriculum."

They trudged through a line of knees to empty seats in the middle of the room and fell into them.

"It's censorship."

"Are you sure you don't just like messing with the vamps?"

Cole turned to Brock and raised his brows. "I wouldn't do that."

"The old Cole wouldn't do that. But you're not him."

"I am so me. Who else would I be?"

"You're new Cole."

"Maybe I'm tired-of-taking-vamp-crap Cole."

Cole caught sight of Rachel, Winston, and Alan across the room and waved. As everyone began to take their seats, Slade and his father strutted down the middle aisle to the front of the room.

"There's Mister Mayor," Cole said.

"They look alike," Brock said. "Do you think a vamp would bite his own kid?"

Cole turned to him, surprised. "What made you ask that?"

"I don't know."

"You should read *The Vampire Dilemma*."

"Why? Does it talk about them biting their own kids?"

"Yep. Krenske considers turning just like murder. The vamp takes the human life and replaces it with vamp life."

"Well, they're still alive."

"No, they're not."

"But technically, they're still alive."

"No, technically, they're dead. Effectively, they're alive."

"What difference does it make? They're walking around and talking and living. So how could it be murder?"

"I think that was Krenske's opinion."

"He's not a vamp is he?"

Cole held up his hand to quiet Brock as Superintendent Pullman called the meeting to order. The members of the school board sat at the front of the room on a raised platform behind a long desk. Pullman was in the middle, flanked on his left by Mrs. Standford and Mr. Drakes–vampires. On his right sat Horace Ackerman and Mrs. Lindell–zombies. Mr. Pullman was a long dead zombie, decayed and deep gray; his eyes were clouded over and he looked around the room with a grim smile.

Pullman seemed to relish in purposely calling up for discussion a long list of concerns having nothing to do with why the crowd was in attendance. New lockers for the middle school, new phys ed equipment for the elementary school. Considering there were only three schools in the school board's region, Cole was surprised at how long and boring the meeting was. Finally, the curriculum came up for a vote. The vamps all stood and formed a line down the center aisle, waiting for their turn to speak, while the zombies and their parents, along with a few regulars got in line behind them.

Mayor Slade's velvety smooth voice began.

"Thank you, ladies and gentlemen of the school board for listening to us. We just want positive, uh, vampirism for our kids in the public school. It's hard enough being a vamp, even though vampirism itself, mind you, is a great thing. But it's tough, you know, living with the, uh–" He paused to look at his palm for a moment. "Uh, stigma, that the regular and zombie people

114

have about it. Our kids need to know that vampirism is a good thing. And they need positive role models."

Mr. Slade droned on for three minutes.

"Our mayor is so...eloquent, don't you think?" Cole whispered to Brock.

Next, Mrs. Welderheim began her high-pitched rant. "Children should not be learned that they are monsters, come down from the likes of Vlad the Impaler. How will they form morals? How can they be good if we tell them that they are bad?"

"Touché," Brock snickered.

"This isn't going to work," Cole muttered. "They'll talk until noon and the meeting will be over."

Suddenly, without realizing even himself what he was doing, Cole strode up the line to the front and shouted, "Give somebody else a chance to speak."

Superintendent Pullman banged his gavel. "You're speaking out of turn, young man."

"We should take turns," Cole shouted, over the booing and hissing of the vamps. "We should go back and forth between the pros and cons."

There was mumbling among the five board members and nodding and shaking of their heads. Suddenly Pullman banged his gavel again and said, "Form two lines, for revising the curriculum on the left, against on the right."

Cole beamed at the vamps.

One of the older vamps shouted, "Which line is for what? Where do the vamps stand?"

There was much scuffling and arguing as the vamps figured out which line was the one they wanted and all settled down again.

"I believe that makes it your turn to speak, Mr. Bertrand," Pullman said.

Cole stepped up to the podium. He held up his hands

to the crowd and said, "Look ma, no crib notes," and began his speech, silencing the eruption of chuckling from the right side of the room.

"Three years ago, before I became a zombie and started attending Darkspur Night High School, the vamps stood before you, begging and pleading for more vampires in the history, literature, and science curricula. Their request was granted, and in addition to all we had to learn of the history of this fine nation," Cole winked at Mrs. Standford sitting next to Mr. Pullman, knowing how she loved her country. "We now had to learn about vampires throughout history. Many great works of literature have had to be shelved so we could read books with vampires in them. All to satisfy their apparent inferiority complex. And now they're back again." Cole waved his hand to the other line where the vamps leered at him. "Because they aren't content. Being ignorant of their own cultural history, they didn't realize that teaching about vampirism would mean teaching about the vile acts of Vlad the Impaler and Countess Bathory. They didn't realize that in the science curriculum we'd learn about the stupidity of the vampire myths in our culture and what people have done, and are doing again, in attempts to thwart the scourge of vampirism. They're not happy because vampires have turned out to be not as cool as they think they are."

With this, the vamps began shouting and spitting and Mr. Pullman banged his gavel again and again.

"They didn't realize that there are no positive vampire role models in history or literature," Cole shouted above the din.

Cole couldn't be sure where the fighting started or who threw the first punch, he only knew that people began screaming. The weak huddled to the floor and tried to crawl out of the melee while the foolish jumped on

116

whoever they saw who was not like them and began pummeling. Mr. Drakes crawled up onto the front desk and punched Mr. Pullman in the chest. Mrs. Standford jumped on his back and wrapped her arms around his face. He bucked and tried to swat her off his back and together they fell off the desk top. Somewhere someone was screaming, "What about Buffy? What about Buffy?"

Cole dodged a blow from Mrs. Welderheim, sending her spinning in her high heels and falling onto Rachel. Rachel had no choice but to push the woman off her where she was trampled by her own vamps. Cole grabbed at Rachel and pulled her out of the fray.

"Get out of here," he called to her over the noise.

"Cole," she screamed. "There's Livia."

Cole turned and saw her, her arms wrapped around her mother, climbing over the backs of chairs, working her way through the push of vamps trying to attack the center.

Cole pushed forward, dodging fists and elbows.

"Tie them up," someone was shouting. "Tie them up. We'll burn them right here."

"Why didn't we bring any hatchets," he heard someone call out.

"Livia," he shouted. He watched in horror as she was elbowed in the face. Her mother began shrieking, lifting her arms over her head. She fainted and fell into the crowd toward the floor.

Cole finally made it to them and pulled Mrs. Duvessa off the floor, flinging her over his shoulder. He put his arm around Livia and led her toward the outer edge of the crowd. Mrs. Duvessa awoke and started screaming and pummeling his back with her fists.

"Don't eat me, please, please, don't eat my brains," she shrieked.

Cole dragged Livia out the front doors into the dark

morning and dropped Mrs. Duvessa unceremoniously onto the grass.

"I don't want your brains. I'm trying to help you."

She cowered before him on the damp lawn of the school board building and began to cry.

"Haven't you done enough?" Livia tore into him. He felt a blistering slap across his face.

"What did I do?"

"Oh, like you didn't intend for this to happen? How could you? People could die in there."

"There aren't very many regulars *in* there."

"What about the burning? They're going to tie us up and burn us."

"No they're...don't be ridiculous."

But from behind the doors, Cole heard screaming and shouting and large pieces of furniture landing on what he hoped weren't heads. He darted back into the room and stared at the scene. They'd lost their dead minds. Even Brock and Rachel were beating up on vamps. Regulars were cowering in the corners at the front of the room. Suddenly Cole caught site of the only person in the room who was calm. Mr. Hood, the gym teacher, stood in the back corner, his left foot crossed casually over his right, leaning against the wall smoking a cigarette.

There's no smoking allowed in the building, Cole thought. He ran to Mr. Hood and grabbed his cigarette.

"Hey."

"Light another one," Cole shouted. "Come on."

Cole dragged Mr. Hood along the outer edges of the fight to the front of the room and climbed onto the long desk.

"Hurry," he shouted. Mr. Hood followed him.

Mr. Pullman was now lying on the desk, playing dead. Cole started to push him off, but realizing what Cole was up to, Mr. Hood pushed him back and stood on top of

118

Pullman's chest, holding his cigarette up to the smoke detector overhead. Cole climbed aboard Pullman, grateful for his size and did the same.

"Smart kid," Hood said.

Cole smiled. "Zombie."

Suddenly they were bombarded with powerful sprays of water. Mr. Hood lost his balance and fell from Pullman's chest.

"Do you mind?" Pullman shouted at Cole.

The screams in the room settled to howls and people stampeded to the exit doors, of which, Cole gratefully realized, there were plenty. He turned to smile at Mr. Pullman, standing in the chaos of the school board's meeting room with a blank, wet expression on his face, before leaving the building. Outside, Cole searched through the dispersing crowd for Livia and her mother but he didn't see them.

"That was some speech," his mom said and she pat him soundly on the back as she passed. "I'll see you back at the house."

"Well, I didn't mean to start a fight," he called after her.

"Uh-huh," she said without turning around.

"You want a fight?"

Cole turned to find Slade posing for a gunfight, his hands hovering over nonexistent pistols in a nonexistent holster around his hips, his elbows holding back his long, dark coat; his dripping hair glistened softly in the school board building's outdoor lighting. Several of the other vamps were behind him, dripping. Cole smiled. Wet vampires.

"I said," Slade sneered. "Are you looking for a fight?"

"No."

"You've insulted us for the last time," Elena Worthington said and bared her fangs.

"Whoah, hoah, put those things away. You don't want to bite the undead You'll hurt yourself."

"You zombies think you're so smart." Ciara Wister said.

"We are smart," Brock said over Cole's shoulder and Cole realized his friends were gathering behind him.

Rachel said, "Cole has a right to speak his mind. If you're insulted, too bad."

"You're asking for it, man." Slade said. "And I'm gonna give it to you."

"That's enough, boys," Mr. Hood called out.

The vamps turned and behind them Mr. Hood and several parents and teachers stood with their arms folded across their chests, drenched and furious.

"Go on home." Mr. Hood said.

Slade leered at Cole and stormed off, the rest of the vamps following him soggily, their wet jeans squishing at their thighs and their shoes sloshing with each step.

"And for the record," Mr. Hood called after them. "Buffy was a vampire *slayer*. Not a vampire." He shook his head. "Idiots," he mumbled and turned to leave.

The zombies stood silent until the vamps vanished around the building.

"Why do you have to start things, Cole?" Alan said. "It's bad enough with the vamps, you have to keep stirring them up."

"He has a right to protest," Rachel said.

"Protesting's one thing. But you called them ignorant. You said vampirism is a scourge. You said they were uncool."

"So?"

Rachel sighed. "You could learn a little bit of tact."

"Maybe we all need a dose of truthful confrontation," Cole said, walking toward the parking lot. "Maybe everybody needs to see just what the vamps are made of."

120

"But maybe they're just as mean as they seem," Alan said. "And maybe somebody will end up hurt, or worse."

Cole turned to Alan.

"You're the one always telling us to hate them, to stop them, not to let them keep us down."

"But not by pissing them off."

"Then how?"

They all stood staring at him. Alan, Stu, and Bill glared in anger, while Rachel and Isabella shook their heads with worry. Winston dug in his pocket protector arranging the pens.

"We can't live in fear." He said. "I won't live in fear. And I won't live inferior to the vamps anymore."

Brock nodded. "No fear," he said, and walked into the parking lot toward Cole's car.

The others hesitated. Alan nodded and twisted his head back and forth as if for strength. Then they all moved forward, and followed Cole.

CHAPTER TEN

After he'd knocked her unconscious, and before he tossed the book into the hole on top of her, Todd flipped through the pages of his sister's copy of *The Vampire Dilemma*. What caught his eye was the word murder.

Murder, according to Dr. Arnold Krenske, was the act of forcefully taking the mortal life from a regular and drawing them into the vampire world through the bite and the drinking of their blood. Ah, good then, Todd thought. Burying Wanda in a hole in the back yard was not murder. She was a vampire, after all. Let her use her super vampire strength to dig herself out. If she still had any strength after he'd smacked her on the back of the head with the spade, anyway.

Lightning lit up the early morning darkness. Wanda's squirty dog yapped inside the house, its tiny paws scratching hopelessly on the sliding door. Wind whipped at Todd's hair and prickled the skin of his arms.

He'd shoveled most of the dirt back into the hole and onto his sister when he heard Rick Slade's Jaguar roar down the street and slow to a purr in front of the house. The horn sounded, sending birds scattering over the roof in the darkness. Todd dropped the shovel and ran around the house and into the street, waving like a lovelorn regular. He grimaced at the thought. When was the coolness going to wash over him? When would he be more like Rick?

Elena Worthington sat in the passenger seat, her usual sour look was tinged with rage, evident even behind her large, round Ray-Bans. Todd instinctively looked to the sky—it was four-thirty and still dark.

"What's going on?" Rick asked. He pulled his sunglasses up briefly to look Todd up and down.

"I was digging."

Rick nodded. "Come on. Change clothes. We're going out."

Once changed, lathered in a new dose of sun screen and wearing his cheap sunglasses, Todd stumbled across the front yard toward the car. He lifted his head a bit and peered under the dark-tinted glasses to see the ground beneath his feet and chastised himself. If he wanted to look cool wearing sunglasses in the dark, he'd have to learn to see through them. He crawled in the back seat between Stephan and Ciara; his face broke into a wide grin at Elena in the front seat. Her long, blonde hair was wet and slicked to her head. He turned to Ciara Wister and she looked down on him through her lightly tinted glasses. Ciara was dark as bitter chocolate, but her lips were deathly white as she frowned at him.

"What's with the smiling all the time?" Rick said, giving him an angry glance through the rearview mirror.

"Sorry."

But he couldn't seem to get the smile off his face. He was riding in Rick Slade's Jag again. And this time, he was sitting next to Ciara Wister, the most beautiful vamp in

124

school. And Elena Worthington was there, the second-most beautiful vamp in school, except maybe for Livia Duvessa. But Rick hated Livia, so Todd hated her, so she didn't count. Slowly, he began to realize that he was sitting between two very wet vampires, the dampness in their clothes seeping into his.

"We don't smile." Rick said. "The glare is part of our image. You're a vampire, for god's sake. Act like it."

"Yes sir," he said and cringed.

"Don't call me sir."

"Yes—" He stopped himself just in time. But at least the smile was gone. "Where are we going?"

"Revenge." Rick said.

"Where's that?"

"Huh?"

"I said where are we going and you said 'revenge.'"

"Yeah." Rick said. "We're out for revenge."

"For what?" Todd was eager to try out a new reason to suck someone's blood.

"The zombies."

"What did they do this time? Is that why you're all wet?"

"They insulted us." Rick said.

"For the last time," Elena said.

"What did they do?"

The vamps were silent and Todd thought maybe they were just stewing, reliving the grave insult that somehow soaked them and sent them away from the zombies and out looking for revenge. But the idea that they'd forgotten why they were mad didn't enter his head until Rick spoke.

"I don't remember exactly," Rick said. "But it was bad."

"Cole Bertrand said we were stupid. And other things. I didn't really understand it all." Elena said.

"He said we weren't as cool as we thought we were,"

Ciara said.

"That's right," Rick said, smacking his fist against the steering wheel. "He'll be sorry."

"All right," Todd said, drawing out the last syllable for cool effect. "So, where are they? What are we going to do to them?"

"We can't do anything to them, yet. But we will."

"Then what are we doing right now?"

"I told you. Revenge."

Rick drove through town and back several times and Todd began to feel a bit nauseated. He wasn't sure that Rick Slade knew what the word revenge meant. And that seemed odd, considering how many more years older than Todd he was. He wondered if the vamp virus somehow muted a person's vocabulary and he tried to remember if he had a good vocabulary or not. He needed a blood box, but he knew better than to ask Rick to stop at the store. Morning was breaking and a storm was looming in the sky. He leaned a bit to his left and whispered to Stephan.

"What are we looking for?"

Stephan shrugged and remained silent, but he looked as angry as Rick. Todd felt small next to Stephan, and oddly irregular. Stephan had a perfectly aligned face with a thin straight nose and neatly trimmed eyebrows. The regular girls called him Vamp Adonis. Todd felt another smile pulling at his lips as he imagined some of that adoration rubbing off onto him. He should try to walk the halls with Stephan more often.

Finally Rick pulled into the mall parking lot and stopped the car, shutting off the engine. He fumed for a moment.

"Well, I don't know where to go," he said. "It's Tuesday morning, almost daylight. Where can we find a secluded place with a few regulars where we won't be seen?"

"Is that how we're getting revenge?" Todd said, his eyes jerking from vamp to vamp. "Biting regulars?"

"It's as good a plan as any," Elena said.

"You know," Stephan said. "You're taking all the...what's that word?"

"What word?" Todd said, seeing a chance to discover if he still had a strong vocabulary or not.

"I don't know. It means, you know, when you do something, like, just do it. Without thinking about it a lot."

"Spontaneous?"

"Yeah, that's it. Rick, you're taking the spontaneousness out of this."

Todd grinned again. He still had it. He remained, basically, a nerd. Then he frowned.

"That's more like it," Rick said, staring at him again through the mirror. "Keep that look on your face all the time."

"So, what do you want to do now?" Stephan said.

"What? Aren't you mad anymore?" Rick said.

"Not really. It was maybe a little funny when you think about it."

"There's nothing funny about my hair." Ciara said. "Look at it."

Todd turned to her with his frowning face. She shoved at him with her shoulder and elbow.

"Get off me." She said and rolled her eyes.

"Well, I'm hungry," Todd said. "Let's get some boxes."

"We're not drinking fake blood."

"Well, where are you going to find fresh blood?" Stephan said.

"Let's go to that little park on Buckley Street." Elena said.

"In the zombie neighborhood?" Rick said. "It's so small."

"But other vamps will be at River Rapids." Elena said.

"Well, we wouldn't find any regulars there, anyway. Not this early." Stephan said.

"Yeah," Todd said. "At Buckley Park, we might find some people out walking their dogs or something."

"Old people," Rick said.

"Well, I'm hungry," Ciara said. "I don't care how old they are."

Rick shook his head sulkily and turned the ignition key. They drove in silence to the suburbs, along Park Avenue, and into the zombie part of town. Rick parked his Jag in the small dirt lot at the corner of Buckley Street and Redwood Drive, where a little playground and picnic tables sat empty.

"Great." Rick said. "There's no one here."

"I vant to suck some blood," Todd suddenly said and slapped a hand across his face.

"What are you, in kindergarten?" Ciara said.

But next to him, Stephan was shaking with silent laughter.

"I get light-headed when I'm hungry," Todd said. "I say weird things."

"Why is he here?" Ciara said.

"Look," Elena said. She pointed ahead, across the park.

Two people emerged from the trees on the other side of the playground with two dogs on leashes.

"We need more sun screen," Elena said.

Surprised at his own energy, Todd crawled over Stephan. "Let's go."

He pulled the driver's side door latch and pushed the door open. He was out before the others and across the park before they'd decided on their prey. Todd leapt on

128

the large one, sank his teeth deep into the man's neck and moaned with pleasure. They fell to the ground together, Todd landing on top of the old guy. After he'd drunk his first fill, he looked up, blood dripping down his chin and onto his shirt, and saw Ciara Wister sitting a few feet from him, the woman cradled in her arms. Ciara's hand gently pet the woman's hair as she greedily sucked the life out of her.

The old couple's dogs yapped and bounced against their leashes.

"This is so not cool," Rick said.

Todd smiled. This was beyond cool.

CHAPTER ELEVEN

In his article, "Love Lives of the Undead," published in *Glamour* magazine the previous year, Dr. Arnold Krenske laid out the difficulties in vamp and zombie dating. Zombies, he said, are calm and thoughtful, for the most part. But in love, unexpected surges of emotion can throw them into stupors in which their brains cease to function adequately. The difference between these love comas and the full zombie are slight and, therefore, great precaution must be taken not to whack the heads off your friends who may look like they've gone brain-crazy, but in reality, are only crushing on some zombie chick who excels in math.

The vamps, on the other hand, are always struggling to control their bloodlust and are more likely to fall in love with a regular, until they accidentally taste a bit of her blood. Once she's a vampire, her appeal is gone. Vamps, naturally, don't have that blood aroma that attracts the opposite sex. Love between vamps does happen, however, out of necessity.

Vamp and zombie girls, he emphasized, being more

powerful than regular girls, are to be respected. Do not cross a zombie girl, or she may whack your head off in a fit of passion. And he advised vamps never to break off a relationship near an open flame, no matter how small. Cole had to assume Krenske, though a regular, somehow knew this from experience.

Krenske said nothing about inter-undead dating. Cole didn't even notice the omission until now.

It was just dawn, the gray sky filled with potential snowfall, when Cole stepped out of his car in front of his house. His thoughts were still racing. What a fight. He'd never seen anything like it. Adults, teachers, board members, students, vamps, zombies and regulars all screaming and fighting and calling names. He smiled inwardly at the thought. Things were changing; he was sure of it. The vamps were losing their place as the coolest kids in school.

"Cole?"

He turned and saw Livia coming across the street, her arms wrapped around her waist, pulling herself tighter into her bulky sweater. He groaned suddenly with the urge to lunge at her and the taste of what he imagined must be brains filled his mouth—something like what he thought liver pate must taste like, with a burning tinge of whiskey in the aftertaste. He craved her. Slowly, he allowed himself to move toward her and met her in the road; he looked down at her pale face and worried eyes and his jaw set hard with desire for her skull.

"Are you okay?" He asked her.

She nodded and stared at him for a few seconds. "Why do you treat the vamps like this?"

"What do you mean?"

His craving was gone, shattered. She rolled her eyes and stared down the road toward the playground.

"You insult them every time you open your mouth."

132

"Maybe they need to be insulted for a change."

"I'm a vamp too, you know."

"But you're not like them."

"Maybe I am."

"No, you're not. They're snobs, Livia. You didn't grow up here. You haven't had to put up with their superiority act. They think they rule everybody. Slade especially. He's nothing but a pharmacist's son, but you'd think he was a prince the way he tries to boss everybody."

"Slade's dad is the mayor."

"The mayor of a po-dunk little town. Big deal."

"Have you no respect for anyone? Just because he's a vamp doesn't mean he's trying to take over the world."

"I'm not really talking about the world. I'm talking about Darkspur."

She rolled her eyes again. "Well, you could be nicer; that's all I'm saying."

"You're not listening to me." He threw his hands up and looked away from her. "We've been nice. And we've let them walk all over everybody. It's time to put them in their place."

"And what is their place, Cole? Huh? You think the zombies are better, don't you? You want the zombies to treat the vamps the way you think you've been treated. You want to humiliate them."

"I didn't say that."

"But that's what you're doing. You're no better than they are. And the way you think of them, is the way you think of me."

She turned away from him and moved toward her house.

"That's not true."

Cole reached out and grabbed her hand; sparks flew up his arm to his heart and it fluttered. He turned her back toward him, taking her by the shoulders. He stared into her amber eyes. He meant to say something—to tell her he didn't think of her at all the way he thought of the other vamps. She was nothing like them. She was special. But instead, he reached up, put his palm against her face and pulled her lips to his Cole's dead heart began beating like it used to. His blood came alive again and began to move through his veins sending a rush of energy to his brain. Her lips were cold against his, but her mouth was slightly warm and tasted like lavender and it thrilled him; what little feeling he still had on his tongue was intensified. He could feel her body against his, cold and hot at the same time and he shuddered.

Finally, he couldn't breathe any longer and they pulled apart, their foreheads touching, each one gasping for air, trying to adjust.

"You're not like them," he whispered.

She shook her head and looked into his eyes, smiling. "No, I'm not."

"Livia?"

She jumped and turned. Mrs. Duvessa stood on her front porch wrapped in a thick pink robe.

"Livia, it's daylight, you'll burn. Get in the house."

Livia smiled at Cole and turned to leave, their fingers grasping at one another until the last second. He stood in the street, his heart still beating, and watched until she was inside her house.

Z

Livia floated through the front door, unable to remove the deep smile from her pale lips. She could still feel Cole's cold lips on hers. She flopped onto the sofa, laid her head back and closed her eyes.

"Snap out of it," her mother yelled.

Livia startled and looked up. Her mother was standing in front of her, glaring down at her, hands on hips, her face red with rage.

"I will not tolerate it. You will never see that boy again, do you understand me? He's a zombie for Christ's sake. A zombie! What do you think it would do to your father if he found out?"

Livia stared, wild-eyed, at her mother and shook her head. Coward, she thought. She should say something. Yell back. Tell her that dad was never home anymore. Ever since he went to work for Welsh he'd spent more and more time away. What would he care if she dated a zombie? He didn't care enough to come home.

"Answer me," her mother said. "What do you have to say for yourself? After all your father has done for you. We had to move here to this god-forsaken place for you."

"But dad's a vampire, too." She said, barely audible.

"He was happy to stay in Florida."

Her mother's voice was rising, becoming shrill. "We only came here for you, so you could go to that stupid school where vampires are not only welcome, but looked up to. And this is how you thank him."

"I didn't ask to come here."

"You did so. All your whining and complaining about how you weren't popular anymore. How nobody liked you and how badly they treated the vampires. Well, here we are in Darkspur and what do you do? Throw yourself at zombie scum."

"He's not scum," Livia mumbled, tears forming in her eyes.

"You will not see him again. And you'll find a vampire to go out with. You hear me? You'll date only vampires."

Tears rolled down her cheeks and she put her hands to her face to wipe them away.

"Dating a vampire is what got me into this mess."

"Yes," her mother screamed, a triumphant look on

her face. "Yes. And I warned you didn't I? I told you to stay away from that one, too. But did you listen? No. You were a little cheerleader snot. Thought you were hot shit. Too cool to listen to your mother, isn't that right?"

Livia cowered into the soft cushions of the sofa and covered her face.

"And look where your rebellion got you? Huh? Here in Darkspur. A vampire, just like your father. If I didn't know better I'd think you planned it just like that. You always wanted to be just like him. Well, now you are. You dug your grave and now you need to get in the coffin. You will date only vampires from now on."

Her mother paused, her chest heaving with anger. She shook her head with disappointment and turned to leave.

"Serves you right," she muttered under her breath before disappearing around the corner into the kitchen.

Z

Cole turned to the house and frowned. He couldn't go inside and see his mother. Not yet. He didn't want to come back down to earth. He shoved his hands into his pants pockets and strolled, almost bouncing, along the street toward Buckley Park. His thoughts raced from one topic to another, always with Livia Duvessa there.

As he neared the park, he was sure he heard the rumble of Rick Slade's Jag roaring down the other side of Buckley Street. What would Slade be doing in his neighborhood? Curious, he lifted his feet and jogged toward the park. He saw the bodies as he approached and fell to the dirt beside the first one. Mr. Epperson's open eyes stared blankly at Cole. Blood spattered his neck and shirt. Cole looked up. Mrs. Epperson lay sprawled a few feet away, her hand still grasping the leashes on which her two, now dead, huskies were tethered.

Cole's mother stepped out of the kitchen and shook

her head, turned and went back in, as Cole came through the front door. When he entered the kitchen, she turned and opened her mouth to speak. But he stopped her.

"The Epperson's are dead in the park. Vamps."

His mother reached for the phone and dialed the police. After two grueling hours of trying to convince them that he'd heard Rick Slade's Jaguar leaving the scene, and being told he was just a kid who couldn't possibly know the difference in engine sounds of cars, which he finally had to admit was true, Cole trudged up the stairs to his room.

His mother was angry, and wanted to lecture him about the school board meeting. His behavior, she said, was out of line. But after his ordeal with the Eppersons in the park, she granted him a reprieve. He didn't care; the meeting was over, the chaos no longer the most exciting thing he'd ever done. Even discovering two dead neighbors and their two dead dogs in the park couldn't spoil that morning for him. Knowing that Rick Slade was definitely in on the feral attacks couldn't dissuade him from his joy. All he could think about was Livia. A vampire. He finally had to admit it to himself. He was in love with a vampire.

He took a brief look at Livia's house across the street before closing his curtains and sitting at his desk. Almost without thinking he turned his computer on, and logged onto the Viral Episodes forum. In the zombie lounge he found a long list of posts about the history of the virus. There was an argument going on, vicious language, threats. It took Cole an hour to sort through it and find the source, where it all began.

It started on Cole's thread, where he asked about history and Cerebellum asked to meet him. Someone named DeadBlood had responded, telling Cole and everyone else to beware of Cerebellum.

"He's a quack," DeadBlood said. "Don't listen to him."

And from there, zombie chaos erupted. Zombies attacking zombies. On one side, a few zombies claimed that Cole had a legitimate question and that the history of the viral outbreak had yet to be told. And on the other side, well, the other side was insane.

"Who cares about how it all started? It started and we have to live with it."

"You zombies need to get lives and stop worrying about why you're dead."

"You zombies need brain scans. LOLOLOL."

Cole could handle controversy; a little argument was always good for moving things forward. But somehow, in the end, Cole had been branded a conspiracy theorist.

"Just for asking about how it all started?" He muttered to himself, fuming.

"Wacko teen zombie nonsense?" He read.

For several long moments, his exhilaration after kissing the most beautiful vampire in school was gone. He fumed and stared at the constant back and forth between the zombies. How could one little question turn half the zombie population into pit vipers?

CHAPTER TWELVE

Livia knew she'd been led into a trap but it was too late to do anything about it. She'd followed Darlene to the vamp locker corner, while Darlene chattered on about inane nonsense, which should have been Livia's first clue. If nothing else, Darlene knew how not to chat. Once at the lockers, Darlene shut up and Livia found herself surrounded by the entire vamp population of Darkspur Night High, which she knew was one hundred forty-eight, not counting herself.

Maybe not all of them are here, she thought. But the air was thick, too many dead bodies crowded in, red eyes glared at her, hisses rose and fell. And Rick Slade came forward, standing close enough for his words to hit her face with his sweet, cherry breath.

"You're the only one here who doesn't smell right," Rick said. "The only one who's got zombie stench on her clothes."

He tilted his head to the right, then left, jutting out his jaw.

"It's time for you to decide, little dead girl. Are you a

vamp? Or are you in hell?"

Livia stared at him, trying not to laugh. Clearly he was serious. He meant to do something awful to her if she didn't behave. But she couldn't get past the posing, the glaring, the head bopping back forth like an emu curious over a peanut.

"You get me?" He said.

Livia nodded.

"She gets you," Darlene said.

"See that she does," Rick poked her with a long, bony finger.

The vampires dispersed, slowly, like you might expect angry, arrogant vampires to do, and Livia turned to Darlene allowing herself to breathe.

"What was that about?"

"Rumors," she said, opening her locker.

"Rumors about what?"

"You and Cole Bertrand."

Darlene pulled her books out, shut her locker and turned to Livia.

"There's something between you two?"

Livia shook her head. "No."

"But you want there to be?"

"No. Yes. I mean. My mom forbids it."

"Smart woman."

Tears filled Livia's eyes and she turned her head.

"I don't get it, you know." Darlene said. "I don't get what you see in a zombie. I mean, sure he's cute and all. But..."

"It doesn't matter," Livia said.

She went to her locker and worked the lock.

"I'll see you in class," Darlene said.

When she closed her locker and turned, Livia was startled by Stephan Hack. He looked down at her, his wide mouth pulled into a gorgeous smile and a lock of

140

dark hair fell across his forehead. His hypnotic green eyes had just a touch of maroon at the edges.

"Sorry," he said. "I didn't mean to scare you. Don't want to get hit or anything."

"I don't hit," she said and realized she was angry. She shook it off and sighed. "Sorry. I didn't mean to snap at you."

"Then we're both sorry vamps," he said and laughed. "Meant for each other and all that."

"Right." What was he saying? "I have to get to class."

"I'll walk you."

They strolled through the halls, the other vamps nodding at them, or rather at Stephan, the regular girls tossing Livia jealous looks. He was cute, she had to admit to herself. As they approached the door to Livia's science class, Stephan took her hand, turned to her and said, "It'll be okay. I'll watch out for you."

She couldn't help but feel a bit comforted by his caress and smile. But she was intensely aware of being watched by every kid in the hallway.

"Uh, sure," she said in a whisper. "Thanks."

Stephan lifted her hand. He better not kiss it, she thought. Not in front of everyone. She winced. But he squeezed it and let it go.

"I'll see you at lunch, okay?"

He left her standing, staring at the wall outside room 110. How lucky was that, she thought. The very evening after she was forbidden to date anyone but vamps, along comes Stephan. She turned and watched the other kids heading to their classrooms. They didn't look back, but she felt that everyone in the school somehow knew she was being set up. What she couldn't figure out was how her mother got to them.

As the clock wound down in science, Livia's nerves wound up. Cole. Cole next class. What would she say to him? She had to say something to him, but not in school. Not in American Lit. She should have called him that evening and told him she couldn't see him again. But she didn't want him to think she thought they were a thing, or anything. If he thought they were a thing, that would be great, she thought. Except that now they couldn't be a thing. Hopefully, he didn't think they were a thing and that morning was just a kiss. Nothing more. Just a kiss.

Between a vamp and a zombie.

Perfectly normal.

The bell rang and she waited until everyone else left the room, slowly closing her folder, putting the cap on her pen, donning her sweater and pulling her purse off the seat back.

"Is everything all right, Miss Duvessa?" Mr. Samuelson yelled, and reached to his ear to adjust his hearing aid.

When the last student left and the door closed behind her, Livia stood and walked to Mr. Samuelson's desk.

"I was just wondering, sir," she said. "What are the differences between zombies and vampires?"

Samuelson's face lit up and his head seemed to fall back on his neck. "Differences? Well, they're myriad. That means many."

"Yes, I know. But I mean, can they...are they still...we're still humans right?"

He shook his head. "Not really, no. Once human, but the virus causes chemical changes within the cells. This is college level material. What's your interest? Planning on a career in biology?" He looked hopeful and nodded yes for her.

"No. I'm just wondering if zombies and, you know, vamps, can date."

"Date?"

"Yeah, you know." She raised her eyebrows and tilted her head hoping he would get the hint. "Date."

142

"But of course. I've seen them dating. I've seen them in the halls. Perfectly normal teenage behavior."

"No, sir. I mean zombies and vamps together. A zombie dating a vamp. And vice versa."

He paused, his mouth open. He sputtered, and said, "Well, why wouldn't they? It seems they've retained the evolutionary social instincts of homo sapiens."

"Yes, but. Well, what about marriage?"

"Marriage? Well, I suppose. But you realize, of course that the biggest difference between them is death. The zombies are dead. In fact, several studies are in progress now and it may turn out that should they be cured of the zombie virus, they may actually die. That is to say, there's debate about whether they'd be dead or alive. Do you take my meaning?"

"Sex, Mr. Samuelson." She blurted out. "Can zombies and vamps have sex together and reproduce?"

His mouth fell open and closed again. Two students for his next class came through the door chatting. Mrs. Roddenberry's voice echoed over the loudspeaker with a message to the janitor.

"Never mind," Livia said and left.

Z

Cole knew not to expect her to smile at him, or talk to him. He knew she was still a vamp and she was afraid of Rick Slade and she wanted to fit in. He knew that during school, they wouldn't be able to walk together, or talk to each other, and certainly not touch each other. But, when she walked into American Lit and took her seat without even glancing at him, he realized from the cloud of gloom that fell over him, that he did expect her to look at him.

This sucked, he concluded. He could now understand what Alan felt, walking around all day moping over girls, regular, zombie, whatever. Alan was always in love with several of them and he and Brock thought it was sick. It is sick, he realized. Was he going to have to go through all his days droopy like a deflated heart-shaped balloon? Would he become stupid?

He tried to think of other things. His class work. His new distinction as a conspiracy theorist at Viral Episodes and the humiliation therewith. Chess. He rarely thought about chess and it didn't help. Whether or not the hobo guy from the mall was insane or brilliant and whether or not he cared anymore. Because, after all, if he couldn't have Livia in his life, talk to her all day and kiss her whenever he wanted, did it really matter if the magick or Welsh Corporation or somebody else was trying to create a new humanity of vamps and zombies just to make a buck?

She wouldn't look at him all day and worse, whenever Slade was around it was clear that he was making sure she wasn't looking at Cole. And that vamp slime Hack followed her around all day gaping at her like a sick puppy whenever Cole snuck a peek. His dead stomach churned and that bite of pepperoni pizza he's sampled days ago decided to burp up and move on. Great, this love stuff was fabulous, he thought.

As Cole left the building, grateful to be heading home where he could finally talk to her, touch her, hold her, kiss her, and find out what the hell was going on, he ran right into them.

"Sure," she was saying, looking up into Hack's face. "Saturday sounds great."

And Hack lifted her hand to his lips and kissed the back of it. Did girls go for that anymore? Was it sixteenth century or what?

"I'll see you then," he said with a goofy smile on his face.

144

"Well, and this week in school." She said.

They laughed together. It was sick, he thought. Hack turned to leave her and she caught Cole's eye. She startled and stared at him. And he stared back. He couldn't move. Anger slowly filled him. Brock's arm slung around his shoulder and dragged him away from her, down the steps into the bitter cold morning, and across the front lawn toward his car.

"It's been all over the school today," Brock said. "They're the new thing. Good for you, though, right?"

"How's that?" He unlocked his car door and pulled it open, tossing his backpack into the back seat.

"Because now you can stop obsessing over her and get back to your normal life."

Cole smirked. "Right. You riding home with Alan again?"

Brock frowned at him. "Look, you're just...you're just not right anymore."

"What's that supposed to mean?"

"Ever since that vamp showed up, you're acting like a fool. You're no fun anymore."

"So, you're riding with Alan then?"

Brock shrugged. "All right, you can take me home. But I'm not going to listen to anymore love stuff."

"I can promise you, I won't be talking about Livia Duvessa anymore."

CHAPTER THIRTEEN

Livia waved good-bye to Darlene and grudgingly opened the door to her house. The last thing she wanted to do was talk to her mother.

"I'm home," she called.

"We're in the den," her mother said.

We? Livia walked through the dining room and into the den to find her father and mother at the table playing cards.

"Dad." She rushed to him and hugged his neck.

"Whoah, watch that vampire strength."

She chuckled.

"Why haven't you been home?"

He shrugged, removed his thick-rimmed glasses and rubbed his red eyes. "It's good to be home. I promise I'll start working more regular hours soon."

"What do they have you doing that's taking so much time?"

He looked at her as if she was a child. "It's not that. They've had some security breaches, that's all. We had to stay there until they could find the culprits."

"And they found them?"

"Livia, dear," her mother said. "Don't attack your father with questions. He just got home."

"I'm sorry."

"Would you like to join us in a round of cards?" Her dad said.

She shook her head. Mother wouldn't let Dad's presence deter her from the cross examinations. Livia left them to their game and stepped out on the back porch in the early morning darkness and wrapped her sweater tighter around her waist. She shivered.

"Pssst."

Livia turned to the sound and peered into the yard.

"Did somebody just psst me?"

"Livia, it's me."

"Me, who?"

"Wanda Quaid. Come over here."

A cold fear swept through her and she shook her head. "You come to me."

"I can't."

"Why not?"

"I can't let anyone else see me. Please."

Livia hesitated. "Who's with you?"

"Nobody. I'm alone."

"Why are you here?"

She heard a loud sigh and Wanda spoke louder. "I don't know who to trust, okay? I figured you were the only one."

Curious, Livia glanced behind her into the house to make sure her parents weren't watching and stepped off the back porch into the darkness of the back yard. As she neared, Wanda's pale face appeared in the dim light of the moon.

"You need a bath or something."

"Yeah, thanks," Wanda said and smirked. Her hair

was uncombed and filled with twigs, and her face smudged with dirt.

"What happened to you?"

"Todd hit me with something and buried me in our back yard."

Livia gasped. "How did you get out?"

"Geraldo dug me up?"

"Who?"

"Geraldo. Our Chihuahua."

Livia laughed.

"Shh. I don't want anyone to find me."

"Your Chihuahua dug you up?"

Wanda let out a giggle. "Well, I wasn't all that deep and I did have to do most of the digging once she freed the top part of me."

"Are you sure Todd did it? It wasn't Rick?"

Wanda shook her head. "Only Todd. He called me out back to show me something and it was just a big hole. The next thing I remember Geraldo's scratching dirt off me and I'm in the ground with a pounding headache. You got any aspirin?"

"Sure, sure. But did you tell your folks?"

"Are you kidding? Something's wrong with Todd. Something bad. My parents weren't even home. He might have done something to them, I don't know. But if they're okay, the less they know the better."

"What are you going to do?"

"I'm leaving. There's a colony out in...I better not say."

"Why did you come here?"

"I need some clothes, and some money. Can you help?"

"Sure. But wouldn't Darlene, or Jenny...?"

Wanda shook her head. "They're too close to Rick. But listen. You have to promise not the say anything to

Todd...or anyone else. Maybe my parents if you think they're really worried. But if you let on you know, Todd might come after you."

"Okay." Livia nodded. "Not a word to anyone. I promise."

Upstairs in her room, Livia stuffed some clothes that might fit Wanda into a drawstring bag and took all the money she could find. She grabbed a jacket out of the front closet and took it all out to Wanda.

"I'll be back when I think it's safe, okay?" Wanda said and hugged her. "Thanks "

"Good luck."

Livia watched Wanda disappear around the house and shivered in the cold, glad she'd finally found a friend.

CHAPTER FOURTEEN

In his book, *Zombie Revolution*, Krenske surmised that the combination of brute strength and brain power of the zombie population would allow them to overpower the vamps, frail in both body and mind, and win out in the coming apocalypse. The zombies would either subdue the arrogance of the vamps and dominate them, or they'd go full zombie and spread the virus across the land, leading to the breakdown of civilization, including, we assume, the synthetic blood factory at Welsh Corporation, thereby eliminating the vamps' only food sources. Either way, Krenske said, the zombies win.

By the time Friday rolled around again, Cole felt he was to the point where he probably would not drive around Darkspur all night Saturday, looking for Stephan Hack's car, with Livia Duvessa inside. Probably. He didn't know if she looked at him at all in school the rest of the week, because he didn't look at her. But Brock and the other zombies were always quick to let him know she wasn't paying any attention to him at all. What are friends for, right?

He followed Brock into the school and decided he didn't need to keep his eyes at waist level anymore, in case he might see Livia and look at her. He walked down the main hall, head held high, winking at zombie girls who smiled at him, like he used to. Maybe his dead heart wasn't in it quite yet, but he'd get used to it.

He rounded the corner to zombie row, grabbed his lock, twisted and turned it, pulled open his locker, stared, and let out a low groan. And he heard the other zombies doing the same. A silence fell upon them all. In his locker, and he guessed he would in all the other zombie lockers as well, Cole found a hatchet, the razor sharp edge dripping in what he could only hope was fake blood. He slammed his locker shut and turned to his friends.

"What do we do?"

Several of the others looked beyond Cole down the hall. He turned to see Livia, dour and gray in the fluorescent lighting, coming toward him. She didn't lift her eyes to his face, but approached him and handed him a folded piece of paper before turning and racing off into the crowded hallway.

Cole unfolded the paper and read aloud: "I dare you to go to Lute."

He looked up at his friends. "It's signed by Rick Slade."

"How juvenile can you get?" Alan said.

"Look," Brock said. "He made an evil grin out of the R in Rick."

"So what do we do?" Rachel said.

"We go to Lute," Cole said.

Fifteen minutes later, the halls were empty except for the several zombies whose lockers were involved, Mr. Lute, and Dean Thompson. Cole realized he would get nowhere.

"I'm sorry," Mr. Lute said. "But we have no proof

that the vampires put these in your lockers and they claim they had nothing to do with it."

"Can't you take fingerprints?" Kyle said.

"Yeah, their prints must be all over the lockers and hatchets."

"This is a school," Lute said. "Not a forensics lab. If you'll all take the hatchets out of your lockers and bring them to my office, we'll make out a report."

"Make out a report?" Cole said. "Is that it?"

"What else can we do?"

Lute and the dean turned and headed down the hall.

Cole grabbed his hatchet, shut his locker and raced to catch up to the principal.

"You can question the vamps again. Ask Livia Duvessa; she'll tell you the truth."

Once in Lute's office they laid the hatchets in a pile on the floor in the corner and received passes to class.

"Aren't you going to do anything?"

Lute sighed and sat in his chair behind his desk. "What do you want me to do, Cole? I can't suspend them just because you and your friends suspect them."

"Don't you suspect them?"

Only Cole and Brock were left in the office.

"Cole, it's getting around that you're trying to find out about the viruses, about how they started."

"Yeah, so? What's that got to do with anything?"

"Quite a lot, to tell the truth. Look, vamps are starting to talk. They're saying that you're accusing them of starting the virus."

"I never said that."

"But that's how it looks."

"But that has nothing to do with this."

"It looks like it does, though."

"What difference does it make what it looks like?" Brock said. "It's the truth that matters, right?"

153

"Yes, of course," Lute said. "But we have no evidence, so we have no truth."

"I bet if you called the police."

"I can't call the police every time a zombie or a vamp plays a practical joke."

"But they're hatchets," Cole felt his blood beginning to pulse through his veins again, his heart did a slow pound in his chest. "It's a threat with a deadly weapon."

"A weapon that, as you well know, is allowed in the event of a zombie outbreak."

The phone on Lute's desk rang shrilly and he picked it up. He mumbled a few times and hung up.

"This conference is over. Please return to your classes. And Cole, I expect this nonsense to stop."

"I didn't have anything to do with this."

"Didn't you?"

Cole stormed out of Lute's office and into the hall, with Brock chasing after him.

"What the hell was all that?" Brock said. "We got detention for crosses and they get nothing?"

"We admitted we hung the crosses."

"Did we?"

"We won't admit anything else, ever again." Cole said.

"Nothing?"

"You heard me."

"Yeah, well, what if Mr. Samuelson put some kind of weird science problem on a board in the hall and you solved it in secret and they wanted to give out an award for whoever solved it."

"What are you talking about?"

"Would you admit it?"

Cole shook his head and turned to leave.

"Would you?" Brock said. "I'm just asking."

"Sometimes I wonder about your meds." Cole said.

After first class, Cole met up with Alan and Kyle on

his way to American Lit. They were somber, and leery. When Slade and five other vamps came toward them in the hall, instead of moving aside as everybody always did, the zombies kept walking.

"They can move over this time," Cole said loud enough for the vamps to hear him.

But Slade and the others smirked and glared at them with pinkish glowing eyes. Neither group yielded and as they came together they started pushing. Slade came right at Cole and shoved him back. Cole put his arms out and knocked Slade to the ground. Someone's arm wrapped around his neck from behind, but before he could turn, whoever had him was pulled off by someone else.

The fight was broken up quickly by Dean Thompson and they were all escorted to their classrooms. It was the same thing after every class—always some group of vamps walking side by side, as usual, through the hallways expecting everybody to step aside. And the zombies refused. By two a.m. the confrontations had escalated from pushing to punches and Cole was summoned back to Principal Lute's office.

"Cole," Lute said. "I don't care what's in your head about the vamps, and I don't care who started what. You and your friends will leave the vamps alone or you'll be suspended."

"Leave them alone?" Cole leaned forward a bit, grasping the back of one of the chairs in front of Lute's desk and wrapping his dead hands hard around it until they went from gray to white.

"How can you be so clueless about what's going on in this school? The vamps have walked around like overlords long enough. We're not doing anything to them besides expecting them to treat everybody else fairly."

Lute shook his head. "Tell your friends to stay out of their way."

He looked tired, deader than usual, and had another patch on his face. Cole loosened his grip on the chair.

"I get it," Cole said.

"Get what?"

"I get who signs your paycheck."

"Not more conspiracy."

"It's no conspiracy. It's just the way things are."

Cole turned to leave, but looked back.

"I didn't really think the vamps were behind any kind of conspiracy," he said. "I just wanted to understand how it all started."

"Well, whatever you did, you're looking like a conspiracy theorist."

That's just great, Cole thought. Even Principal Lute is on the Viral Episodes message board.

Early Saturday morning after school, in the chilled, dewy air Cole and his friends stood in the parking lot staring at the hoods of their cars glistening in the parking lot spotlights.

"What is it?" Alan asked.

"It's blood, I think." Cole said, reaching out and putting his finger in the sticky red goo. He looked around the parking lot. "I think it's real."

The other kids were leaving, car engines raced, chatter floated off in all directions. Cole followed a trail of blood across the parking lot toward the road. His friends followed him to the small corner of the lot where the squat green dumpsters sat inside an open chain link enclosure. Even they could smell the rotting corpse.

"What do you think it is?" Rachel said.

Cole sighed and walked up to a dumpster and looked in. He winced and walked quickly back to his car, his friends following.

"Rabbits," he said.

"So, we go to Lute?" Alan said. "We have some

evidence this time."

"What evidence? Who's to say we didn't kill the rabbits ourselves? No. We don't go to Lute anymore."

"The cops?"

"We don't do anything unless we have real proof. But this proves one thing."

"What?" Rachel said.

"The vamps are out to get us."

"You don't mean like high school out to get us," Rachel said.

"No," Brock said. "He means like out to get us."

"Like slasher film out to get us?" Kyle said.

"Yeah, like that."

Rachel snorted and they all looked at her. Cole realized she'd laughed.

"Aw, come on," she said. She looked back and forth and all around the group of zombies standing at Cole's car. "Come on, they're not going to try to kill us. That's just. I mean, they're just high school kids like us."

"Some of them have been high school kids for thirty years."

"But you don't have any reason to think they really mean us harm, Cole. Come on, guys."

"Rachel's right, man." Brock said.

Cole shook his head. "I hope you are right."

Cole and Brock got in his car and watched as Rick Slade came out of the school building, swaggering and pushing his posse around. That little twerp Todd Quaid bounced around him like a cheerleader.

"Slade looks really irritated by Todd." Cole said.

Brock was silent. Cole watched as Todd climbed into the passenger seat of Slade's Jag, forcing Elena, Slade's girl, to the back seat with Stephan.

"I'm going to follow them, are you with me?"

Brock nodded.

Cole started his engine and pulled his car out of the school parking lot behind Slade's.

"Maybe if we confront him, we can get him to admit it." Cole knew he was lying as he seethed with hatred. Slade should pay.

"What good will that do?"

"We'll know for sure."

"Don't we already know?"

Cole was silent for a long time until they neared Brock's turnoff.

"I'm going to keep following, okay?"

Brock shrugged. "He's just going to the park."

"Okay, maybe I want to break his face on the hood of my car."

"Now you're making more sense." Brock smiled.

"I wouldn't mind forcing him to take off that stupid Matrix coat and wiping the blood off my car with it, either."

"I'm in," Brock said.

They followed Slade's car up Park Avenue, past Cole's neighborhood and onto Grommet Lake Drive. They drove along the river, under the highway and up the mountain, twisting and turning among the colorful trees, leaves twirling through the air as they past.

"Where's he going?"

"I don't know," Cole said.

He slowed his car and backed off. Where would a thirty-year old teenaged vampire go after school on a Saturday morning in the opposite direction of down town? This wasn't about beating the guy up anymore. Now, Cole was curious. Slade turned off Grommet Lake onto Cascades Drive.

"You know where this road goes?" Cole said.

"Everybody knows where this road goes."

They followed as Slade drove into the main parking

lot of the huge Welsh Corporation complex and continued on, through a gate at the other end onto a dirt road and disappeared into the woods. Cole stopped his car.

"Are you going in?"

"There's nothing in there but the woods."

"So, it's perfect. We beat the shit out of him and nobody sees it."

Cole shook his head. "I don't like it."

"What's not to like?"

Cole turned his car around and headed home. "You're really smart about math and science, Brock, but I don't think you know much about vamps and fighting them."

"What's to know? We're evenly matched."

"Not exactly. The four of them are about as strong as the two of us. But we're deader than they are."

"Deader." He said.

"Exactly. Things sometimes break down. We have to be careful."

"And they don't?"

Cole shook his head. "You should really read some of this stuff I've researched. Especially Dr. Krenske. He wrote a whole book on vamps."

"You're chicken."

Cole put his foot on the break and turned to look at Brock. "We don't know who else is out there."

"You think they're feral, don't you?"

"Yes. And through those woods, on the other side of the mountain is where they found Tina West and her friends. Dead."

"Then we should go check it out."

"And then do what? If they don't whack our heads off to start with, you think the police will believe us?"

"So, you want to go to the mall or something?"

Cole seethed and shook his head slightly. "I can drop you off if you want."

"You're afraid she's going to be there."

Cole said nothing. What if he was right?

The next afternoon, Cole woke to his mother calling him down for breakfast.

"Cole, hurry, the news," she said.

As he thumped down the stairs she said, "It's all over the news. Huge feral attack in Stone Creek. Some seventy people were bitten last night. Most of them killed. They're listing the names in a few minutes. Hurry, hurry."

His mom and Craig ate as the three of them sat watching the scrolling list of people in the small town northwest of Darkspur who'd been killed or turned.

CHAPTER FIFTEEN

What's happening?" Rick Slade threw his hands up and glared at the vamps huddled around the fire out in the woods by Hidden Lake.

Todd shrugged. What was the problem? He turned to the others, standing with their arms wrapped around themselves, their eyes downcast.

"What do you mean?" He said, wondering why he was the only one willing to speak.

"Why are you killing people?"

Rick's eyes were wide and rabid. He looked at them each in turn until his frantic expression found Todd.

"It's you." He said and slowly pulled an outstretched hand around to point at Todd. "You started this."

Todd shook his head. He used to think Rick Slade was the coolest kid in school. Slade had been at Darkspur Night High for some twenty-odd years and maybe it was that experience, the timeworn wisdom, that attracted him and all the other regulars. He was like a god–a pale, moody, skinny statue of a god. And he led a posse of demigods, beautiful, slender and ghostly white. They all wished they could be just like them.

When Wanda, grudgingly, led him out into the woods at Hidden Lake that day a few months ago and offered him to Ciara Wister, Todd, though scared out of his pants, was thrilled. He could be one of them. And why not? Wanda shouldn't be the only vamp in the family.

But now, Todd was struck by the inconsistency in Rick Slade.

"We're vampires," Todd said. "It's what we do."

Rick's head shook back and forth. "No, no. We drink blood, but we don't kill people."

"Why not? They're of no use to us. You want that old couple and their dogs in the bloodline? Those jerks in Stone Creek?"

"No," Rick said and rubbed his hands through his hair. "But..."

The others began to look up and around, as if coming out of a blood stupor.

"He's right," Ciara said. "We have to be choosy about who we turn. We don't want just anybody."

"But if we kill too many people, we'll get caught. They'll put us in jail, or kill us."

"They can't catch us," Todd said. "We're vamps."

"Yeah," Stephan said. "We're the...what's the word? The tops, the best."

"The elite," Todd said. "We're it, man. And the more we turn, the more power we have." He gave Rick a disgusted look. "Isn't that what you wanted?"

"Yes, yes." Rick said. "But so many dead."

"Exactly. While you were busy daintily sucking on a few regulars, we did what had to be done."

They all turned to him and Todd felt a surge of importance.

"Now, wait a minute. I did what I ordered you all to do. You're the ones who didn't obey. If we kill people,

162

I'm the one who gives the orders. Got it?"

He posed for effect and Todd had to smile. That was the old Rick Slade he knew and loved.

"Got it," Todd said. "When can we do it again?"

"We have other problems," Rick said. He stepped closer to the fire and put out his hands to warm them over the flames. "I know someone who has a way to get the zombies off their meds so we can hack off their heads. You guys interested?"

Deathly white smiles erupted all around.

CHAPTER SIXTEEN

Finally, Saturday night. All night and no school. Cole picked up Brock, Alan and Rachel and they drove to the theater in the mall. Everything felt like it used to for a while, talking, laughing, joking. It was as if there wasn't a problem with the vamps. And maybe, Cole thought, maybe there wasn't. Maybe it could all just die now. Maybe he could forget about the start of the virus and getting back at the vamps. Maybe he could forget about Livia Duvessa.

But there she was, in the theater lobby with the vamps, Stephan Hack's arm slung carelessly across her shoulders. Cole felt as if another zombie had punched him in the chest. As they came closer and Slade leered at him, Cole nearly salivated, yearning not only for Livia Duvessa's juicy brains, but Stephan Hack's skull crushed between his hands.

They both turned to see him and the other zombies and Cole's dead stomach tightened. Seething, he followed the zombies through the lobby, past the hissing group of vamps.

"Hey, loser," Slade called out. "Your heart's dead; it can't be broken."

The vamps snickered. Brock grabbed Cole's arm and pulled him forward into the theater.

"Just forget them," Brock said.

"I didn't do anything. Tell them to forget."

They took seats up front and slouched low.

"Tell me what you got from the weird guy." Brock said.

"Now you're interested?"

"I am. Tell me."

"I don't know what it was. Just a bunch of nonsense. The guy was crazy."

"So what was it?"

"I told you I don't know. I didn't read it."

Brock turned to look at him. "What do you mean you didn't read it?"

"It looked like crazy man ravings. I didn't read it."

Brock stared at him. "All this time you've been trying to figure out what's going on with the virus and all the sudden it's crazy and you don't even try?"

"The guy's a lunatic."

"Hey, you don't have to convince me. I'm just saying." Brock turned back to the screen where ads for the local mortuary and music teachers rotated space.

"Saying what?"

"You've lost your focus."

"What's that supposed to mean?"

"It means if you weren't drooling all over Livia Duvessa you'd have read the guy's rantings. You'd have read them three or four times, convincing yourself there must be something in it you're missing."

Cole said nothing for a few minutes. Rachel was on his other side and he could see her glancing at him several times, but he didn't turn to look at her. Even in the dim

166

light of the theater, he didn't want to see the hurt and disappointment on her face. Thinking she must have really loved him, Cole felt a pang of regret hit is gut.

"I told you, it was nonsense." He said, uncomfortable in the silence.

"I'm sure it was. But you said yourself you didn't read it so how do you know?"

"Maybe that stuff isn't important anymore. We need to be thinking about what we're going to do about Slade and the vamps."

"What's to do?"

Cole turned to glare at him. "We have to make it stop. We have to put them in their place."

Brock shook his head. "Lute told us to stop."

"They won't stop until we make them stop."

"If we retaliate, it'll only make it worse."

"We don't have a choice."

"Yes, we do. Listen to yourself, man. This isn't about the vamps; it's all about Livia. It wouldn't have even gotten this far if it weren't for her. We would have let them have their Jello brain joke and they'd be over it now."

"This isn't about Livia; it's about us. Aren't you tired of taking it from them?"

"It never bothered you before. It's always been about the vamps being stupid and immature and playing their stupid childish pranks. Why does it matter now? Because you want Livia."

Rachel stood suddenly. "Excuse me."

"Where are you going?" Alan said.

"Ladies room."

She scooted in front of them and Cole looked up into her face as she passed. She gave him a weak smile.

"I don't want Livia," Cole said, while Rachel could still hear him.

The lie hit him hard and he winced. He wondered if Brock was right. Before Livia Duvessa moved in across the street he was ready to do whatever he had to do to find out what was behind the viruses. Before she showed up, he knew the vamps were just stupid. Annoying, sure, but zombies didn't stoop to the vamp level. But it had gone way beyond annoying this time

"We have to end it."

"Why don't we just ignore it? Won't that end it?"

"You wanted to beat Slade up, too."

"That was before I figured out that this was all about Livia Duvessa."

"Oh, and when did you figure it all out, genius?"

"Just now in the lobby, brain dead."

"You're calling me brain dead now?"

"Could you two shut up? The previews are starting soon." Alan said. "Rachel's going to miss them."

"I'm telling you it's not about Livia." There was, after all, the possibility that it wasn't. "It's about standing up for zombie rights. We have to show them they can't just take over."

Brock sighed. "What do you have in mind?"

"We need to humiliate Slade, in front of everybody. If we can loosen his grip on the other vamps, we'll have a chance for normalcy."

"You'll never get the others in on it."

"Why not?"

"Too immediate. They don't mind anonymous stuff like hanging stupid little crosses. But they don't want anything up close. They don't want to be identified."

"We'll see."

The lights went down and the previews started. Rachel didn't return until the movie had begun and Cole was uncomfortably conscious of her beside him for the next two hours.

168

The next Wednesday morning, the school board took an un-advertised vote to leave the Darkspur Night High School curricula unchanged. The vamps could not erase Vlad the Impaler from their history class. On Wednesday night, when Cole and Brock arrived at school, they stood with the other students and watched as police swarmed the campus. The school was trashed. A dozen windows were broken; desks, chairs, books and office supplies littered the front lawn; and the two Franks were stuck on the roof, dazed, with no memory of how they got there.

CHAPTER SEVENTEEN

In his book *Zombie Revolution*, Dr. Krenske explained the dangers of cold weather on the zombie. Stiffness, numbness in the extremities, and complete loss of smell and taste were to be expected. But the zombie must take great care to wear protective clothing to prevent fingers, toes, ear lobes, even noses from breaking off, depending, of course, on the state of decay of the individual zombie.

Cole was, of course, one of the lucky ones. His mother knew he'd been bitten before he died and he was prescribed a pre-death dose of Zom-be-Gon. The chances of losing an appendage were fairly slim for him, but he wore the gloves, the leather shoes over warm fuzzy socks, and the jacket, anyway. He didn't want to rub it in to Alan and Rachel, after all. But he wouldn't go as far as the ear muffs and he flatly refused to wear the nose guard.

"Come on, man," Alan let out a muffled whine.

Of the zombies in the advanced state of decay—Rachel, Alan, Stu Martin and Isabella Rothstein—only their eyes could be seen. They wore scarves wrapped around their faces, ear muffs, and on top of their heads, heavy fur hats. The hats, zombies were willing to admit, were just for show. But Cole supposed they did help hold the scarves on.

"I told you meeting in the cemetery is too creepy."

"We needed someplace really secret," Cole said. "I want us to hit back at the vamps. Hard."

"Can't it wait until after winter break?" Isabella said.

"That's two months from now. You want to wait two months?"

"I'd rather not get expelled so early in the year. I like my classes."

"Yeah, me too." Stu said.

"We're not going to get expelled. We can't wait until after the break. They're putting cameras up because the vamps trashed the school."

"We don't know it was them," Isabella said.

"We know." Cole said.

They all shrugged. They did know.

"We have to do it before they install the cameras."

A few of them nodded.

"All right then, here's my plan."

On Friday, Alan and Kyle were to sneak into the vamp neighborhood during the day while they were all sleeping and let the air out of one of Slade's tires. It was a well-known fact that Slade showed up to school just in time because he thought it was cool. They wanted him to be late.

Cole, Brock and Stu waited in their cars in the parking lot at school that night. The lot was full; the last of the students ran into the building before the bell rang. Another car pulled into the lot and they all ducked down.

"He's not very late," Cole said.

"It's only Trevor," Brock whispered.

172

Cole, hunched low in his seat, tried to peer over his steering wheel. Trevor stood at his window, staring at him with a wide grin. Cole jumped.

"Go away."

"Who are you hiding from?"

"Go away."

Trevor's eyebrows shot up. "What's going on?"

Cole sat up and rolled down his window. "We're waiting for Slade. Now go away."

"No way, man. I want in."

"No you don't. We'll probably get expelled."

"I don't care. I want in."

"Fine," Cole said. He reached behind him, unlocked the door to the back seat and let the werewolf in. "Get down so he doesn't see us."

"What's the plan?"

"Shh," Brock said. "Here he comes."

They hunkered down as far as they could. Cole heard a car door slam.

"He sounds pissed," Trevor said.

"We let the air out of his tire," Brock said and snickered.

Cole peeked over the dashboard and saw Slade walking up the front walk. As soon as he entered the school he said, "Let's go."

When he was out of his car and running up the front walk he heard the slow, limping stomps of deader zombies behind him. Silently Cole cursed the cold weather.

"What's the plan?" Trevor said.

"Grab him and haul him into the nearest bathroom. We have to keep him quiet, though."

They all entered and headed straight for the vamp lockers. The halls were empty; Mrs. Roddenberry's voice over the loudspeaker was finishing up the morning's news. They slowed as they neared the vamp lockers and crept to the corner. They heard Slade slam his locker door shut and walk toward them.

Before Cole could give a signal, Trevor leapt forward and a loud thud echoed in the hallway.

"I got him," Trevor whispered loudly. "You got tape or something?"

Cole stared at the floor. Trevor was on top of Rick Slade, completely overpowering him, with his arm wrapped around his face. The only things moving were Slade's feet, back and forth, back and forth, like he was trying to swim with them.

"Jesus, Trevor, you're suffocating him," Rachel said.

"Yeah, well get out your tape or something, hurry. If he passes out he can press charges against me for aggravated battery."

"Can't he do that already?"

Alan and Kyle took out the tape and as soon as Trevor released Slade's head they slapped it over his mouth silencing his screams before they were heard.

"Make sure he can breathe," Cole said. His heart had begun to beat again and he trembled with the small surge of blood through his veins. Cole and Brock tied Slade's hands and together with Trevor, they hauled him into the boys' bathroom around the corner. Rachel and Isabella stood watch outside.

Slade was breathing hard, screaming against the tape and kicking wildly. Trevor grabbed his feet and held them.

"Let's do it," he said with a wide grin.

Cole undid Slade's jeans and he and Brock stripped him clean of clothes, cutting his shirt off him with scissors.

"That's just unhealthy," Brock said with a smirk.

Slade's skin was deathly white, smooth and hairless. His ribs rumpled against the skin on his torso. Pale blue

174

veins pulsed on his arms. He huddled in the corner, surrounded by the zombies, his eyes a blazing fire of hatred.

"Don't worry, won't be long. Just sit tight." Cole said to him.

"What's the plan?" Trevor said.

"We let him out as soon as the bell rings," Brock said.

They stood staring at Slade.

"You guys go on," Trevor said. "They'll suspect you."

"What about you?" Alan said.

"I don't have a class first period. I just came in to use the library."

Cole smiled. "I'd shake your hand, Trev, but we've all just touched naked vampire."

They laughed.

Cole sat in Calculus and watched the clock tick toward eight-twenty-five p.m. Nobody had cared when he slipped into class late; he hoped the same could be said for the others. When the bell rang, he tried not to hurry and was now thankful for the cold weather. None of the zombies would move too quickly. Once in the hallway, he heard the screams and laughter. He rounded the corner to the front lobby and watched Rick Slade's naked backside run out the front door, down the steps, past the flag pole and into the parking lot.

Trevor passed him and whispered, "I let him have his keys."

Cole could only stand amid the crowd and laugh with them.

"I want you to understand, Cole," Mr. Lute said with a frown as Cole, Alan and Trevor took seats in his office. "Rick's accusation against you three is very serious. However, after interviewing the other vampires, we have determined that there is no proof against you."

Cole said nothing. All the zombies had agreed that

175

the time for being truthful and forthright with the administration had passed.

"I asked you to make this stop," Mr. Lute said. "Was this how you intended to do it?"

Mr. Lute paused as if he actually expected a reply.

"I thought you were smarter than this, Cole. I thought you were a serious student of history. Surely you must have known that a stunt like this would only pull the vampires closer together in their unity against you and the zombies."

Now Cole dropped his eyes to Lute's desk in front of him. They'd humiliated Slade. They'd shown him to be nothing but a scrawny little coward. Would the vamps still follow him?

Principal Lute sighed. "That will be all, then."

The disappointment in his voiced touched Cole. But he couldn't think of what to say to him to make Lute, or himself, feel better.

"You think he's right?" Trevor asked outside Lute's office.

"Maybe," Brock said. "I'm not sure it makes any difference."

"Exactly," Cole said. "The vamps hate us. So we gave them one more reason. Big deal."

"Yeah," Trevor said. "And it was a lot of fun."

"What was with Slade's body, though?" Brock said as they headed back to their classes.

"Very odd," Trevor said.

"Why do the regular girls go for that?" Cole said.

"Well," Brock said. "They don't go around naked, so the girls don't realize they look like albino lizards."

Cole chuckled. "I know what I'm drawing when we do full figures in art class."

"Aw, man," Brock said. "Tell me you're not going to start drawing naked guys."

176

"Do naked vamps count as naked guys?" Trevor said.

"Good point, dude."

Slade showed up in school later that day, fully clothed, and just a tad pink in the face, very unusual in a vamp, and, Cole hoped, very embarrassing. The vamps hissed through the halls, muttered vamp threats to the zombies, and strutted from class to class seething with vengeance. A typical day at Darkspur Night High School.

After dropping Brock off after school, Cole pulled his car along the curb in front of his house and sat inside it. Darlene Chriss' car was in Livia's driveway. He watched as Livia got out and waved to Darlene. Darlene backed out and drove away as Livia stood on the front walk. She waved once more; then she turned to Cole's car and glared at him before going inside.

Cole breathed again. His mom was home and she called out a hello from the family room as he went up to his room. He turned on his computer and logged on to the Viral Episodes forum. Suddenly, his Windows Messenger box popped up. It was CookieMist345.

"Remember me?" She said.

Cole sat, his hands poised over the keyboard, trying to think of when he'd chatted with a CookieMist in the past. Nothing. She must just be another zombie from the forum.

"Sure," he typed.

He perused the forum for a few minutes, glad to see his infamy as a conspiracy theorist seemed to have been pushed into history by the discussion of the practice of brain fetishes.

"Did you ever read Cerebellum34's stuff?" Cookie said.

Something struck Cole as odd, but he couldn't get at what it was. His fingers paused as he considered how to answer.

"Cerebellum's insane," he wrote and hit enter.

He waited, staring at the dialogue box. He could almost feel the frustration somewhere else in Darkspur as CookieMist struggled with her words.

"Maybe," she said. "But it can't hurt to look, right?"

Cole sighed with relief.

"What do you think I'll find?"

"Confirmation."

"Of what?"

"Of what you think you know."

"What do you think I think I know?"

Another pause. Longer this time.

Finally, she wrote, 'Dr. Krenske isn't in charge of Welsh Corporation any more."

A pang of sadness stabbed at Cole's dead heart and it fluttered. But Dr. Krenske must be ancient by then. Naturally he'd want to retire at some point.

"So?"

"So, he was forced out."

"I haven't read anything about it."

"You won't. Nobody knows."

"But you?"

Long pause. Cole waited, but she didn't respond.

"How do you know?" He asked.

"There are others," she wrote. "Former employees, now working on the outside. They could figure out the stuff Cerebellum gave you."

"Who are you?"

Nothing. CookieMist345 was offline.

Cole dug Cerebellum's folder out from under papers and books on his desk and looked at it. He'd have to read it later.

Z

Rachel's house on Pine Grove Lane was decked out

with orange and purple lights, orange and black streamers, plastic pumpkins, witches' brooms and orange balloons. Rachel loved a good party and she took the zombies' teasing with a smile.

"You're never too old for Halloween," she said, smacking Cole on the shoulder.

"Just so long as you don't expect me to bob for apples."

"My face would fall off," she said. "So, no, we won't be playing that game."

"Oh, I see how it is," Brock said, winking at her.

Every zombie in school and then some was at Rachel's. Her parents had warmed the house up so nobody's nose would fall off, despite the chill in the October night air outside. And they'd barricaded themselves upstairs to let the kids have free rein below. It was not a pretty sight. They played darts in the dark, losing plenty in the walls, and in several of their friends' faces. They littered the rooms with confetti, stomped plastic cups flat for no reason and danced on the furniture. The music pounded and the walls shook, lights flickered on and off to the beat. After two hours, Cole was disoriented, high on laughter and mayhem. And then it happened; none of the zombies realized what was going on until someone knocked the stereo to the floor.

Cole saw Rick Slade a split second before the fist smashed into his face. Vampires grabbed him from behind and held him while Slade pummeled his face and chest. The lights went out. Zombies screamed. Cole leaned against those that held him, lifted his knees high to his chest and kicked Slade, sending him across the room where he fell into the frantic crowd.

Cole beat his way through the vamps until he found Slade again. He punched him hard across the cheek, but Slade turned back to him with a sneer.

"You're going to be the first to go," Slade said. His arm swung around but Cole ducked and landed his fist in Slade's stomach.

Cole pulled back to punch him again but two zombies and a vamp locked in a stronghold fell into him pushing him to the floor. Slade's foot smashed into his forehead. Cole pulled his arms to his face for protection and watched as Slade tripped over his own feet trying to kick him again.

"You're all dead," Slade screamed. "Stupid, stupid zombies. I'll see you all dead."

Strong arms had hold of Cole, pulling him to his feet, and the house lights went on. Everybody paused to blink.

Cole winced as Rachel's dad yelled near his ear, "Out. All you vampires, out."

Mr. Maddox unceremoniously dropped Cole and charged after a few vamps as they fled. Cole followed and he and several others stood outside on Rachel's front lawn in the early morning darkness watching the vamps get into their cars to leave. Livia Duvessa stood next to Stephan Hack's car under the streetlight, staring at him, worry etched clearly across her face. Hack opened the passenger-side door and put her in his car before jogging around to get in behind the wheel. He sped off after the rest of the vamps.

Z

"I told you to stay in the car," Stephan said with a sneer.

Livia turned away from him, watching the houses rush past her in the dark.

"What did you think you were doing?" He said.

"Nothing."

Their silence hung in the air, but Livia relished in it. She couldn't think if Stephan was chattering on about something; and she needed to think. It made some sense that Rick would want to break up the party and even beat up on Cole. What Cole and his friends did to him was awful, even if it was juvenile. Still, the violence was overdone. The vamps were more than just angry. Rick had stirred them up into a frenzy. They wanted more than revenge. They wanted blood. Well, they couldn't get it from the zombies, so why bother?

Stephan drove down Livia's street.

"Are we going to my house?"

He nodded. "I'm taking you home."

"That's good."

"What's that supposed to mean?"

"Nothing. My dad's finally home from work for the weekend that's all. I'd like to spend some time with him."

They were both silent as Stephan pulled his car along the curb in front of Livia's house.

"Aren't you coming in?"

He shook his head. "I have to meet up with Rick and some of the others."

"And naturally I wasn't invited."

He shut off the engine and turned to her.

"Rick thinks you're a spy. He thinks they only reason you're going out with me is to keep tabs on him and the other vamps. Is that true?"

"No."

"But you still like Cole."

She turned her eyes away.

"I don't get it," he said. "He's a zombie. They're disgusting."

Livia rolled her eyes. "They are not."

"Their faces are falling off."

"Only some of them. And they paste the pieces back on."

"Okay, I'll grant you that Cole is the least decayed of

181

all of them, but..."

They were silent again for a time until he said, "So, you're not just going out with me to spy on Rick?"

"No," she said.

"Good. 'Cause they're going to have to be dealt with. And if you get in the way, Rick won't just be mad—he'll be crazy."

"What do you mean?"

"I'm talking killing crazy."

Livia smirked at him.

"I'm serious," he said. "You don't know what he's capable of."

"And you do?"

He hesitated. "Yes. Well, maybe not Rick. But there are others who will do it for him."

"You mean Rick's friends are the ones killing people?"

"I didn't say that."

"Do you know who's doing the killing?"

"Are you sure you're not a spy?"

"I'm a vamp, same as you. Why would I spy on you guys?"

"I don't know."

"So, tell me. It's not you is it? You're not killing regulars."

Stephan shook his head slowly. "No."

"But you know who it is?"

"I can't tell you. Just be careful and stay out of Rick's way. And stay away from Cole and the other zombies. Or we could both end up dead."

She rolled her eyes.

"I know it sounds crazy."

"It does." She said.

"But you have to trust me. This is bigger than just high school pranks. And you have to stay out of it."

She reached over and put her hand on his thigh. "You really do care about me, don't you?"

"Did you think I didn't?"

"I thought you were only going out with me to keep an eye on me. Because Rick told you to."

"Rick did tell me to ask you out. But I wanted to do it."

She nodded absent-mindedly.

"You believe me, don't you?"

"Yes."

He leaned forward and she held her breath. As he pressed his cold, dead lips against hers she froze. His mouth was dry and he held the kiss without movement, too long. She smiled up at him as best she could when he pulled back.

"I'll IM you later, when I get home, if you'll give me your ID."

"Okay," she said. "I'm CookieMist345."

"Wait," he said before she could get out of the car. "I need to write that down."

He made her wait while he dug a torn and wadded piece of notebook paper from under the passenger seat behind her feet, and then a pencil stub from the glove compartment, then had her repeat it three times, then had her spell it twice. Finally, she got out of the car and hurried into the house.

"How was the party? You're home a bit early."

Her mother sat at the kitchen table in her nightgown, her reading glasses perched on the tip of her nose and a book open in front of her.

"It was okay," Livia said.

"You enjoyed your date then? He's a sweet boy. Your father and I like him."

That was what was important, after all, she thought.

"Do you like him?"

"I like him well enough," Livia said. Well enough to put up with him for a while, anyway. "Where's Dad?"

"He was called back into work just a few minutes ago."

Livia's dead heart sank and tears welled up in her eyes.

"I never see him anymore."

Her mother shook her head. "He works very hard." And she went back to her reading.

Z

Cole couldn't sleep. He stood at his bedroom window staring across the street at Livia's house. She'd be sleeping and the thought piqued his anger. How could she sleep after what the vamps did at Rachel's? At least she didn't take part in it. And she looked upset when she saw him. He almost thought it possible that she still wanted him.

What happened? His heart twisted into knots. One night they were kissing and the next they hated each other. It all happened so fast he couldn't remember the transition. All he knew was that he had her in his arms one minute and then she was accepting a date with Stephan Hack, the jerk. All the vamps were jerks. Violent, arrogant, brainless jerks. He thought she was different; but she was just another vamp.

He turned to his bed where he'd tossed the large envelope full of Cerebellum's nonsense. Why not? What else did he have to do? It wouldn't hurt his history studies to learn as much as he could about the viruses. He dumped the contents onto his bedspread and picked up the first page of several yellow legal papers, covered in writing. After reading over half of it he realized it was snippets of a diary. Cerebellum had apparently hand copied someone's journal. It couldn't have been his own, it was too disconnected. Unless Cole was right the first

184

time and Cerebellum was insane.

The last line on the page was, "Clues, clues, clues. There are clues."

The hair on the back of his neck stood on end and his blood began to flow easier in his dying veins. He reread the page. Each entry must have been something Cerebellum thought was a clue to a mystery. The reference to tea and the lab now made sense. All the entries were about food and drink. He took tea in the lab. He had cake in the library. He ate dinner on the balcony. And after he said there were clues, he tested the coffee on his dog.

Poisoned? That's it, Cole thought. The person writing the journal thought he was being poisoned. The architectural drawings on the index cards looked like room layouts, apparently those of the Welsh mansion and business complex. Included in the envelope was a map of the grounds with a note on the spot that Cole knew was deep inside Hidden Lake woods north of the big house.

The note said, "Search for victims."

In a standard white envelope, Cole found folded newspaper clippings about Herb Slade, Rick's father, and his pharmacies. They were awarded an exclusive contract in Darkspur for the distribution of Zom-be-Gon, and the vampire mood drug, Calm. Another article said that Slade had purchased a share in Welsh Corporation to help develop pharmaceuticals for the vampire population. Another was about the celebration of Welsh Corporations thirty-fifth anniversary. Dr. Arnold Krenske stared out of the weathered piece of newsprint at Cole, old, tired, defeated.

Cole's eyes were thick with sleep when he started stacking the papers to return them to the envelope. One set of notepad pages, folded together, fell from the bunch and out of them, an index card fluttered to the floor. Cole unfolded the papers and read a long list of names with notes and dates next to them. He recognized many of them as vamps. He was about to reach to the floor for the card when the name Duvessa caught his eye. He sucked in a breath and read. "Orel Duvessa, three years ago. Didn't work. Had to go for daughter."

"What?" Cold said aloud.

He reached for the card and on it the word genius popped out at him. He read the handwritten note.

"Krenske, genius, youngest man in the world to start and run multi-million dollar corporation. At 13, created Welsh Corp, named for his mother Marion Welsh, who suffered from rare blood condition. He set out to find the cure."

Suddenly Cole wasn't tired anymore. He dumped the envelope contents again onto his bed and found the white envelope, ruffled through the clippings and pulled out the one with Krenske's picture. He was an old man. Very old. Thirty-five years. That would make him only forty-eight. But he looked eighty. He was poisoned! Or something. Something had happened to him. And that picture was taken five years ago at least. Was he even still alive?

Cole knew he had to find out.

CHAPTER EIGHTEEN

ole woke late on Sunday; it was nine o'clock that evening before he was ready to go out. He and Brock were supposed to track down some of the other zombies and head over to Rachel's to help clean up after the party disaster. But he needed to think before he talked to Brock.

He walked down his dark street, his hands in his pockets against the cold, recollecting all the information he'd found in Cerebellum's envelope. It had to mean something, he thought. But he hated the idea of the zombies calling him a conspiracy theorist. No self-respecting zombie wanted to be labeled stupid. He found himself in the playground at the end of the block. When he looked up, suddenly aware of his surroundings, Livia was sitting on a swing looking at him in the moonlight.

"Hi," he said, without thinking. "Sorry. I didn't know you were here."

"It's okay." she said. "I mean, it's a free country and all."

"For the time being."

"What's that mean?"

"Nothing."

"I can leave," she said. "I've already been here a while."

"That's okay."

"Well, you can stay, too. I mean. We can be in the same park together, right?"

"Sure," he said. He looked around, looked up, looked down, and finally walked over to the swing next to hers and sat in it. The seat was cold and the chain colder. He let out a shiver.

"Are zombies colder in the winter?" She asked.

"Definitely. And parts fall off."

"Not you."

He shook his head. "I got the vaccine before I died, almost immediately. It makes a big difference."

"You know, you think the vamps are the coolest kids in school, but I know some regular girls who really go for zombies."

Cole laughed. "Sure you do."

"I do."

"Well, we don't see them lining up for autographs or anything."

"They're intimidated, that's all."

"Intimidated by what?"

"Your brains, silly. You guys talk about important stuff."

"Yeah, I get it. Great gray skin isn't enough to overcome their distaste for science."

"Well, you guys could work on your social skills."

"We have more important things on our minds."

"Exactly," she said, smiling at him.

After a pause, he said, "I've been meaning to apologize, you know, for that night."

"What night?"

He nodded slightly. "You forgot."

"You mean, *that* night?"

"Yeah, I didn't know you liked Stephan Hack. I mean, I wouldn't have, you know, kissed you, if I'd known. I didn't mean to step on anyone's territory."

"I'm nobody's territory," she said. "And anyway, I didn't like him."

"Then why did you go out with him?"

"I mean, I didn't like him when you kissed me."

"But you liked him the next day."

"Yeah."

"Wow," he said. "That's really, I don't know...fickle."

"Fickle? Did you just say fickle?"

"Is there a better word?"

They were silent for several minutes. The creaking of the swing chains irritated Cole. He wrapped his arms tighter around his waist.

"You cold?" He said.

"Nah."

They went silent again. The wind whispered through the pine trees lining the western edge of the park. A dog barked in the distance. Cole suddenly remembered the Eppersons and their dogs, lying dead in the playground sand. He shivered.

"My mom and dad told me I couldn't see you anymore," she said.

He nodded. "Well, it was lucky you had Stephan to take up the slack."

Her feet patted the ground below her swing.

"Did you find out any more about your research? You know, about the virus?"

"Maybe."

"What did you find?"

"Why are you interested?"

She shrugged. "I don't know. I thought maybe you

189

could find out if the vamps' virus has anything to do with violence."

"What do you mean?"

"I don't know, really," she sighed. "It just seems like they're getting meaner."

"That's just because of the fights, the pranks. Lute was right; we should have just left it alone."

"No, I think it's more than that. I know I've only been here a couple of months, but they're just getting agitated, more and more. And Rick is feeding off it. They keep talking about killing zombies."

"Maybe they're just mad. And you're right. You haven't lived here long. They've never been a happy bunch."

"You didn't feel that way before."

"What do you mean?"

She shook her head. "When I told you before you said I should go to the police."

He shrugged and looked away. "I don't know what I think anymore."

They were silent for a while, only the creaking of their swings against the wind echoed between them. Cole fought the urge to tell her everything he'd been thinking. If something was going on, he didn't want her involved. But his curiosity tightened his chest.

"Did your dad want to work for Welsh?" He said.

She hesitated before answering. "What do you mean?"

"I mean, when they offered him a job, did he take it? Or did they have to, you know, work to get him."

"They offered him a job years ago, before he was a vamp. I remember because my mom didn't want to live here. They offered again after he was turned, but he still said no."

"So, it wasn't until you were turned that he accepted a

190

job with them."

She nodded. "That's right. Even my mom thought it would be better for us here after that. Why?"

"What did you say your father did for them?"

"He's a chemist. Why?"

Cole shook his head. "Just wondering."

"I wish I could go back to Florida."

"Really?"

"I don't know. Maybe I need a whole new place. A place where nobody cares if you're a vamp or a zombie or a regular."

"Does a place like that exist?"

She turned to look at him and his heart thumped a couple of times in his chest.

"I hope so."

They sat staring at each other in the dark for several minutes. Cole's fingers froze on the swing chain but he didn't want to move. He wanted to look into her eyes forever.

"I have to go," she said.

"I'll walk you back."

He wanted to be near her, take her hand.

"You better not. If my mom sees us together, I'll be in big trouble."

"Oh."

He felt a gnawing, gaping emptiness inside him as he watched her walk into the darkness down the street. He still wanted to crush her skull and feel her brains in his mouth; but he wanted to hold her, kiss her, and comfort her first.

Z

When Livia returned to school on Monday the vamps' pecking order had clearly changed. Wherever Rick was alone, he was the god. The vamps lowered their eyes and nodded their yeses whenever he spoke. But when Todd Quaid was with him, Rick had less swagger, he was less bold, and less witty–though Livia never saw as much wit in him as the other vamps in the first place. Livia could barely keep herself from mentioning Wanda whenever she was in Todd's company. But she knew Wanda was right. If he could knock his own sister senseless and bury her, he wouldn't think twice about doing worse to Livia. She wondered if Stephan might have meant Todd, when he claimed Rick knew feral vamps who killed regulars. But she looked at him and decided against it. Burying his sister, sure. Hurting Livia, yes. But sucking the blood out of a regular until she was dead? That took the kind of intimacy she didn't think Todd was capable of.

At lunch, as she walked through the cafeteria to the vamp tables, Livia glanced several times toward the zombie corner where Cole sat with his friends. He returned her look, but neither of them smiled.

As she approached, she heard Darlene saying, "Right after school. 112." But as soon as she pulled a chair from the table, Darlene and the girls she was talking to startled and exchanged fearful looks.

Livia sat across from Rick and Stephan. She smiled, but clearly Stephan was angry with her. Rick nudged him. Stephan gave him a shocked look. Rick nudged him again and turned to Livia.

"He's mad."

"Why?" Livia squeezed her blood box straw from its plastic wrap and stuck into the box.

"Why do you think? You're still hung up on that zombie."

Livia felt the blood in her face pool at her cheeks and she lowered her eyes.

"How can you even think it?" Rick said, glaring at

her.

"I don't see the big deal," Livia told him.

"It isn't normal," Elena said.

"What's not normal about it?"

"We stick to our own kind," Rick said.

"What kind?"

He rolled his eyes. "You're a vamp. You can't go around with zombies. It's just not right."

"We're people, just like everyone else," Livia said. Her voice trembled and her eyes remained on the table in front of her.

"We're not like everyone else and you know it."

"We are. We're just afflicted differently."

"There she goes again."

"What?" Livia challenged him, finally raising her eyes to his.

"You know what. You act like we're sick. But we're not sick. We're turned. We're transformed. A new species."

"We're afflicted. And so are the zombies. They're no different than us."

"They are different," Jenny Salts said.

Livia turned to her, hurt.

"Come on," Jenny said. "You have to admit it. We're different and, well, you just don't go around with zombies."

Livia shook her head. "We're both undead. So what's the big difference?"

"Well, you eat blood and he eats brains, for one thing."

"He doesn't eat brains."

Rick laughed shortly. "Only because he's on his little pill."

"We're just not that different. I think you all just don't like the zombies because they're smarter than us."

"That's part of their virus," Elena said. "We can't be jealous of something they can't control."

"They aren't all that much smarter," Jenny said. "Look at you, Livia. I mean, you're smart."

"Yeah, that's probably why he likes you," Elena said.

Rick laughed loud this time and looked around the table at them all. "He likes her for her brains," he said.

Livia rolled her eyes. "He doesn't like me."

"Good," Rick said. "Maybe he is smart. But staying away from vamp chicks isn't enough to save him from what's coming."

"What's coming?"

Rick eyed the other vamps and smirked at Livia. "Nothing you need to worry about. Just don't get attached to any zombies, if you don't want to be disappointed."

The Wister twins sat down and started chattering. Ciara liked to scold her brother and quizzed him on his classes. Livia tuned them all out until the bell rang. She waited until Rick and Stephan left, Stephan giving her a slight smile and a nod, before she gathered her books in her arms.

"See you at the meeting," Ciara Wister said. She gave Livia a sly smile.

"What meeting?"

"Never mind," Darlene said.

"Oh, weren't you invited?" Ciara said and let out an uncharacteristic, high-pitched chuckle.

"I said never mind." Darlene gave Ciara a hard look. "You're mom's picking you up today, right?"

Livia nodded. Darlene and the twins left and Livia looked at Jenny. "What meeting?"

Jenny looked around the cafeteria before replying.

"Rick's called a meeting after school." She looked apologetically at Livia.

194

"Am I the only vamp not invited?"

"I thought it was for all of us."

"Well, I should go then. Where's it at?"

Jenny's eyes darted nervously to the floor.

"I don't know if I should tell you. Rick would have told you if he wanted you to come. But..."

"It's okay, it's room 112, right?"

Relief flooded her face. "Yeah, that's right. So you do know."

Livia tried to smile at her. She took another brief look at the zombies before she left.

When the last bell rang, Livia hurried to room 112. It was one of the two science rooms that were connected to a lab in between. She caught up with Jenny at the door and they walked in together. The room was dark, but dozens of pink eyes glowed at her when the vamps turned to stare.

"What is she doing here?" Rick sneered.

Jenny looked at Livia, fear on her face, and turned to Rick. "Isn't this meeting for all of us?"

"She hates her own kind."

"Oh, come off it, Rick." Darlene said.

Though she'd said it with hesitation and some fear in her voice, Livia was grateful for the defense.

"What's the big deal?" She said, letting herself slide in behind a desk in the back row. "What are you meeting for?"

"We're not talking about this in front of her," Rick said to Jenny.

"Why not? What are you planning?" Livia said.

Rick seethed and glared at Jenny.

"All right, I'm leaving,"

"I'm sorry, Livia," Jenny said.

Livia shrugged. No big deal. She left the classroom, walked next door to the lab and entered quietly. She put her backpack and umbrella on a desk and crept up to the adjoining door, thankful that it was only opaque plastic; holding her breath, she pressed her ear to the small space between the door and the wall, listening. Rick did all the talking and when she'd heard enough, she turned, grabbed her backpack, and slipped out the door and down the hallway, realizing too late she'd left her umbrella behind. She started to turn around but heard the door open and the others leaving the science classroom. She darted down the hallway out of sight and waited until they disappeared before turning around and going back into the lab room. She found her umbrella on the floor under the desk and grabbed it. When she turned to leave, Jenny stood in the doorway.

"You were in here listening." She said.

Livia said nothing, but stared at her.

"I'm in big trouble because of you. All because you followed me into the meeting."

"Jenny, you're not going to kill zombies," Livia said. "Tell me you're not going to take part in this."

"What did you hear?"

"Enough."

"No, not enough. Nobody's going to kill anyone unless they've gone full zombie. It's not just legal to kill a full zombie, it's necessary."

"There aren't any full zombies."

"But there will be."

"How do you know that?"

She hesitated, started to speak and stopped, and finally said. "There's going to be a zombie outbreak. Rick wanted us all prepared. I...I don't know why he didn't want you in on it. I shouldn't have told you."

"How can he know about an outbreak before it happens?"

"I don't know."

"But you believe him?"

"Why wouldn't I believe him?"

"Are you sure Rick even knows what full zombie looks like? What if he's lying to you? What if he gets you guys to kill people who aren't full zombies?"

Jenny sighed and glared at Livia. "You know, I knew you didn't like Rick when you first came to school; but this is ridiculous. I mean, you're talking murder. You really think Rick would just kill zombies whether they're full zombie or not?"

Livia stared at her.

"How far does your hatred go?" Jenny said.

"I don't hate him; but I don't trust him."

"Well, I do. Rick doesn't like zombies. But he's no murderer."

"Then why are you all afraid of him?"

"What?" She shook her head. "You're imagining things. We're not afraid of Rick. We're afraid of your friend Cole and the other zombies. You should be afraid, too. You would be if you didn't hate..."

"Hate who?"

"Rick is right about you. You hate your own kind."

Jenny turned and left the room, leaving Livia shaking with nervous energy. She was sure she'd heard right. Rick was planning to somehow make the zombies go full zombie so he could kill as many as possible, Cole especially. But how?

She headed out of the now empty school. The front lawn glowed in early morning moonlight and the lamp posts highlighted the wet shine on the icy asphalt of the parking lot. The vamps were getting in their cars to leave and she hoped they wouldn't notice her as she walked to the flagpole to await her mother. She was about to take a seat on the bench when she realized Rick strode toward her from the lot. Fear rose up from her toes into her chest and her breathing quickened. Just as he reached her, her mother's car came through the front gate and she felt some relief.

Breathlessly she said, "My mother's here, I've got to go."

He stood only inches away, leering into her eyes. "She'll wait," he said. "Jenny tells me you listened in on our little meeting."

She nodded. "So?"

"So you listen up. One word of it to any of the zombies and you're dead."

"I'm a—"

"Yeah, yeah, I know. You're already dead. There are ways. You know there are ways. I promise you, your mom will never see you again. You got that, zombie lover?"

Without thinking, she nodded.

"If I so much as see you going near a zombie, you're dead. You got that?"

"Yeah, sure. Sure." She said.

He stepped aside and she dashed to her mother's car.

"Was that Rick Slade?" Her mother said with a smile as she drove away. "Such a handsome boy."

"Yeah, right," she said quietly.

"Well, if things don't work out with Stephan...well, there you go."

There I go, she thought.

ole knew something was going on with the vamps. All the zombies knew it. The vamps were slithering around, doing a lot of whispering, and huddling together in little groups watching the zombies as if they expected something. But what?

"Okay," Brock said after school later that week. "I'm back to believing in the conspiracy theory again."

Cole laughed. "Which one?"

"You had more than one?"

"I don't think I ever completely formulated any theory."

"Well, the vamps are definitely up to something."

"I agree, but I'm not sure we're talking about the same vamps."

"Why?"

"That crazy dude's papers."

"You mean the list you told me about?"

Cole nodded. "A list of people who just happen to be vamps now."

"And the idea that there were victims in Hidden Lake

Woods."

"There's definitely something going on. I'm just not sure if our Slade problem has anything to do with it."

"You mean Mayor Slade?"

"It is hard to believe. Let me just see Dr. Krenske and we'll know more."

"You're finally going to see your hero."

Cole shook his head and sighed. It was true. What could he say?

"And you think he's going to tell you that vampires are trying to take over the world?"

"This is no time to refrain from a rush to judgement." He said with a smile.

"You're serious? The vamps are trying to take over the world?"

"It's probably just our imaginations gone crazy."

"Our imaginations? Speak for yourself."

"Maybe we don't know the history of the viruses because it just hasn't been written yet. And I'll be the one to write it."

Brock nodded. "We can always hope."

"What could they be planning anyway? Another fight?"

"I thought you said they were taking over the world."

"No, not the Welsh vamps. Slade."

"Another fight? I enjoyed the last one."

When Cole called the Welsh Corporation, asking for an interview with Dr. Krenske, he'd been shuttled from person to person until he was finally told no. But a simple appeal to Mrs. Moody from the school newspaper got his foot in the door and an appointment on Thursday morning after school. After all, Krenske and the Welsh Corporation founded Darkspur and the high school. Certainly they would let the student newspaper have an interview.

200

Cole was ready with a short list of questions regarding Krenske's mother and her blood condition and what a cure may have to do with the viruses. It was just a hunch, but if he played the questions correctly, he'd know if Krenske was hiding anything. Wondering how he might handle the age question, he opened his front door to leave and found Livia Duvessa standing on his front porch.

"Cole," she said, her face frantic, her eyes darting up and down the dark street. "Cole, the vamps are planning something, something awful. I wish I knew how, but I think Rick is going to get you to go full zombie so he can kill you. It sounds crazy, I know. But you have to believe me."

"What?" He stared at her.

"Please, just be careful. I can't stay here. If someone sees me talking to you..."

"He can't make us go full zombie, don't worry about it."

"I hope not. I know it sounds insane. But what if he kills you anyway, and just says you were full zombie?"

Cole shook his head. "He wouldn't risk it. He's immortal. Can you imagine life in prison when you're undead?"

"But his father has so much power. In the town. At Welsh. I know, I know, I shouldn't accuse him if I don't know all the details. But I heard him say there would be a huge zombie outbreak and the vamps are ready for it."

She looked so small and deathly cold standing in the porch light. His first thought was to comfort her, to smooth her hair, caress her skull, and imagine her juicy brains in his hands.

"Don't worry about it." He said. "It's just high school pranks."

"Please, just be careful."

She turned and ran across the street to her house, slamming the door shut behind her.

As he drove to the Welsh mansion he considered what Livia had said. Would Slade and the vamps really kill the zombies? She'd tried to tell him before that they were planning something. He should have made her to go to the police. He should have called the police himself. But what would Slade do to Livia if he found out she'd tried to warn people? He shuddered at the thought. Slade was dangerous, that much he knew. But if his suspicions were correct, the whole vampire population needed to be stopped.

He was shown into a carpeted, lamplit, front room in the Welsh mansion where he waited for twenty minutes before the door opened and through it rolled a wheelchair carrying a tired, withered old man covered by a plaid blanket. The chair was pushed by a tall, sleek, frowning vampire. He pushed Dr. Krenske to a small round table. Behind him, a woman pushing a tea cart entered the room; she poured steaming tea and set a cup on the table for Dr. Krenske.

"Would you care for tea?" The dour vampire asked. His voice was like silk and echoed slightly in the room.

Cole shook his head.

"Very well. You may begin."

Cole sat down in a chair next to the table and leaned forward toward Dr. Krenske. He looked at him for several seconds, peering at his face. It did look like the guy in the picture.

"Dr. Krenske?" He said quietly.

The old man turned slowly, his head bobbing a bit back and forth, to look at him. His round moist eyes settled on Cole's and he smiled. He looked like a zombie, but Cole had never read anything about Krenske being a vamp or a zombie.

"I'm Cole Bertrand, Darkspur High newspaper staff."

"Eh?" Krenske's voice rang loudly through the room. "Speak up," he yelled.

Cole raised his voice as loud as he dared. "I'd like to ask you some questions."

"Yes, yes," he said. He pulled an arm from under the blanket and pointed a wrinkled, bony finger at Cole. "Go on."

"I understand you started the Welsh Corporation hoping to find a cure for your mother's blood condition."

The old man nodded. The vampire moved from behind Krenske's chair to stand beside him.

"Did you succeed?"

He shook his head.

"Are you still trying?"

He opened his mouth and snapped it shut again. "No," he said.

Cole looked up to the hovering vampire and back to Dr. Krenske.

"How did the zombie and vampire viruses start?"

Dr. Krenske tilted his head and leaned forward toward Cole.

"I don't know." He said. "Nobody knows."

"Are you trying to find out?"

"No."

"Why not?"

Krenske leaned further. "What difference does it make how it started?"

"But aren't you curious?"

The old man coughed and the vampire pushed him forward, swatted him several times on the back and pushed him back again. Krenske looked up at the ceiling.

"We must concentrate ourselves on helping vampires and zombies live with their afflictions. The past is past. What's done is done."

"What do you know about the magick?"

Dr. Krenske looked back to Cole and smiled.

"Magick? There's no such thing as magic, son."

Cole fidgeted in his seat and glanced quickly again to the brooding vampire and back to Krenske.

"Sir," he said. "In your book, *Zombie Revolution*, you seem to say that, in the end, zombies will rule the world and either drive the vamps underground, or destroy them."

"Yes, yes. Naturally," Krenske said with a wave of his wrinkled hand. "If the vampires turn too many, they'll be left without a food supply. But they don't seem to care about long term consequences."

A low hiss escaped the vampire and he laid a slender hand on Krenske's shoulder. Krenske's eyes darted toward it and he looked back to Cole.

"You can only expect them to understand so much, you see."

"Well, do you think...that is to say, sir," looking up to the vampire, "with all due respect," and back to Krenske, "do you think the vamps are trying to kill off the zombies and take over the world?"

Krenske looked at him, stared for several seconds. A clock somewhere in the room ticked louder and louder. Finally, Dr. Krenske sucked in a long breath and laughed loud, spittle spewing onto his plaid blanket. He sucked in another breath and started coughing again. The vampire beat him on the back until he stopped. Krenske laughed some more until Cole was laughing with him.

Well, that was that. Now he'd have to pretend to conduct the rest of the interview for the school newspaper. As he flipped through his list of questions, voices erupted outside the room and another vampire entered.

"Rollings, come quick. Trespassers."

204

The vampire bowed slightly at Cole and patted Krenske's shoulder.

"I'll be back shortly," he said and Cole thought it sounded a lot like a threat, rather than a promise.

As soon as he left the room, Dr. Krenske sat up, pulled his other hand out from under the blanket and rolled his chair closer to Cole.

"It's like this, listen quick. It was meant to be the cure, but it killed the first test subjects. Well, not entirely, they were zombies, you see. And the next formulation caused the vampire outbreak. I wouldn't mind so much, myself, if we all could've just lived with it. We were making a fortune off the blood boxes, Zom-be-Gon and, of course, Calm for the vampires' aggressiveness; but the vampires turned out to be somewhat, I don't know what you'd call it, let's say, arrogant, and I fear they want to use the virus to, well, to put it bluntly, take over the world. They've been turning certain regulars by design, and of course, they encourage the ferals. Do you think you could do something about it all? I'm afraid I haven't much time left. The dog died, you see."

Just then, Rollings returned and Krenske's shoulders fell, a bit of slobber rolled down his chin, and his eyes glazed over nicely.

Rollings looked at Cole and wiped Dr. Krenske's chin with a handkerchief.

"You look like death. Did he say something to upset you?" Rollings said.

"Oh," Cole shook himself out of his shock. "No, no. He just fell forward and started drooling and mumbling."

"I warned your Mrs. Moody that he'd likely not be able to offer much. But I'd be happy to answer all of your questions."

Rollings face slowly formed into a smile.

Ten minutes later, Rollings escorted Cole to his car

and folded his arms across his chest. Storm clouds had formed in the predawn darkness seeming to cast Rollings in a paler shade of white. But his blood red lips still curled in a placid smile as a cold wind ruffled his hair.

"What's wrong with Dr. Krenske?" Cole asked him.

"Nothing."

"Nothing?"

Rollings shoulders raised and lowered slowly. "He's a very old man."

Cole nodded. Sure he was.

A car engine raced and Cole turned to see Alan's car fly out of the woods, cross in front of the mansion, kicking up dirt, and race down the road toward town. A black sedan followed shortly after, but stopped at the boundary of the yard.

"Your friends, I presume." Rollings said.

Cole's mouth fell open. "I don't know what you're talking about," he said and got in his car. He couldn't help smiling as he drove off the property.

Alan and Brock were waiting for him at his house, their faces beaming with grins.

"Did you see us?" Alan said. "That was the scariest thing I ever did."

"What were you doing?" Cole said.

"Brock figured they wouldn't let you see the old doctor alone so we staged a diversion."

"Did it work?" Brock said.

Cole smiled. "Genius."

"We're not zombies for nothing. What did you find out?"

"There's definitely something going on with the vamps. But I didn't learn much. Something about trying to take over the world is all."

It was still not daylight and the early morning sky was filled with dark clouds, promising a dark day. A shrill scream echoed through the neighborhood and chills sped down Cole's dead spine.

CHAPTER TWENTY

The three of them turned, looking for the source of the scream; it was easy, the woman screamed again and again, running out of her house—fourth on the left down the street—and across her lawn. She screamed as she struggled to get into her car. But she turned back toward her house, screamed again and ran toward the park at the end of the block.

"What's got into Mrs. Sheffield?" Cole said.

Another scream rang out, this time farther down the street.

"What the...?" Brock said.

Cole put up a hand to silence him. Winston Sheffield lumbered down his driveway four doors down.

"Oh, no," Alan said. "Is he...?"

"Maybe he just needs a hypo."

Alan ran to his car and pulled his emergency kit out of the glove compartment.

"Let's go," he said.

"Prep one, just in case," Cole said as they ran down the street toward Winston.

"It's still too dark," Brock said. "How can we tell?"

"We need more light. Get him under the street lamp."

They ran to one of the few poles on the street and called out to Winston. He turned, a low groan escaped him, and he limped toward them.

"Cole?" Alan said, his voice trembling. "There's another one."

Mr. Hanson came out of the dim morning toward them, followed by Mrs Albrecht and little Cindy Lou Peterson. Cole swallowed hard. They were definitely full zombie. They'd gone almost greenish, blue gray; skin peeled away from muscle on their faces, patches of hair fell off as they lurched forward, dragging dead legs. And their eyes! Deadened, gray, lifeless orbs rolling in their sockets.

Suddenly Mrs. Peterson stomped down the street, her enormous torso pounding up and down under her silk pajamas.

"Cindy," she cried.

"No, Mrs. Peterson," Cole called.

"Cindy."

The large woman grabbed her little girl and turned her toward their house. She let out a horrific scream and pulled away without her left arm. Cindy turned back to the boys and spat her mother's fat, juicy arm to the road.

"We didn't bring our hatchets." Cole said.

"Shit," Brock said.

"Can we be sure?" Alan said.

"Snap out of it, Alan," Cole said. "This is happening."

In chapter eighteen of *Zombie Revolution*, "Is it Dead Yet?," Dr. Krenske listed the signs of a full zombie:

- Stiffness in all joints; difficulty in movement
- Deader than usual appearance in the skin
- Eyes completely whitened and/or rolled up

210

into the head

- Mouth open, enlarged tongue, drooling
- Spasms and tics, especially in the neck and shoulders
- Deep, resonating groans that may, or may not, sound like the word brains.

Unfortunately, the intended audience for Krenske's book, namely everyone, didn't read it. This was probably because of the title, and the picture of a zombie carrying an enormous axe on the cover. It could also have to do with the fact that Dr. Krenske's writing style was academic and dull. Even the zombies didn't read it. And while full-zombie spotting was included in the required high school level class, "Now you're a zombie, what next?," obviously, reading about a full zombie attack and experiencing one were two very different things.

The boys backed out from under the street lamp as Winston lurched into the light. His eyes were deadly white, his skin greenish grey and parts of his face curled and fell off. Stiffly, he moved toward them, moaning.

"Did he just say brains?" Alan squeaked.

"Hurry," Cole said and darted back toward the house, weaving in and out between the other zombies. "I have two hatchets under my front seat."

"Me, too," Alan said.

Several more zombies careened toward them from the other end of street and Cole's mother's car screeched to a halt behind them. In the light of a street lamp, Cole could see his mother's horrified face. She maneuvered her car around them and pulled into the driveway.

"Get inside, Mom. Hurry."

"Cole, be careful. I'm calling your step dad."

"Just get inside," he yelled.

"Cole," she screamed.

He turned to see Mr. Lawrence, the eighty-year old pervert from next door lunging for him. He swung the hatchet around hard; it caught in Mr. Lawrence's head. Brock screamed a war cry, ran forward and sunk his hatchet deep into Mr. Lawrence's neck. The old man's head fell forward, held on by a thread of skin and muscle, and his body crumpled to the ground.

They stood over him staring for a few seconds.

"Let's go." Brock said, finishing off the cut with one more hack.

Cole rescued his hatchet from old man Lawrence's skull and ran into the growing hum of groaning zombies, hacking off their heads one by one.

Z

Livia heard Mrs. Bertrand's screams and pulled the curtain from the front window. She let out a gasp when she saw Brock lop off Mr. Lawrence's head and turned from the scene covering her face with her hands. She trembled violently for a moment, then forced herself to shake it off. Falling to the floor, she frantically searched under the coffee table for her shoes.

"What's wrong?" Her mother said.

"They need help. There are zombies loose."

"Zombies?" Her voice quavered with fear.

Mrs. Duvessa pulled aside the curtain at the front window and peered out at the massacre.

"Oh, dear lord. You're not going out there."

"I have to help."

"What are you going to do, chop off zombie heads? Is that the kind of story you want to tell your grandchildren? Is that what you want haunting your dreams?"

Livia stared at her mother, incredulous.

"What are you talking about? I have to help them."

212

"What for? They're already zombies. What more could happen?"

"They can be killed, mother. Killed. I have to help."

"You're not leaving this house, young lady."

"It's my duty to kill full zombies as much as it is yours."

"That's a lie. It's your right, certainly. But no one is expected to leave the safety of her home to put her life at risk. You can be killed just as easily as they can."

"No, not quite, mother. I'm a vamp. We're... Oh, I don't have time to explain this to you; I have to get out there."

Her mother stood in front of the door, her arms outstretched.

"I know you think I'm stupid about vampires, Livia. But I've seen zombies rip them apart in seconds. You *can* be killed."

"I'm helping Cole."

"Over my dead body."

"Don't be so melodramatic, mother."

There was a knock at the door and her mother jumped and let out a short scream.

"The zombies."

Livia rolled her eyes and stepped around her to peer out the window. Rick, Todd, and Stephan stood at the door with a couple of unfamiliar vamps.

"Who is it?"

"Nobody. They'll go away."

"I said, who is it?" Her mother shoved her aside and pulled back the curtain. "Why it's Rick and Stephan, probably here to see if you're safe. That's sweet of them."

"No, don't open the door."

"Why not?"

Her mother pulled open the door and let the vampires in.

Z

Cole was several doors down the street when he heard Mrs. Duvessa screaming. He turned toward her house and saw her on the front lawn, her hands on her head, running in circles.

"Get back inside," he called to her and was nearly grabbed by Mr. Keefer full zombie. He lopped off his head with his dirty hatchet and moved on.

The three of them finally came to the point they dreaded. Winston was limping toward the playground, harsh moans echoing around him. His mother stood by the pines, still screaming.

"Winston, baby, no. No, Winston." Then another piercing shriek.

"Turn around, Mrs. Sheffield," Brock called out.

"No," she screamed.

"Alan," Brock said.

"Got it." Alan ran across the playground, grabbed Mrs. Sheffield and pulled her through the trees into the Robinson's back yard.

Her screams filled the neighborhood as Winston turned to Brock and Cole

"Oh, man. Winston, what happened?"

He was decayed, rotting flesh hanging from his face, one ear dangling from his head. He opened his mouth and his gray, dead tongue pushed its way out between his blue lips, speckled with rotting spots. The tongue slipped back in and Winston bared his teeth while his unseeing eyes rolled back in his head. He lurched forward and moaned.

"Winston," Brock mumbled.

Cole swung his hatchet and whipped it across his friend's neck. Tears filled his eyes as he watched Winston fall to the ground. Cole raised the hatchet to sever the

214

head but Brock stopped him.

"Let me."

Cole looked at him, shocked.

"I don't want you to be the only one to have to do it," Brock said.

Cole nodded and let Brock whack Winston's head off.

Another zombie limped down a driveway in the distance.

"This is going to be a long morning." Cole said.

CHAPTER TWENTY-ONE

Todd jumped into the back of Rick's Jag with his hatchet; he gave what he hoped was a casual, careless nod to Elena in the front seat and smiled at Stephan and Liam Wister.

"This is going to be fun," he said. "Where's Ciara? She's going to miss it."

Liam shrugged but didn't answer.

"She's following with Jenny," Elena said.

They drove out of Noche de Sangre and along Park Avenue.

"You like my sister," Liam said, frowning.

Todd smiled at him.

"She hates you."

Todd shrugged.

At the entrance to Crane Park, three zombies limped out into the road. Rick slowed the car, swerving to avoid hitting them.

"Stop," Todd said.

"We're going to Buckley Street."

More zombies teetered into the street.

"Come on," Todd said. "Stop here. Crane Park is full of them."

"Yeah," Liam said. "There's plenty here."

Rick sighed. "Okay, but just for practice. Then we head over to Buckley."

He pulled the car to the other side of the street in the grass and they all got out, swinging their hatchets.

"Damn," Elena said. "I need more sun screen."

"Ah, come on," Todd said. "It's cloudy enough."

She rolled her eyes at him and pulled her sunglasses off the top of her head to cover her eyes.

"Twit," she mumbled before running across the street and hacking the head off a zombie.

Three other cars skidded to a stop and Todd saw Ciara and a bunch of other vamps join in. He whacked off the heads of the first two zombies he came to and jogged over to Ciara, making her way down Crane Street.

"Hey, Ciara," he said.

She turned to him, her dark curly hair bouncing around her head and her lips pursed in a smirk. "What do you want?"

"Nothing," he chuckled. "Just thought we could fight together. You know, shared experience and all."

"Huh?"

"What are you doing?" Liam called out.

Todd turned to watch him hack the head off an undead.

"We're fighting together."

"Stay away from my sister."

"Liam, be careful," Ciara yelled and turned to whack the head off another zombie.

"There are a lot of them, aren't there," Todd said.

"Don't bother me."

"Sorry." He said. "I don't mean to distract you. I just thought—" He swung around and notched the head off another one. "I thought we could hang out, you know."

"Leave my sister alone," Liam called.

Todd turned to tell him to chill out, but instead, saw two zombies take him from behind.

"Liam," Ciara screamed and started toward him.

Todd grabbed her and held fast as she clawed at him, screaming, "Liam!"

The two zombies each grabbed one of Liam's arms and a third lumbered over and took his head. They pulled and Liam's screams echoed through the neighborhood. Suddenly the zombies fell, each with a part of Liam in its arms, and began eating.

A piercing shriek escaped Ciara; she vomited synthetic blood, and Todd let her fall to her knees. He stood, stunned, watching Rick and Stephan run forward, and then stop, realizing they could do nothing more. He turned and attacked two zombies coming for him and Ciara, and then pulled her to her feet.

"Get off me," she wailed. "Leave me alone."

"We have to fight."

She sobbed and stood, and swung her hatchet at him. He ducked and fell backwards.

"Not me." He said.

"I could have saved him."

"Nuh-uh," Rick called. "He was a goner."

"What the hell was that?" Stephan cried.

"I told you," Rick sneered. "Zombies are dangerous."

"You never said they could do that."

Ciara was straddled on top of Todd; she drew back a hand and slapped him hard across the face leaving a deep pink mark against his white cheek.

"It's your fault."

"No," he mumbled and covered his face.

"Why did you stop me?"

"I was protecting you."

"You killed my brother."

She sobbed and climbed off him, staggering toward a clutch of three zombies. She let out a deep-throated scream and attacked them. One, two, three, their heads thudded to the ground. Then she turned back to Todd, raising her hatchet high overhead.

"I should kill you."

"Ciara," Rick said. "Leave Todd alone and let's finish this."

She turned to hack up a zombie behind her as Todd got off the ground and whacked off a few more heads. Dang, he thought. There went any chance he might have had with Ciara.

Z

Eighty-six zombies had gone full out on Thursday morning for no apparent reason. Vamps were on the news, in the Crane Park neighborhood, hailed as heros for saving the area from the brain-eating undead. The news vans didn't show up on Cole's street. There were only twenty zombies killed there. But Cole and Brock watched from his bedroom window as the Darkspur Monster Squad, wearing bio-hazard suits, wrapped the bodies of the newly-dead undead and took them away.

The Monster Squad patrolled the hallways at school Thursday evening. Half the regulars didn't show and the vamps huddled in their groups leering at the zombies with a mixture of loathing and terror; the grisly story of Liam Wister's demise had spread.

"Do they think we had an outbreak on purpose?" Rachel said, sliding into her seat in the cafeteria at midday break.

"That's just it," Brock said. "All the news reports say that the zombies were taking their meds. They've counted their pills and the pharmacies checked out their prescriptions."

"You're saying people are going full zombie even on the Zom-be-Gon?" Alan said.

"They must be. We all knew how anal Winston was about the pills."

There was a pause as they all turned to Winston's usual seat, empty.

"And even if he did miss a pill or two, we would have noticed, wouldn't we?" Cole said.

"Somebody would have noticed," Rachel said.

"So we could be next," Alan said. "The virus in us is mutating or something."

"We don't know that." Cole said.

"But whatever it is, it can happen to us."

"He's right," Rachel said. "Why else would the Monster Squad be here today?"

Trevor brought a tray to the table loaded with food and sat beside Rachel.

"Do you mind if I eat?"

"Why would I mind?"

"Isn't it bad form to eat when you just had to kill your friend in a zombie outbreak?"

"Are you sure you're not a werewolf?" Brock said.

"Go ahead and eat," Rachel said. "Before I was zombified, I would eat to feel better, too."

"Oh, I don't need to feel better. I'm just hungry."

"I can't believe you had to axe Winston," Stu said.

"Can we not talk about it?" Cole said.

He sat back in his chair and let his eyes wander around the cafeteria. The magick tables were empty, except for that little witch who never got along with anyone. She caught his eye and winked at him. The few regulars at school huddled together and cast furtive glances at the zombies. They're afraid, he realized. He turned to the vamp tables where they all sat posed, but

221

cautious. It was a heady, powerful feeling, he realized, to cast fear into one's enemies.

"She's not here," Brock said.

Rachel rolled her eyes. "You're such an embarrassment, Cole. The vamps are watching."

"They're gloating," Brock said. "They're heroes after all."

"Yeah, but isn't it weird that they just happened to be in Crane Park when it happened?"

"They might know some vamps there," Rachel said.

"There aren't any vamps in Crane Park," Brock said.

"I wish they'd stop staring at us like that," Alan said. "What are they so pissed about?"

"Liam."

"We didn't do it."

"We're no different from the zombies who did," Rachel said.

"They don't look pissed," Brock said. "They look...excited. Like they're expecting to get to axe us any second."

"Maybe," Cole said. "But they're mostly afraid."

Cole turned again to the vamp corner where Slade sat glaring at him. There was something in his expression that made Cole think he knew where Livia was. Before his mother dragged him into the house Thursday morning after the slaughter, Cole tried to find out if Mrs. Duvessa and Livia were okay, but Mrs. Duvessa wouldn't open her door. She called to him through the door and said they were okay, but he was sure something awful had happened. What would have caused the woman to run around her yard screaming like that? If there was a zombie in her house, she wouldn't have gone back inside. And how would a zombie have gotten into her house anyway unless she opened the door and let it in? Cole had gone so far as to walk around their house looking for

222

broken windows or smashed-in doors and it was completely in tact. Maybe Mrs. Duvessa was just crazy. But where was Livia?

The next morning after school, instead of waiting for Brock in his car, Cole walked to Darlene Chriss' car and tried to look uninterested, pacing around in circles, until she showed up.

"Have you talked to Livia?"

He lunged toward her a tad too quickly sending her into a defense pose, her backpack falling from her arm and her purse flying around to hit her on the back. She leered at him, hands raised, fangs bared, and Cole could sense her fear.

"I haven't seen her." She said, her lips twitched uncomfortably around her canines.

"When did you talk to her last? Did you go to pick her up this morning?"

Darlene relaxed her stance, letting her hands fall to her waist. "Her mom told me she's sick. Look I'm not supposed to be talking to you, could you just go away?" She bent to pick up her backpack.

"You heard the vamp."

A shiver raced down Cole's back as he turned to see Slade and his vamps posing in the parking lot like gunslingers. Confidence and hatred oozed out of their faces. Surprisingly, Todd Quaid stepped forward, just ahead of Slade and raised his chin at Cole.

"It's only a matter of time, Bertrand," Slade said with something of a hiss. "I got plenty of use out of my axe yesterday. It'll be nice and dull when you go full zombie. I'll be sure to hack your head off nice and slow."

"And maybe you'll just happen to be in my neighborhood when it happens?"

Slade flinched, his brow furrowed almost imperceptibly and his eyes darted to Todd before finding their way back to Cole.

"Maybe." He said. "Maybe I can smell zombie flesh."

"I haven't seen your sister around lately," Cole said to Todd. "She sick, too?"

"Too?" Todd said, caught off guard.

"Like Livia."

When Todd's leer turned slowly into a menacing grin, Cole shuddered.

"Yeah," he said. "She's sick. Like Livia."

Cole said nothing more and walked a wide path around the vamps, stepping up his pace once out of their zone. Brock was leaning on the hood of his car.

"What was that all about?"

"I was just curious about Livia, that's all."

"Are you out of your mind?"

"Maybe."

Cole drove into Crane Park to drop Brock at his house.

"My neighborhood looks like a war zone, huh?"

Glass spotted the street; boarded up windows and torn sod greeted them at Brock's house. Cole left the car running and waited for Brock to get out.

"So, you think one on one, a zombie could kill a vamp?" Brock said.

"Why?"

"Just wondering. I mean, I thought you had to burn them."

"Apparently just pulling them apart and eating them will do the trick."

"Yeah, but I mean, a zombie like you or me. Could we kill one?"

"Just one on one?" Cole shook his head. "I don't know. They're skinny and all."

"But they're strong."

"Not strong enough to get away from a few full out

224

zombies."

"Yeah."

They sat in silence for a moment until Brock finally got out and waved good-bye. As Cole neared his house on Buckley street, his heart skipped a few worried beats when he saw a police car in the Duvessa's driveway. He parked quickly and ran to her house just as the cops were coming out the front door, with Mrs. Duvessa, nervous and worried, rubbing her hands together, following them to their car.

"What happened?" He said. "Is Livia okay."

"That's him," Mrs. Duvessa said. "That's the boy I was telling you about."

"What is it?" Cole said. "What happened?"

"We'd like to ask you a few questions, son." The larger cop said. He smiled briefly, and then let his face return to its natural dull expression.

"Is it Livia?" he said. "What happened?"

"When was the last time you saw Livia Duvessa?"

Cole looked back and forth between the policeman and Mrs. Duvessa. "You said she was okay, just sick."

"Like I'd say anything to a zombie in the middle of an outbreak."

"Full out zombies don't talk."

"I don't trust zombies," she shrieked.

The other cop took Mrs. Duvessa by the arm and led her back into the house.

"I'm going to ask you again, son," the large cop said. "When was the last time you saw Livia Duvessa?"

"Thursday morning, just after school. She came to my house. Must have been 3 a.m."

"Why would she do that?"

Cole's mind raced. "She told me the vamps were planning an attack on zombies."

"An attack? You mean a street fight? Like the fight

you started at that party."

"The zombies didn't start that fight, the vamps did. But no, not like that. They're behind it. The zombie outbreak. They started it, somehow, so they could kill zombies. That's what Livia was trying to warn me about."

"Really now? And what did you do when you heard about it?"

"I...nothing. I had an appointment with Dr. Krenske."

"We'll check that out."

"There were witnesses."

"About the fight at the Maddox's."

"The vamps started it."

"And you saw Miss Duvessa there?"

"She was with her boyfriend. The other vamps were there."

"Mrs. Duvessa tells me you thought you were her boyfriend."

"What? No. I mean, we...I liked her and all. But no. She's going out with Stephan Hack."

"And this made you angry, I guess."

"Yeah, well. I guess. But what does this have to do with—what happened to Livia?"

"Well, son, we don't know."

"She told me he wouldn't like it if she was caught talking to me."

"Who wouldn't like it?"

"Slade. Rick Slade. He's the one who's behind the zombie attacks."

"Now, son." The cop stuck his right thumb behind his belt and pulled his polyester pants up a bit higher around his belly. "They went full zombie. The vamps in Crane Park saved lives."

"It was set up. Somehow they made them go full zombie."

"Now, that's a mighty harsh accusation you're making

226

there, son. Do you have any proof?"

"Well, no, not exactly. But Livia told me and she said Slade would make her disappear if she said anything."

"And now she's conveniently vanished."

"Convenient? Aren't you getting it? Slade and the vamps at the high school are trying to take over the world and they've done something to Livia."

The cop chuckled and his belly jiggled.

"Now, son, for all we know Miss Duvessa just spent the night, er, or the day, with a friend and she'll be home by dinner time, or lunch?" He turned to his partner who came down the walk. "You just can't talk normal anymore, can you? What with vampires sleeping all day and the school day being in the night. It's all so mixed up." He turned back to Cole. "I get turned around. Anyway, son, there's no need to be making accusations against the Slade family."

"Aren't you even going to look into it? Ask questions or something?"

"Ask questions about what? This is a simple missing persons investigation. And it seems that you were the last person to see Livia Duvessa, other than her mother, who says she went out to help you with the zombie uprising here on this street. She hasn't seen her daughter since. What do you have to say about that?"

Cole felt himself go very cold as he stared at the cop.

"I was with Alan and Brock. My friends. I heard Mrs. Duvessa screaming. But I didn't see Livia."

"And Alan and Brock, your friends, can verify that you were with them?"

"Yes, sir. They stayed at my house after, until the bodies were taken away and Alan's father came to follow them back home in Alan's car."

The officer scribbled notes in his little notebook and stuffed it into his pocket.

"Are your parents home now?"

Cole nodded. "My mom's car is in the garage."

"Well, what are we waiting for?"

Cole fumed. They interviewed his mother briefly, and then called on Alan, his father, and Brock. They even talked to Mrs. Sheffield in the middle of her funeral arrangements for Winston.

"I know you didn't have anything to do with this," his mom told him.

"But what about Slade and the vamps? Do you believe me about that?"

"I think it's possible. But the families of the dead undead say they were taking their meds. How could they have interfered?"

"I don't know. But I think we should change pharmacies, just in case."

His mother looked at him with a gentle smile. "Cole, honey. It's just not likely that important people like the Slades would do something so awful."

"I know, Mom. And you're probably right. But just humor me. What can it hurt?"

"I can tell you're really scared. And well, it must have been awful, with Winston. So," she patted his arm. "We'll toss your pills and I'll go get you some fresh ones from the Glenwood Springs pharmacy right now."

Cole relaxed with relief and after a quick meeting at the cemetery, all the zombies agreed to convince their parents to do the same. Cole arrived home very late for bed and crashed.

That evening, Slade and most of the vamps were absent and the regulars still hadn't returned to school. Classrooms were almost empty. Mr. Lute told the school that all would be back to normal on Monday night. Cole wasn't convinced.

He arrived home early Saturday morning, a feeling of

228

dread and remorse hanging over him. Livia was still missing and now Slade was in hiding. He went straight to his room and logged onto the Viral Episodes website and entered the Zombie Forum. The place was abuzz with the zombie outbreaks, three threads were dedicated to those undead who perished, where zombies left notes of sorrow at their losses. Cole sat, staring at the screen, daring himself to post about his theories: the vamps were responsible for the outbreak; they may have tampered with Zom-be-Gon; they want to take over the world; and they'd kidnaped Livia Duvessa. But the zombies on the forum weren't just the zombies he knew in school. They were all over the country and the world.

He sighed and rubbed his tired eyes. He couldn't do it. What if he was wrong? What if Dr. Krenske was just a crazy old man? What if Livia had just been overreacting? But where was she?

"Cole, let's go," he heard his mother call.

He lugged himself down the stairs and shoved his hands in his pants pockets.

"Are you sure you want to go out?"

"Yeah, it's okay."

"Once a month," his stepfather said. "Movie. It's a rule."

"But the outbreak..."

"...is over," Craig said. "And you could use a little family time. Right?" He turned to Cole.

Cole nodded. The mall and the theater were out of the neighborhood and that was where he needed to be. He let his mom think it was because of Winston; but he needed to stop staring out his bedroom window looking for signs of Livia. His stepfather drove them to the crowded mall where he was forced to park in the outer rows of the lot.

"See?" He said. "Everybody's out. It's all over."

229

"It's not over for the families of the dead," Cole muttered.

Craig put his arm around Cole's shoulders as they walked through the lot. "I'm sorry. You're right."

He stopped walking and looked at his wife.

"Should we forget the movie this month? I thought it would do Cole good, but maybe it's too soon."

"Nah, it's okay," Cole said.

Shrieks filled the early morning air and Cole turned this way and that. "Where are they?"

Craig turned in circles, "What is it? Another outbreak?"

"There," Cole shouted.

From the mall and through the parked cars, full zombies were loping toward them.

"Why are they moving so fast?" Craig said.

"They just do sometimes. It depends on how dead they were. Or how undead. Whatever. Let's get back to the car."

More screams echoed through the night as they ran.

"I can't believe I didn't bring the hatchets. I can't..."

"It's not your fault," his mother said and then she screamed.

Zombies rounded the cars in front of them, lumbering toward them. They turned, but more zombies came at them, forcing several other people into the center of their zombie circle with Cole and his family.

"What do we do?" A small, old woman cried, grasping Cole's arm. "What do we do?" She wore a wool suit, wide-heeled maroon shoes and a green leather handbag and dug her fingernails deep into Cole's left arm.

A father and his son in matching camouflage pants and hunting hats put their backs together and pulled machetes from their belts.

"All right, Kevin," the man said. "Take your time and

230

whack 'em good."

CHAPTER TWENTY-TWO

Cole struggled to free himself from the panicked woman's grasp.

"Do you have your hatchet?"

"Hatchet?" She let go of him and pulled open her purse; her trembling hands fumbled and the bag dropped to the ground. "I have a knife," she said.

Deep, rumbling groans echoed around them.

"Run," Cole said. "Hide."

The woman danced away in her thick high-heels, shoved her purse at a zombie on the left edge of the circle, knocking him back; she reached a pick-up truck and fell to her hands and knees, trying to scoot herself under it.

"Way to go old lady," Cole mumbled.

"I have a machete," a tall, blonde man in a knit cap said. "It's in the car."

Suddenly, a war cry rang out and Cole saw two men and a woman running at them with long swords.

"Aawaawaaaah," they screamed and began slashing at the zombies.

Cole stood frozen as pieces of zombie flesh smacked at his face and chest. He didn't recall he, Brock, and Alan killing the zombies on Buckley street with quite so much enthusiasm.

The hunters launched their own attack and the old lady was trying to lie on the ground to roll under the truck. The blonde guy turned and ran through the mayhem.

"Run." Craig scolded, grabbing him by the arm.

They dodged zombies left and right and were at the back of their car when Cole heard his mother scream. He turned to see her on the ground, struggling to get up.

"Jane!" Craig called.

"My heel broke," she cried. "I twisted my—" She screamed, turning to push herself along the ground to get away from a female zombie teetering toward her, spitting dried blood.

Craig ran for his wife and pulled her to her feet.

"Craig," Cole yelled and darted toward him. The zombie grabbed Craig's arm and pulled him backwards. Before Cole could reach him, the zombie's mouth chomped down on Craig's shoulder. Craig let out a painful scream.

"No," his mother shrieked. She lunged toward Craig but Cole grabbed her and pulled her back to the car. He pushed his mom into the back seat and pulled an axe from under it. He raced back to Craig who was limping to the car, the female zombie, energized by the bit of flesh she'd secured, chasing him.

Cole let out a cry and slashed at the zombie's neck with his axe. He hacked at her several times as she lay twitching on the ground and turned to the other zombies.

"Get to the pharmacy," He called out to his Mom. "Hurry."

"You come, too. I need you."

234

She was outside the car, leaning over Craig's body, now slumped partially on the back seat, his knees on the ground.

"Help me," the old woman in the red shoes screamed. She'd climbed into the back of the pickup and two zombies were reaching for her. Cole would have to take her with them. But before he could start toward her, one of the zombie's grabbed her by the leg and started chomping on her. He pulled her off the truck and three more zombies joined in, pulling her apart before Cole could get to her. Sirens filled the air, drowning out the screams.

"Hurry, Cole, hurry." His mother pleaded from the car as zombies closed in on him.

Dodging lumbering brain-eaters, Cole hit the ground in a roll, tripping one of the undead, sending him to the ground where he rolled back and forth with loud moans. After shoving Craig into the backseat, he got into the car, slammed the driver's side door and sped off to the pharmacy where they were forced to wait in line with a hundred others who were bitten in the onslaught.

Mayor Slade assured them that Craig received the serum in time and would rise from the dead, very shortly after he died, which, Slade told them, would be at about ten that morning.

His mother helped Craig upstairs to lie down and await his death while Cole, still suffering the aftereffects of adrenaline crossed the street and knocked on the Duvessa's door.

"Go away," Mrs. Duvessa said, looking out the front window at him.

"Is Mr. Duvessa home?"

"No. Go away." She pulled the drapes closed.

"Please, Mrs. Duvessa. Tell me what happened to Livia."

He knocked again and leaned his forehead on the door. "Please."

"I don't know what happened."

Cole turned to the window. "You must remember something."

She leered at him for a few seconds, then her face relaxed a bit and she rolled her eyes. She disappeared and the door opened a few inches.

"I'll tell you what I told the police and then you have to leave me alone. I don't like zombies, you know. And stop watching the house. You think I don't see you from your upstairs window?"

"Okay, I promise. Just tell me what happened."

"You were out in the street killing zombies and Livia wanted to help you. There was a knock at the door and I opened it."

"Who was it?"

"I don't remember."

"You must remember something."

"I don't remember I tell you. I...well..."

"What?"

"I thought it was that nice Rick Slade boy. But I just don't remember."

"Okay, then what happened."

"I don't remember."

"But I saw you out in the yard screaming. What were you screaming about?"

"I don't remember." Her voice trembled. "It must have been awful. All I do remember is standing in my living room and realizing she was gone. I looked everywhere and couldn't find her. I thought...I thought." She choked back a sob. "I thought you'd killed her."

"Me?"

"I thought you were a zombie. There were so many of you in the street. But I was too afraid to go out and

236

look for her body."

Mrs. Duvessa covered her face with her hands and cried.

"I've tried to contact my husband, but they said he's in some kind of vault. I just don't know what to think. I don't know what's happening to the world anymore."

Cole sighed. "It'll be all right, Mrs. Duvessa. I'll find Livia, I promise. And we'll get all this straightened out. Really, it'll be okay. You'll see."

She looked at him and nodded, sniffed, and closed the door on him.

Z

The next Monday night at school, Slade was back, taunting and swaggering as usual with his little nerdy toad Todd by his side. Cole felt the deep rumble of a growl inside him and his teeth gnashed together at the sight of the vamps shoving others out of their way in the hall. Cole had had enough. He stormed across the hall, to the crowd of vamps in their locker corner, grabbed Slade just as he turned toward him with a smirk on his face, and slammed him against the lockers.

"Where is she?" Cole shoved his fist into Slade's neck and felt a surge of satisfaction as the stupid arrogant vamp drooled a bit and turned to his friends with fear in his eyes. From the corner of his eye, Cole saw Brock and Alan and a few other zombies several feet away, a guttural hum drowning out the vamps' hissing.

"Tell me where she is or I'll crack your larynx."

Slade's eyes darted from his friends, to the snarling zombies, and back to Cole, alarmed.

"What did he say?" Ciara Wister, donned all in black, presumably in mourning for her brother, said. "He's going to crack his what?"

"His larynx," Alan said. "You know, his voice box."

A vicious smile crossed Alan's face and Cole turned full at him, confused. Were they all getting meaner, or just the vamps?

"We have boxes with our voices in them?" Another vamp said.

Cole pulled Slade away from the lockers and slammed him hard against them a second time.

"Where is she?"

Something of a pitiful whine edged his voice and hoped Slade hadn't noticed. He loosened pressure against Slade's throat so he could speak

"I don't know what you're talking about." Slade said, sputtering.

"Well, I'll tell you then. You and your friends are tampering with the zombie meds. You're causing the zombie outbreaks. You're the reason Winston is dead. And when Livia tried to warn me about it, you took her. What did you do with her? Tell me."

He slammed the wiry vamp again into the lockers. Slade let out a squeak.

"You can't prove any of that."

Cole turned to find Todd Quaid, looking up at him, smiling menacingly. Ignoring him, he turned back to Slade.

"Tell me where she is or I'll–"

"You won't hurt him." The little squirt vampire seethed with delight.

"I will so."

"Then do it," Todd said.

"What?" Slade squealed.

"We don't know anything about your little tramp. So, you'll just have to kill Slade."

Cole stared at Todd, puzzled. Who was this little upstart, anyway?

"You're not helping, Todd." Slade said, wriggling

against Cole's grasp.

"Rick doesn't know where Livia is, but last we heard she was planning to kill herself."

Cole's grip on the vampire loosened as he took a slight step back.

"She what?" Of course he didn't believe it.

"No, no. It wasn't suicide. It was zombie." Todd's smile widened. "That's right. She wanted to become a zombie. So, for all we know, she's the one behind the outbreaks."

Slade smirked, grabbed Cole's arm and twisted his hand off his shirt. Cole looked around at the other vamps and his eyes fell on Darlene.

"Do you know where she is?"

Darlene's brow furrowed, but she lowered her eyes to the floor.

Cole turned to the others, "What did he do with her?" But they all looked away from him.

"They won't tell you anything." Todd said.

"All right, break it up," Principal Lute's voice rang through the hallway. Vamps and zombies scuttled away to class and Slade glared at Todd before turning away.

"You want to tell me what your problem is Mr. Bertrand?" Lute said, standing in the now empty hallway with two members of the Monster Squad.

"It's the vamps. Livia told me. Slade and his friends are behind the zombie outbreaks. They planned them so they could kill zombies."

Lute motioned for Cole to follow him and they walked in silence to his office, where he closed the door, leaving the Monster Squad outside. The principal sat heavily in his chair and scooted it closer to his desk. He'd changed his Skin Like New patch and now it matched his gray face, but Cole saw the signs of decay that excessive stress brought him.

"Do you have any evidence?" Lute said.

Cole slumped into one of the chairs in front of Principal Lute's desk and rubbed his eyes with the heels of his hands. He shook his head wearily.

"No, of course not." Lute said.

"But Dr. Krenske said the vamps were using his formulas to try to take over the world. And Livia came to me to warn me and now she's missing."

Lute peered at Cole with suspicion on his face and tapped a pen rhythmically on the desk.

"Krenske's a very old man."

"He's only forty-eight." Cole said.

"He's suffering from some debilitating condition."

"He was fine when the vamp goon guarding him left for a minute. That's when he told me what they were doing."

Lute shrugged, but didn't take his eyes from Cole. "He's crazy."

"But what about Livia? She told me the vamps were planning to make us go full zombie."

"And she conveniently disappears."

"Is there a new definition of convenient that I don't know about?"

"Maybe she's been killed by the zombies."

Cole started, and stared at Principal Lute in despair. He put his hands on his eyes again and rubbed.

"Or, you could be right." Lute said.

Cole's head popped up and he stared, amazed, at Lute. "You think I could be right?"

The tapping of his pen on the desk ceased and Principal Lute rested his elbows on the large desk calendar.

"The Science Club discovered something last week and it was only brought to my attention this morning."

Lute hesitated and Cole sat forward in his chair.

240

"What?"

Lute sat back, reached his arms up and clasped his hands behind his head.

"One of the students got into Winston's locker and brought his spare pill box to the lab. Apparently, Winston was very organized and rotated his spares regularly with his regular pill box. Anyway, this student, Rachel, you know her. She claimed that the pills in his spare box were new. So, they tested them."

"Sugar pills," Cole said. "Placebos."

Principal Lute shook his head. "No. No. That wouldn't work. It takes two or three days without any pills to trigger a symptom. Or, as with your friend Bill, about a week of haphazard dosing. And the symptom is mild enough to be caught and treated with the hypo. No, they found something much worse."

"Something that triggers full zombie quickly?"

"A high dose of the original Krenske formula. The one that started the first zombie outbreak."

"How would they know that?"

"They weren't supposed to know. But Mr. Samuelson once worked with Dr. Krenske and has several samples of their research. But this doesn't make any sense." He shook his head. "They're just making more zombies. They can't take over the world that way."

"But, that's what Dr. Krenske told me."

Lute smiled. "More evidence that the vamps aren't big in the brains department. Don't tell anyone I said that."

The next evening, Cole brought Cerebellum's envelope to school and gave it to Mr. Samuelson.

"Where did you get this?"

"Some homeless guy in the mall."

Mr. Samuelson raised his brows.

"It looks like inside information." Cole said. "I don't

know what to do with it."

Samuelson emptied the envelope on his desk and ruffled through the papers and cards. "Very interesting, indeed," he mumbled.

"It makes sense to you?"

He looked up at Cole as if surprised to find him standing there.

"Yes, yes, it does."

"Then you can do something about all this?"

Samuelson smiled. "I'll do my best."

Z

Wednesday morning, after school, the zombies gathered at Wakefield cemetery to bury Winston. The Sheffields had called in Frat Boys Recovery Service and even after they were told it wouldn't work, they paid three thousand dollars to have Winston's head sewn back on. Arms, legs, and other appendages were their specialty, but, the Frat Boys' spokesman said in his interview with the evening news, this was the first time they'd ever attempted a head.

The Sheffields waited almost a week, hoping that Winston would get up and be undead again. But in his chapter, "Head Whacking," Dr. Krenske confirmed that after the head is hacked off, the zombie is gone.

Brock, Alan, and Cole received special funeral notices telling them they weren't to blame for Winston's death and his parents held no hard feelings.

"Mine said they wondered, though, if Winston was really full zombie, but they wouldn't question it." Alan said.

"Mine too," Brock said. "It said, we don't blame you, but we wonder if you really had to do it."

"Yeah," Cole said. "But we won't go to the authorities because it looks like there were full zombies around so it's possible."

"So, you think we should really be here?" Alan said.

"He was our friend." Cole said. "I can understand his parents not really wanting to accept it. But we're the ones who had to hack his head off."

"Well, you two," Alan said. "Not me. I mean, I held his mom back, but I didn't kill him."

"The vamps killed him," Cole said.

They joined the other zombies, and Trevor, at the grave site where the coffin was set next to its hole.

"You're going to get seriously hurt the way you're going around accusing vamps." Alan said.

"So what am I supposed to do?"

"If you don't have any evidence, you need to keep quiet."

"Maybe there is evidence."

"Like what?"

"Maybe I've been sworn to secrecy until the authorities have checked it out? Maybe me telling you would jeopardize the criminal case?"

"Then maybe you shouldn't be mentioning it." Alan said.

"Really?" Brock said. "There's a criminal case and you've been sworn to secrecy?"

"No. But what if there was? I thought Alan, at least, would understand. He hates them more than any of us."

"Yeah, because they think they're so cool and they get all the chicks, brainless. Not because I think they're trying to bring on a zombie apocalypse."

"Shh."

Several of the mourners turned to glare at them. As they stood grave-side and listened to the tearful speeches about how wonderful Winston was, how neat, how organized, how anal retentive, and what a good thing you would normally think that would be for a zombie on medication, Cole couldn't stop thinking about Livia and feeling her cold lips against his. A low, rumbling moan escaped him and he flinched under Brock's elbow hit in the side. He had to get her off his mind, and yet, he had to keep thinking about her. Where could she be? What would they have done to her?

His eyes wandered over the cemetery and the several mounds of dirt from previous burials. There was Mr. Lawrence, the old pervert; and one for Mr. Hanson; and that small one was little Cindy Lou Peterson next to the big one for her mom. Three more swells of freshly packed earth rose gently in the distance. Three funerals Cole's mother had forced him to attend already in the past three days. As he started to turn back to Winston's proceedings, he caught sight of another hill of dirt, in a far corner of the cemetery, near the big oak tree. Who was buried there?

"He was such a lovely boy," Nurse Frommer was saying. "Always handy with a pen; he carried several in one of those plastic pocket protectors. He didn't have pockets all the time. But he wore the protector anyway, pinned to his shirt. I told him it would ruin the material." She burst into tears. "But he said he'd rather risk it to always have a pen handy The dear boy. The dear boy."

Cole nudged Brock.

"Who's buried in that one way over there?"

Brock shook his head and lifted his shoulders.

"That grave's been there," Alan said. "It was there when they buried Cindy Lou on Friday."

"Must have been someone who died naturally," Brock said and turned back to listen to Winston's music teacher tell about the time Winston helped him set up for a recital and was gracious enough to rearrange all the chairs in the auditorium for effective feng shui.

Once the funeral was over and the mourners filed

slowly away, Cole stood with Brock and Alan and watched as the cemetery workers lowered the casket into the hole with a machine.

"This place isn't so bad in daylight," Alan said.

Cole nodded. "C'mon, let's go see who's buried over there under the oak."

"Just because I said it's better, doesn't mean I like looking at graves or anything."

"Aw, just come on."

They approached the lightly packed mound of dirt and stood looking down at it.

"So." Alan said. "Now what?"

Mr. Roginaldi, the rotund, mullet-sporting, plaid-suited cemetery director approached from behind them and sighed.

"You boys have been here every day, haven't you. You knew all the deceased."

"Except this one." Cole said. "Who's buried here?"

The cemetery director looked to the ground as if he hadn't noticed the grave until that moment.

"Well, I don't know. I'd have to look at my records. But with the rate of the zombie deaths lately, it doesn't surprise me that I'd have no clue. I hope I don't have to see you boys again, any time too soon."

"Why isn't there a headstone?" Cole said.

Mr. Roginaldi put out his short, fat arm to lead them all away. "The headstone has to be ordered, you know."

"Would you mind finding out who's buried there?" Cole asked him.

Mr. Roginaldi smiled. "Oh, sure. I'll try to look it up later and I'll give you a call."

"I could look it up for you."

"I'd rather not have other people going through my files. Just wait for the headstone and then everyone will know."

Mr. Roginaldi patted him on the shoulder. "Go on now. And let's hope I don't see you again any time soon." He waddled off toward the cemetery office leaving Cole, Brock and Alan at the parking lot.

"Don't you think it's strange that he doesn't know who's buried there?" Cole said.

"Is he supposed to know all the names?" Brock said.

"But whoever it was, was just buried recently."

"Why do you care?"

Cole turned to look at Brock. He raised his eyebrows; he could feel his dead eyes glaze over slightly as he imagined Brock's response.

"Oh, no. No way. You don't think...?"

"What?" Alan squeaked. "What does he think?"

"Do you?" Brock said.

Cole let his head fall slowly into a nod. "I think it's possible."

"What? What?" Alan said bouncing on his heels.

"He thinks Livia Duvessa is buried under the oak tree."

"They killed her?" Alan's voice reached the cracking point, his face lit with fear and horror.

"She's a vamp," Cole said. "She'd still be alive."

"They could have killed her," Alan said.

"But why bury her, then? She'd just be charred remains."

"You could bury charred remains."

"But Alan, think about," Brock said. "Just calm down and think."

"Okay, okay," he continued bouncing. "Calming down."

"There's a mound of dirt. That means there's probably a coffin in the ground. Why would they call attention to the spot by putting the remains in a coffin?" Brock said.

246

"Why would they put it in the cemetery?" Cole said.

"Okay, okay," Alan nodded and looked this way and that. He lowered his voice. "But why do we think it's Livia?"

"No clue," Brock said. "Look, she'll turn up."

Cole turned and walked toward Alan's car. "You think so."

"I do think so. If they've got her, they'll let her go eventually."

"Why would they do that?"

"Why would they risk killing her? You know how hard it is to kill a vampire."

"Why wouldn't they kill her?" Cole said.

Alan let out a terrified squeak as he got into the car with them.

"Listen to yourself," Brock said. "This is Rick Slade you're talking about. He's not smart enough to pass keyboarding and you think he's somehow masterminded a vamp takeover and the murder of another vampire."

"There's a big difference between ignorant and stupid," Cole said. "And it's not like we haven't heard rumors of him burying vamps alive before. And anyway, I think that little brat Todd Quaid is a lot meaner than Slade."

"Yeah, well, if you think you're going to get me to dig up a grave or something, you're ignorant and stupid."

"I'm not planning on that...yet." Cole said. "First we need to drag a vampire out into the sunlight."

Alan snorted with a choked laugh.

"Take us to Darlene Chriss' apartment," Cole said.

Alan squeaked again.

CHAPTER TWENTY-THREE

Cole stood at the window in Darlene's darkened bedroom; the shade was drawn and haloed by a sharp band of light along the edges. Darlene was an older vamp and rumored to live alone in a second-story apartment with a pet tarantula. The tarantula was the reason Alan stayed behind in the car. Cole could only hope she kept it in a cage of some kind as he and Brock broke in through her front door and found their way through the apartment. Standing by her bed, Cole nodded to Brock who stood on the other side, ready to grab her when she woke. Cole pulled hard on the shade, flooding the room with daylight.

Darlene shrieked and rolled toward Brock to cover her face. Brock grabbed her and pulled her to the foot of the bed, off it, and into the bright light of the window.

"Where's Livia?" Cole said. He was stunned at the calm viciousness of his own voice.

Darlene screamed, then hissed; Brock, holding her from behind, turned his head away, avoiding her fangs. Her white hair, rumpled in sleep, stood out all around her ashen face like a halo. Deep, glowing red eyes raged at Cole.

"I don't have my sun screen. I'll burn. You jerks."

"Where is she?"

"How did you get in here?"

"Did you really think you could keep a zombie out with a dead bolt?"

"Get out." She screamed and writhed, trying to force Brock off of her.

"Just tell me what you did with Livia and we'll put you back in the dark."

"I didn't do it. Todd said he put her away. He said she's dead and buried. Close the shade; I'm burning."

Cole drew the shade down and turned to see Darlene whirling around to slap Brock hard across the face.

"There," she said. "I hope your face rots off."

"It was Cole's idea," Brock said.

"Leave me alone." She stomped across the room in the dark and rummaged through drawers in her desk. "Where the heck is my aloe vera?"

Cole looked around, but he couldn't see much with the sunlight blocked out. He left the room, found Darlene's bathroom down the hall and turned on the light. From inside her medicine cabinet, he took her tube of Burn Away and brought it to her.

"Here," he said. "Do you need help?"

"Of course not. Stupid zombie."

"Are you sure? We could put it on your back."

"I don't need it on my back." She snorted and choked back anger as she squeezed a glop onto her left arm.

"Brock, fix her door."

"What did you do to my door?"

Cole offered her a sheepish grin.

"Great," she said. "You better fix it good."

Darlene sat back onto the pillows on her bed as she

rubbed the ointment into the skin of her bony left arm.

"You can leave now." She said.

"Do you think he put her in the cemetery?"

She rolled her eyes at him. "I think so."

She squeezed another glob of ointment onto her right arm and rubbed it in.

"Do you need some on your face?"

"Why? Does my face look bad? You know I'm the palest vamp in the world. Damn virus. I burn way easier than the others."

He took the tube from her and put a dot of ointment on her nose and one on each cheek.

"It looks a little red. Sorry."

"Do you expect me to thank you? When Todd and Rick find out I told you, are you going to save me? Hah. I doubt it."

Cole smiled at her in the dim room. "Sure we will."

"Have you saved Wanda Quaid, yet?"

"Wanda Quaid?"

"She's been missing since that school board meeting and the big fight."

"Well, we didn't know. How were we supposed to save her?" Cole said.

"You wouldn't anyway. You just want to save Livia."

"I didn't know the rest of you needed saving."

"We don't."

Cole smacked his hand against his head. Were all vamps this crazy? "We're leaving now. Just go back to sleep and pretend we weren't here."

"Find her," she said and Cole turned back to look at her.

He watched as she rubbed the dots of lotion into her cheeks.

"I will." He said.

He found Brock at the front door looking helpless.

"I can't fix this. Let's just leave before she comes out and screams at me again."

They propped up the front door as best as they could and headed down the stairs from the second floor.

"We're insane, you know that?" Brock said. "We just attacked a vampire. And not just any vampire. One of Slade's vampires."

"It wasn't that bad. And I'm not sure she's one of Slade's, really."

"That's it? That's all you can say?"

"Did she tell you anything?" Alan said when they got back in the car. "Did you see the tarantula?"

"When can we dig up the grave?" Cole said.

The timing of a grave dig in Darkspur was crucial, but almost impossible. Mr. Roginaldi ran the cemetery in the early morning hours and his twin brother, the other Mr. Roginaldi, opened it up at dusk for a few of hours. Zombies buried their dead in the mornings and vamps after sundown. In the afternoon, no one would likely be in the cemetery, but the daylight wouldn't give the zombies any cover against the occasional regular who might drive by. And after all, they went to Darkspur Night High and slept all day. They'd be dead tired trying to dig up a body.

In the dead of night they'd be wide awake and primed for digging up a grave. But zombies and vamps would be out and about during the night and the chances of being caught were good, especially with all the recent deaths and the likelihood of a visitor in the cemetery. But they chose the dark, anyway, meeting at the cemetery on Wednesday night at eleven.

Alan, Stu, and Rachel, bundled in their jackets and scarves, arrived and approached Cole.

"This is bad. I've never skipped school before." Rachel said.

252

"Well, we can't do it during the day." Alan said.

"Why not?"

He laughed. "You can't dig up a grave in daylight. That's just wrong."

"Is this illegal?" Stu said as he shoveled the first clump of dirt and tossed it at the oak.

"Of course it's illegal." Alan said.

"It's not illegal if Livia Duvessa is buried in here." Brock said.

"You mean if she's buried in here illegally," Rachel said.

"How else would she be buried here?" Cole said.

"Maybe she died and her parents buried her."

"Don't you think we'd have heard about it?" Alan said.

"You'd think, sure," Rachel said. "But maybe we didn't. So, if she's in here and she's dead and buried, well, and burned to ashes, because she's a, you know—"

"Or pulled apart by zombies." Alan said.

"Do you think her parents would have arranged her body parts, back together like, in the coffin?" Brock said.

"Could we just dig, now?" Cole said.

They continued to dig, the slither of the shovels into the earth and clumpity-clump of the dirt hitting the ground at the base of the oak, rattled Cole. He shivered. What if Livia really was in the ground? He felt his chest tighten as his dead heart struggled for a few beats.

"I find this strangely natural," Brock said.

"I do, too," Rachel said. "It's as if a small cadre of zombies digging up a grave in the middle of the night is perfectly right with the universe."

"It was Dr. Frankenstein who dug up bodies, not zombies." Alan said.

"Technically," Stu said. "It was his servant Igor who dug up the body."

"But wasn't Frankenstein's monster a zombie?"

"Don't say that," Brock said. "Cole will have Frankenstein in the curriculum at school."

They laughed.

"Aren't you supposed to be quiet when you dig up bodies illegally?" Cole said.

"You said it won't be illegal once we find out Livia is in here alive." Stu said.

"Yeah, but we don't know for sure if she's in there yet, do we?"

"Oh, that's just great," Stu said. "You mean we could be digging up some headless zombie corpse?"

"What's the big deal?" Rachel said. "If you've whacked off a zombie head, you can look at a headless corpse."

"A headless corpse that's been under ground for a few days."

"But it's been embalmed and all. It's not like it's going to be covered in worms."

"Could we just shut up and dig?" Cole said.

They dug quietly for a time, shovels sliding in, clumps of dirt hitting the ground, the cold wind singing through the pines.

"Do they embalm zombies?" Brock said.

"Sure, why not?" Rachel said. "There's some stuff in there, you know."

"Just wondering. I bet we look nicer after we die. All plumped up with embalming fluid. Too bad we didn't get to see Winston or the others."

"Well, their heads were whacked off and all," Alan said.

They were only three feet down when their shovels hit something hard with loud thuds. They all turned in unison, those in the hole looking up, to Cole; their faces somber and knowing.

254

"It's got to be her," Rachel said. "A real coffin would be much deeper."

"And much nicer," Brock said, shining his flashlight on the wood crate in the hole.

"Shh," Cole said. They paused. "I don't hear anything."

"Let's get it open," Stu said.

"I can't look." Cole turned away. He heard the creak of wood and nails as they pulled the lid off. Then silence. No one spoke. Cole could only hear the cold autumn wind whisper through the pines and oaks surrounding the cemetery.

Rachel said. "Is she...?"

"I can't tell. Let's get her out."

Finally Cole turned to see Brock and Stu standing in the box in the hole, lifting a limp body out onto the ground.

"She's not stiff," Alan mumbled with a squeak.

"She's cold," Stu said.

"She's a vampire, you idiot." Brock said. "They're always cold."

"Well, how the hell do we tell if she's alive?"

Cole's weak legs carried him, trembling, to Livia's body. He knelt beside her and took Brock's flashlight, shining it into her face. Her eyes were open, her mouth screwed up in a silent scream and the skin of her cheeks scratched open, exposing blue and white flesh. Cole took one of her hands and examined it in the light. Her fingernails were broken and her fingers covered with splinters from the wooden crate.

"She was alive when they put her in the hole." He said. "I think she's still alive."

He choked back the urge to cry, but when he heard Rachel begin to weep, he rose and turned away, pounding his fist into his forehead to keep his strength.

"Did she just blink?" Rachel said.

Cole turned back and fell to the ground, shining the light in her eyes again.

She blinked.

"She's alive," he said.

"Okay," Brock said. "Fill the hole back in so they don't know we got her out. And put her in the car. We'll take her home."

Cole winced when Brock picked her up and carried her over his shoulder like a sack of corn. But he couldn't bring himself to carry her; he knew he'd cry if he had to.

"Here's your undead daughter, Mrs. Duvessa," Stu said. "We dug her up for you."

To Cole's surprise, Alan laughed. "Where'd you dig this one up, Cole?" He said.

Z

Screaming, screaming, screaming. Livia couldn't stop the screaming. Even after she'd screamed for several hours and knew she'd long before stopped actually making any noise, she kept hearing herself screaming. She'd screamed when they grabbed her and even managed to scream when they stuffed the rag in her mouth. She screamed through the fight, and managed to force the two vamp bystanders to help Rick and Stephan hold her down while Todd put thick tape over her mouth. Then they tied her hands and feet. She nearly choked on the rag, but she kept screaming.

When Stephan carried her out of her house and down the street, she saw Cole and Brock in the distance, hacking the heads off zombies, and she screamed some more, but he stuffed her into the trunk of an old car, apparently without anyone noticing. Except her mom. Dear, trusting, zombie-hating mom ran out of the house screaming. But it was too late. The trunk lid closed and the car puttered to life. She screamed and screamed. And she screamed some more.

When they dragged her out of the trunk at the cemetery, she was still screaming. She screamed the loudest when they pulled out the hypodermic. After they poked her and she figured they'd injected her with something that would kill her, she kept screaming. They untied her; they pulled the rag from her mouth, and she screamed, though by that time she was hoarse. They pushed her and she fell into the hole and before she could get up to scream some more, they'd covered the box. Hammers pounded nails into the lid and dirt fell through the cracks. She knew she was in big trouble. But she kept screaming. She suddenly thought of Geraldo. He could dig her up. But what were the chances?

Even as she fell into what she could only call a zombie state, strangely enough, she was screaming. Maybe she slept, maybe she didn't, but if she did, she dreamed of screaming. Once aware again, she scratched and clawed and fought off a dizzying paralysis, and she screamed, though she knew she'd stopped making noise. Eventually, she'd stopped moving completely. She stared at nothing, though she was aware of everything–although, everything at that point was a tiny, dark, enclosed space. She was frozen, and yet still screaming away in her head. She wished she could make it stop.

This must be vampire hell, she thought. She'd lie in the dark like that for all eternity with her own screams ringing in her head. At some point, though, she reasoned, she'd go completely insane and maybe it wouldn't matter so much.

And when she was rescued, you'd think the screaming would stop; but it didn't. She just kept screaming. She watched as Cole fought back horrified tears, looking at her body, asking if she was alive. She screamed like mad.

What if they burned her thinking she was dead? Well, it would only be awful for a few seconds, she figured. And they would never know. Unless Rick told them. And of course Rick would love to tell them that she wasn't dead when they'd burned her. She couldn't bare the thought of the guilt Cole would feel. If only she could stop the screaming!

And finally she was at home in her own bed, but then she had to hear her mother's screams along with her own. Would it never end? There was a fight about her. Cole told her mother not to call the police—the vamps couldn't know that they'd found her or they'd kill her. But her dear zombie-hating mother wouldn't listen to him. How could she believe a zombie, after all? No, she called the police and then she had the nerve to stand there in the bedroom, right in front of her catatonic daughter and accuse Cole of doing this to her. Cole!

How stupid could her mother be? Even if it was possible, which clearly it was not, why would he bring her back in such a state?

"You'll be arrested," her mother said, with this triumphant look on her face.

"She's right," Brock said.

And so Cole left, probably to go on the lam for the rest of his life, because obviously Rick Slade had shot Livia up with something that would leave her in a catatonic state for the rest of her life, which was, of course, forever, because damn it, she was a vampire. And she'd never be able to tell the police who really did this to her. If she could have rolled her eyes in disgust, she would have. Hell, if she could close her eyes more often than every ten seconds and save her eyeballs from drying out and having to be removed, she would.

And then her mother, bless her poor ignorant soul, came to the bed, laid a hand over her face and closed her

258

eyes and they stuck shut. Ah, peace at last. Except for the incessant screaming.

CHAPTER TWENTY-FOUR

On Thursday evening, most of the kids were back in school and they held a brief memorial that morning for the zombies who'd lost their heads the week before. Posters went up in the halls throughout the day with pictures of the few students, friends, and parents who lost their undead lives.

The vamps paraded in the halls warning people that the end of the zombie culture was near.

"The zombie revolution is over," Rick Slade called out, standing in the main hall after third period. "Their superior brains are no match for the sharp blade of an axe."

"Where'd he steal that from?" Rachel said, walking with Cole to chemistry class. "He couldn't have thought it up himself."

Cole shrugged. "He probably thinks he's talking about Krenske's book. But, if anything, the outbreaks are the beginning of the revolution."

"A zombie revolution? Is that what the book is about?" Stu said, coming up from behind them.

"That's the title of the book, brainless."

"So, we're supposed to have a revolution? We're the ones who take over the world?"

Cole nodded. "Sort of. Either way, the zombies win. The full zombies are creating new zombies by the hundreds every time there's an outbreak. And if we all go full zombie because of their meddling, they can't control the numbers."

"But they can, Cole." Rachel stopped him outside the chemistry lab. "Think about it. They're immortal and much harder to kill. Full zombies can't organize and think well enough to kill vampires. All they have to do is whack off all our heads and they win."

"I saw three zombies rip a woman apart and eat her last week," Cole said. "And they killed Liam Wister somehow, too. The vamps don't stand a chance."

At lunch, the zombies and Trevor huddled around the grave-digging team as they told them about their escapade in the cemetery and their time at the police station under suspicion of kidnapping and attempted murder.

"I can't believe you didn't get arrested."

"There was no evidence." Brock said.

"You say that like you really did kidnap her." Bill said.

"Well, we didn't." Cole said. "Do you think the cops interviewed the vamps?"

"I doubt it," Stu said. "The cops in this town are afraid of the vamps."

Most of the zombies turned at that point and stared across the lunchroom at the vamp tables.

"Stop looking at them," Rachel said.

When the bell rang, the zombies sat, waiting for the vamps to leave. But instead, the vamps gathered themselves together into a mob and followed Slade to the zombie tables.

"I hear your little girlfriend went insane over the

weekend," Slade said with a smirk. He put his hands up to his face and wiggled them around. He said, "looloo," and laughed.

"She's traumatized," Cole said.

"And when she comes out of it," Brock said. "She's going to have a story to tell to the police."

"It won't matter," Slade said. "After today, none of it will matter."

Slade and the vamps turned and tried to walk out of the cafeteria through the heavy door, but their mob got stuck with Slade at the back.

"Come on," Todd Quaid said. "Move it."

Slade pushed through, tossing vamps out of his way. "Me first, Todd. I should have been at the front anyway, stupids."

Cole laughed but he turned back to the zombies and they all stared at him.

"You heard him," Rachel said.

Nodding, Cole said, "Yeah, I heard him."

"Well, what are we going to do?"

"Keep your hypos with you. Get together in groups, choose a house on each block. Stockpile your weapons."

"You mean...?" Alan said.

"Yep. I mean."

"Zombie apocalypse." Trevor said. "Cool."

"Cole, you said you knew what was going on." Stu said.

He nodded again. "Someone's tampered with the meds, making us go full zombie really fast. Any pill we take could be the one."

"What do we do?" Alan said.

"Stop taking the pills," Brock said. "Stick with the hypos."

"Are you crazy?" Rachel said. "The hypos only work if you're going slowly into zombie mode. You take it with the meds in your system and you could overload."

"So, wait until you start into full zombie and then stick yourself."

Rachel shook her head. "That's too risky."

"Taking the damn pills is too risky," Trevor said.

They all turned to him.

"They control the means of production," he said with a grin.

"Not all," Cole said. "Our parents all went over to Glenwood Springs to get pills."

"You think the vamps' control is only local?" Trevor said.

Cole nodded.

"Another risky move."

The zombie horde milled around Cole's table for several minutes, fearful and alert.

"Well," Cole said, "Let's get back to class."

In the parking lot that morning, Cole caught sight of Slade, leaning on the hood of his car in the dark. Rachel, Alan, and Brock met up with him and followed his gaze.

"Is that guy an idiot, or what?" Cole said.

Slade was pointing at his own pink, glowing eyes, and then pointing back at the zombies.

"He's an idiot," Brock said. "But that won't keep him from turning us full zombie and whacking off our heads."

At home, Cole stood at his bedroom window, cautious and on edge. He'd had little sleep, most of it in a chair at the police station the day before. And he knew he wouldn't likely get more for some time. Dawn was still almost four hours away. The dark would help them.

"Mom," he called. "Is Craig on his way?"

"Yes." He could hear her running all over the house, pulling weapons out of the closets and from under the beds, stockpiling them in strategic locations throughout the house. "Do you see his car? Do you see anything?"

264

Craig pulled his car onto the grass, pushing the front end up against the hedge on the left side of the house. Cole's mother's car was already positioned this way on the right side of the house with Cole's behind it, at an angle with the back end toward the street.

"He's here."

"When is Brock expected?"

"Any minute." He called.

Cole looked to Livia's house. If the zombies came, he'd go for her. He ought to go then, he knew. But if he dragged Livia out of the house without her mother's permission, he'd get arrested for sure. He'd have to wait until their situation was clear; only then would the police finally understand what was happening in Darkspur.

"Are you sure?" Craig said, coming into his room.

"No." He turned to his stepfather. "But Slade made a threat and we have to take it seriously. How are you feeling?"

"Good," Craig said. "Strange, but good."

Cole smiled. "It takes getting used to. Especially the dying part. But you're past the worst of it."

Craig nodded. "Yep. I only vomited rotten food and pieces of my stomach once today."

Cole turned back to the window. "My hope is that Slade's as stupid as he seems. Isolated outbreaks, he can do. But on a massive scale? Even if his father's in on it...maybe he's just too incompetent to pull it off."

Alan and Brock arrived and Cole went out to direct Alan on parking his car behind his dad's and help them with their cache of weapons. Their parents showed up seconds later and pulled their cars along the curb, creating a barrier to the house. Zombies were terrible climbers, especially over slippery car hoods. In the back yard, their chain-link fence, up against the Baxter's wooden fence behind them, would deter all but the hardiest, newly-dead

265

undead.

The parents greeted one another and discussed their expertise. Alan's parents, the Pattersons, tall and lanky just like their son, were sharpshooters, only recently took the qualifying classes, after they finally came to terms with Alan's zombiism. The Hansons were zombies, turned the same time as Brock in a small outbreak years ago. They were well practiced at the art of the axe and machete. Cole was astonished to hear his own mother list her qualifications, both in zombie and vampire killing, but also in bomb making and poison. Poor Craig sat, dazed, when they all looked at him.

"I can't quite remember any training," he said.

"It should come back to you if you're attacked," Cole said, but he and his mother exchanged knowing looks.

Dying brought certain challenges for the zombie. Some things were lost forever.

"If you have any problems, just hide in the closet until it's over, okay?" Cole said.

Craig looked at him and shook his head. "I may not remember what qualifying classes I took, but I think I can still wield an axe."

Cole smiled. "Good."

"And we've all had our qualifiers on identifying the full zombie?" Mrs. Hanson said.

Everyone nodded.

"We're talking about a mass outbreak," Jane said. "Anything that comes at us that isn't screaming for help is going to get hacked."

"Whoa, dude," Brock nudged Cole. "You're mom's kickass."

They all startled at the distant sound of breaking glass followed by screaming.

"What is it?" Mrs. Hanson said.

"To the windows," Jane said.

The sharpshooters ran upstairs, and Brock, Alan, and Cole followed, finding the windows in Cole's room. In the early morning darkness, a few doors down on the opposite side of the street, five zombies surrounded a car and had broken out the windows. The man and woman in the car screamed as they were pulled from it and torn apart.

"I'm going for Livia," Cole said. "Who's with me?"

Brock nodded. "Let's do it."

"Alan?" Cole said.

Alan managed a nod, but his gray face ran deadly white.

"We've done this before," Cole said and pat him hard on the shoulder.

Alan stood taller, swallowed hard and nodded. They armed themselves with axes and headed to the door.

"Be careful," Jane said as she followed them outside.

"Where are you going?" Cole said to her.

"We're covering you," she said as Craig and Mr. Hanson joined them.

"We've got your backs," Mr. Patterson shouted down at them from one of the open second-story windows. He lifted his rifle and saluted them. Cole watched as Mr. Patterson chewed off the tip of a cigar and spat it to the ground below.

"Let's go," Cole said. "Hurry."

They leaped over the cars and darted across the street. Cole turned to see his and Alan's parents standing in the road, prepared for attack. He ran up to Livia's house and tried the door but it was locked. Not wanting to draw the attention of any nearby zombies, he rang the bell. He caught Mrs. Duvessa peering out of the front curtain.

"Mrs. Duvessa," He said as lightly as he could. "There's another zombie outbreak. Come over to our house where we can protect you."

"Go away," she shouted. "Go away or I'll call the police."

Cole looked at Brock and Alan and they all nodded. He stepped back and threw himself at the door. It burst open and he landed in the Duvessa's foyer. Mrs. Duvessa let out a prolonged screamed until Brock grabbed her and wrapped his arm around her face.

"Shut up, the zombies will hear you. Aaah! She bit me."

Mrs. Duvessa began her screaming again and ran up the stairs. Alan ran forward and tackled her.

"You two take her, I'll get Livia."

"Where's Mr. Duvessa?" Brock said.

But the woman only screamed.

"Shut up you old bat, you're just calling zombies."

Cole raced up stairs and into Livia's room where she lay on the bed. Her mother had turned the room into a shrine of sorts—candles cast eerie shadows against Livia's face and her stuffed animals were propped up all around her body. Livia looked peaceful, asleep, a slight smile at her lips. Cole reached to scoop her into his arms and stopped when his face drew near hers. He hesitated, and then brushed his lips gently across her mouth, realizing he may never get the chance to kiss her again. He picked her up and carried her downstairs.

Mrs. Duvessa's screams, somewhat muted most likely by Alan's arm, echoed out in the street. Cole prayed the full zombies were long dead and slow. He heard gun fire as he turned to get Livia out the front door without hitting her head or feet on the jamb.

"Cole," his mother screamed. "Run."

He did as he was told, and blindly ran across the street toward the house. Craig was on the hood of Mr. Hanson's car pulling the kicking and screaming Mrs. Duvessa up. Alan jumped up and took the crazy woman again, dragging her over into the yard. Another shot rang out.

Mrs. Duvessa broke free and screamed, "You're trying to kill us."

Just as Cole made the car and Craig reached down to take Livia from him, Mrs. Duvessa leaped over the hood, slid across it, and landed on the pavement. Cole grabbed her before she could run from him. She screamed—a deep, horrifying shriek—and Cole knew she'd finally seen the zombies. He turned, and nearly let out a scream himself. There were no longer five zombies a few doors down. Dozens of zombies, down the street on the left, and down the street on the right, and coming through the yards out of the darkness, all attempting to converge on the screams they heard out of Mrs. Duvessa's mouth. Cole grabbed her and shoved her back to the car where Alan took her, helping her over.

"Hurry," he said.

"My husband," she cried.

"Where is he?"

"At work."

"We can call him," Cole said.

Shots rang out from the windows above them as she finally allowed herself to be helped through the yard and into the house.

Cole took Livia from Craig, carried her up the stairs and dropped her unceremoniously onto his mother's bed. He showed Mrs. Duvessa the closet and the small cache of weapons in the corner—two hatchets, a butcher knife, and a pistol.

"There's a zombie hypo kit, too, if anyone needs it. If the worst happens," he said. "Barricade yourself in this room and stay completely quiet."

"What if they get in?" She wailed.

"Hide in the closet and be very quiet," he said.

"They're full zombies, remember? They can't smell you and they can barely hear you as long as you're not screaming."

"Cole," Brock called to him from downstairs. "It's Rachel and Kyle. They need help."

He left Mrs. Duvessa with her panic and ran back downstairs, following Brock out the door. Mr. Patterson called to them from the upstairs window.

"There are still more coming down the street. I don't know if we have enough ammo. We'll never hold them off."

"The cars will keep them out," Brock called.

Mr. Patterson shook his head. "They'll fall all over themselves, and some of them will climb across the others and over the cars."

More shots rang out. Cole ran across the front yard amid the panic and shouting of the parents, as they stood atop the cars shooting the heads off zombies when they got too close.

"We need to barricade ourselves in the house," Craig shouted.

"I have to get to Rachel," Brock said.

"Where are they?"

Cole climbed up onto Alan's car and saw Rachel's old two-door surrounded by zombies, with Rachel screaming inside.

"What's with Kyle?" Brock said.

"He's been bitten," Mr. Hanson said. "We have to get to them."

"It's too late," Jane said. "He's a zombie. Twice bitten."

"We have to try," Cole said.

In his book, *Zombie Revolution*, Dr. Krenske warned that twice-bitten full zombies led very short, very violent undead lives. Two hours at most. Two hours of hell

270

before they chewed and ripped their own appendages off and pulled off their own heads with their savage strength.

Brock and Cole and their parents jumped off the cars and into the street and began hacking their way through zombies toward Rachel's car.

"They're long dead," Brock cried out. "Slow."

"How can they all be long dead if it was the vamps messing with the meds?" Cole said, bringing his hatchet down into the neck of Mr. Ricker from down the street. "Sorry, Mr. Ricker," he said.

"I don't think this is a good time to argue about that," Brock said.

Cole pulled open the driver's side door and grabbed Rachel. "Let's go, in the house."

Brock had Kyle, weak as death, in his arms and they all ran back to the house, climbing over the cars.

"Maybe Krenske's original mistake created really slow zombies." Cole said as he shoved Rachel aside to hack at one.

"And maybe these guys came from the cemetery."

"What are you guys talking about?" Rachel said, grabbing Cole for protection.

"Brock still doesn't believe this is Slade's doing."

"I didn't say that."

They climbed over the cars and crossed the yard into the house.

"Rachel," Cole said. "Take Kyle upstairs to my parents room. Mrs. Duvessa has some hypos you can use. He needs two of them. Hurry."

She nodded and took Kyle from Brock, pulling his arm over her shoulders, bearing his weight easily as she hauled him upstairs.

"Cole, it won't work," his mother said. "You need to whack off his head."

"Dr. Krenske theorized that a double hypo of Zom-be-Gon might restore them. He just never managed to get them dosed in time."

"Vampires!" Mr. Patterson called from upstairs.

Cole looked at Brock and without words, they both darted back outside and jumped up onto the roof of Alan's car. Two houses down, Slade, and his usual posse—Stephan, Todd, Elena, and Ciara—and a few other vamps sauntered down the middle of the street wearing trench coats with hoods pulled over their heads and dark glasses despite the early morning hour, hacking at zombies.

"Oh, man. Who's that?" Cole said and laughed.

One of the younger vamps had a spinning umbrella hat shoved over his hood

"What are you, a comedian?" Brock called out as the vamps neared the house.

"I told you not to wear that stupid thing," Todd said.

"Get back inside," Mr. Patterson called from the window. "There are hundreds more coming."

"We'll handle them," Slade said to Cole. "You sissies go on inside. We'll deal with you when we're finished."

"You can't touch us," Brock said.

"Don't worry," Slade said. "You'll be full zombie; you won't know what's happening."

A low growl echoed in the street and Cole turned to see a batch of zombies limping toward them.

"You see, they're faster." Cole said to Brock.

"Okay, okay, whatever."

"So you agree that I know more about zombies than you?"

"Well, you read the book." Brock said.

"Do we help them?" Cole nodded toward the vamps, posed like ninja assassins waiting for the next round of zombie hacking.

"Are you kidding?" Brock said. "And give them a chance to whack our heads off in the chaos?"

272

The vamps moved forward, dropping to the ground in rolls, whirling around in circles toward the crowd of zombies lumbering down Buckley Street as Cole and Brock headed back into the house. Before they reached the front door, a piercing scream rang out. They turned. Cole saw a mass of zombies ripping and tearing and growling. The vamps around them fought strongly, whacking off heads as fast as they could, but another went down with a scream.

"Too many," Elena called out.

The zombies took them from front and behind, pulling them down and ripping them apart.

Brock rolled his eyes at Cole. "All right, let's get them in the house."

They jumped onto the cars and into the fray just as their parents hit the yard. Shots rang out as the Pattersons fired at the zombies on the outskirts of the battle. Cole whacked off a few heads and found himself next to Slade. They put their backs together and flung their axes wildly at zombie heads.

"You guys need to get into the house. You're overrun."

"All right, all right," Slade said.

"Never!" Todd Quaid said. "We won't surrender to zombies. Stay and fight."

"Don't be an idiot, Todd. Get in the house." Brock said.

"Todd Quaid," Cole's mother shouted. "Get inside the house this minute."

"To the house," Slade yelled and the vamps darted, dodged, and hacked their way through the zombie crowd.

"Fine," Todd said, jumping atop Alan's car in one leap. "But under protest."

Once over the cars and inside the house, Cole turned on Slade.

"What the hell were you thinking? You don't go out and fight zombies during a huge attack like this."

"What do you call what you're doing?"

"You only go out when necessary," Brock said. "Like we just did to rescue your sorry butts."

"Enough bickering," Craig said. "Get a shotgun and get to a window. Blow the head off anything that gets on one of the cars."

"I don't think the vamps can be trusted with weapons." Cole said.

"We don't have a choice," his mom said. "There are a thousand zombies out there."

Cole glared at Slade and twirled his hatchet in his hands as his mother handed Slade a shotgun. Only Elena, Todd, Stephan, and Slade stood in the living room and Cole realized the other vamps with Slade were all dead.

"You haven't just killed zombies," Cole said. "Your friends are dying, too."

Suddenly Mrs. Duvessa screamed in terror. Cole and Brock ran upstairs and stopped, stunned, on the landing. Kyle, his eyes glazed over, stumbled out of the master bedroom, groaning and drooling. Cole pushed past Brock, leaving him to deal with Kyle and ran into the room. Livia was still lying, unmoving, on the bed, while Mrs. Duvessa cowered in the corner by the window, Rachel limping toward her, moaning.

"Rachel," Cole yelled at her. "Rachel, turn around. Turn around or I'll...Rachel."

She didn't answer. He reached for her and pulled her by the arm. As Rachel turned to him, her arm swung and knocked the hatchet out of Cole's grip. She looked at him with unseeing eyes, patches of her face dangling by thin wisps of skin. Drool trickled down her chin and her white eyes rolled back into her head. Something of a smile crossed her lips as she grabbed Cole's arm and pulled him

274

toward her, wrapping him in a powerful hug.

Cole let out a shout. Rachel pushed his head down onto her chest and he knew she would open her strong zombie jaws, crack open his skull and slurp out his brains. He fought her, but she was too powerful. Suddenly he felt a thud on her back. Rachel let go of him and stumbled backward, gurgling and sputtering, turning around to where Mrs. Duvessa now stood. A hatchet was sunk deep between Rachel's shoulder blades. Cole grabbed it and used it to pull Rachel backward, away from Mrs. Duvessa.

"Get Livia and find a place to hide," Cole yelled. He yanked several times at the hatchet Mrs. Duvessa had hit Rachel with, surprised at how deep she'd penetrated. Finally it jerked free. When Rachel turned to him, he lifted the hatchet high, swung it around, and whacked off her head.

Mrs. Duvessa was carrying Livia in her arms when Cole lifted Rachel's feet and dragged her headless corpse out of the room.

"Where to?" Brock said on the landing, standing over Kyle's body.

"Spare room," Cole said.

They dragged the bodies into the room where Mr. Patterson stood poised at the window shooting zombies, cursing, spitting, and occasionally shouting out, "Yee-haw."

"Excuse us, Mr. Patterson," Cole said. He picked Rachel's body up and shoved it out the window. Brock did the same and they each went back for the heads. In the master bedroom, Cole lifted Rachel's heavy head, turning his eyes away, vowing to kill Slade if he could prove this was his doing. The room was empty.

Cole tossed Rachel's head out the spare room window and raced downstairs to search for Mrs. Duvessa and Livia. His mother had the television on and the

275

vamps and zombies were huddled around it watching the news.

"Where's Mrs. Duvessa?" Cole asked.

"Aren't they're still upstairs?"

Fear pricked at Cole's heart; he turned and took the stairs three at a time. He checked the spare room, the den, and his own room. All empty. He returned to the master bedroom. Empty.

"Mrs. Duvessa?"

No answer. The closet door was closed and he approached it.

"Mrs. Duvessa, are you in there?"

He pulled open the door and heard a gunshot. He stumbled backward with the force of the blow and looked down to his chest.

"You shot me." He said.

Mrs. Duvessa stood in the closet, panic on her face, her hands shaking. She dropped the gun and Livia began to scream.

CHAPTER TWENTY-FIVE

Cole watched, as if looking through gauze, as Livia pulled herself to standing in the closet, stared at the hole in Cole's torso, then turned to her mother and pummeled her with her fists letting loose a series of hoarse curses Cole figured must only be found in the vamp dictionary.

"It's okay," he said, pulling her off her mother. "Livia, I'm okay."

Footsteps raced up the stairs and Jane, Craig, and Brock burst into the room.

"It's okay, mom," Cole said, walking Livia to the bed and sitting her on the edge. "Mrs. Duvessa shot me, that's all."

"What's happening?" Livia said, dazed.

"We're in the middle of a massive zombie outbreak. There were zombies in the house. Your mom was just really scared, that's all."

"But she shot you."

"I'm fine. I'm a zombie, remember?"

Cole shuddered and rubbed his face, trying to get his

eyes to focus and stop the spinning feeling in his head.

"You don't look fine."

"She's right," Jane said, laying a hand across Cole's forehead.

With the touch of his mother's hand, Cole realized he was dizzy and, strangely enough, nauseated. He hadn't been nauseated since the day he died. He sat next to Livia on the edge of the bed and tried to steady himself.

"I don't feel so good, Mom," he said.

"Well, you've been shot in the stomach. We'll have to try to get the bullet out."

"The Monster Squad's here," Mr. Patterson called from the spare room. "They've got an axe machine. Oh, my god, they're hacking at them, chopping them up. Oh my god."

"This I gotta see," Brock said and ran from the room, followed by Craig.

There was a commotion downstairs, people yelling, doors slamming.

"What's going on?" Jane called.

More steps pounded up the stairs.

"The vamps left out the back and over the fence. I tried to make them stay, but they were determined," Alan said.

"Stupid vamps," Cole muttered. His head felt heavier than usual and his heart ceased its slow pulse.

Mrs. Duvessa came out from the closet, still trembling violently.

"I'm so sorry. Will he be all right?"

"You shot him, Mother."

Cole grabbed the edge of the mattress and forced himself to stand, towering over his mother and Mrs. Duvessa.

"I don't feel so good."

He reeled.

278

"Oh, my god," his mother said.

As the world around him went white, Cole heard his mother scream, "Hypo!"

Z

When Cole opened his eyes, he found himself lying on his mother's bed in the master bedroom. Standing around the bed, staring at him with goofy, relieved expressions were Livia, Brock, Craig, and his mom.

"What happened?"

"Our Zom-be-Gon was tampered with." Craig said. "We're on hypos now, until we can get it straightened out."

"You got shot, man," Brock said. "What's it feel like?"

Cole instinctively reached for the hole in his chest and found a large adhesive strip stuck to his skin under his shirt.

"Mrs. Duvessa dug the bullet out for you," his mom said with a smile. "She's a nurse, you know."

"I know. What about the outbreak?"

"You should've seen the street, man," Brock said. "There were dead bodies everywhere."

"I like that song," Cole said. "I remember now. The Monster Squad arrived. But is the outbreak over?"

"It's on the news," Brock said.

"What is?"

"Everything," Livia said. "The vamps at the Welsh complex were caught trying to leave town. Rick's father was arrested."

Mrs. Duvessa called up the stairs. "They're at the mansion, come watch."

Craig helped Cole out of bed and down the stairs where the Pattersons, the Hansons, and Mrs. Duvessa were huddled around the television set in the family room. The regulars noshed from an enormous bowl of popcorn and sipped sodas. Livia dropped into the recliner and pulled one of Jane's afghans over her feet. She closed her eyes and yawned.

"Is she going to be all right?" Cole said walking to her and putting his large hand over one of hers.

"She needs sleep," Mrs. Duvessa said and reached for a fistful of popcorn. "There's my husband on television. Hi, Orel." She waved.

"She knows he can't hear her, right?" Brock whispered.

Cole stared at Mr. Duvessa on the screen as he held up his hand to shield his face while being led out of the Welsh mansion.

"That's odd," he said. "If you put a beard and mustache on Mr. Duvessa, and put him in a homeless guy's coat and hat...he'd look just like..."

"Like a homeless guy?" Craig said.

"What would happen," Brock said, "if a zombie was bitten by a vamp?"

"Happens all the time," Jane said.

"I thought they died from sucking up air," Alan said.

"Don't be silly," Mrs. Duvessa said.

"What do you get, then?"

"A zamp. Not much different." Jane said.

"You get a vambie," Mrs. Duvessa said.

"What's the difference?" Brock said.

Mrs. Duvessa smiled and winked. "The vamp bit the zombie. Vambie. Now if Cole here were to bite Livia, she'd be a zamp."

"Or maybe a zombire," Stu said. "As long as we're making up names."

"So, it's a matter of reciprocity," Cole said.

"Shh, the news is back on. Look," Mrs. Duvessa said. "It's Dr. Krenske."

280

Dr. Krenske's gray head bobbed up and down amidst a sea of reporters and their microphones. He waved his hand at them and tried to cover his face.

"In his statement to police, Dr. Krenske denied any part in the zombie outbreak and police say the lab at Evan Slade's home appears to have no link to the Welsh Corporation."

"Krenske had nothing to do with it," Cole said.

The reporter continued. "Evan Slade denies any knowledge of the conspiracy against the zombies, however, all the pharmacies in town, owned by Mayor Slade, have reported that their supplies of Zom-be-Gon have been replaced by a different formula. Thanks to scientist Richard Samuelson, former Welsh chemist, fired over a disagreement within the company several years ago, all the pharmacies' supplies were tested yesterday."

"You were right, dude," Brock said. "It was Slade all along."

"I really didn't think it was his father, though."

"They were probably working together."

"Maybe. We'll know soon enough when they arrest Rick."

"Does Mayor Slade own the Glenwood Springs pharmacy too?" Jane asked.

"Apparently," Craig said.

"I'm sorry, Cole. I should have taken this more seriously." His mom said.

"It wasn't your fault."

"I know. But I should have gone all the way to Denver for meds."

"Well, the body parts have been cleared off the streets," Mr. Patterson said. "I guess we can get back to normal now."

"We need to make a run to the pharmacy. There'll be a long line for the new Zom-be-Gon." Craig said.

"I should get Livia back home so she can rest." Mrs. Duvessa said. "Cole, will you help me?"

"Are you sure you're strong enough?" Jane said.

Cole nodded and Mrs. Duvessa smiled at him. He took Livia in his arms and carried her to the front yard. He held her there, with her mother standing beside him, patting Livia's head, while Mr. Patterson moved the cars.

"She'll be all right soon enough," Mrs. Duvessa said with a worried grin. "You'll see."

Cole nodded. Once the path was clear, they walked into the street.

"Are you sure it's over?"

Before Cole could answer her, Mrs. Duvessa let out a deep-throated shriek. He twisted and turned, tossing Livia over his left shoulder.

"It's just a head, Mrs. Duvessa."

He took her by the arm and moved her around it.

"What is it?" His mother called, running out of the house and into the street, followed by Brock and Craig.

"The Monster Squad missed one," Cole said and absent-mindedly kicked at the severed head, before turning again toward the Duvessa's.

He carried Livia upstairs and laid her in her bed. Her eyes were closed, the dark circles under them deeper than usual against her deathly white skin. Mrs. Duvessa sat on the bed next to her, gently placed a hand on her cheek and looked at Cole.

"She'll be all right. Really she will."

"Are you trying to comfort me? Or yourself?" Cole said with a smile.

"You, of course," she said.

Cole was surprised that her voice was sweet and kind, unlike he'd ever heard it directed toward him before. Mrs. Duvessa took a brush from the bedside table and began brushing Livia's hair out across her pillow.

282

"I talked to Dr. Rapier. He's a vampire, you know. He said that she likely won't remember much."

Cole nodded.

"But, I want you to know that I believe you."

"You do?"

"Yes. You couldn't have hurt Livia. And thank you for finding her."

"What changed your mind?"

She shrugged. "You're a zombie. And I suppose I've been a bit on edge since Livia and Orel were turned into vampires. And today. Well, I've never been so scared as I was today. But you were there to help. And I shot you for it."

Cole laughed. "I don't think you did that on purpose."

"But I did." She looked up at him with a smile. "I thought you were going to rip me apart and eat my brains, of course."

"You were panicked."

"Exactly. And you were there to help."

They stared at one another for a brief moment, until Cole nodded again.

"Come back later." She said. "I'm sure Livia will be up and about in no time."

Z

Todd slammed the Jag's passenger door and stomped over to the dead fire pit; he kicked at the pine-needle covered ground.

"What did we run for?" He said, turning on the others as they approached.

"Livia woke up," Rick said. "She'll turn us in."

"What are you, chicken? We're vampires. Nobody can touch us. Nobody."

Stephan furrowed his brow and shook his head. "You know, I think you're thinking of vampires in a different

283

kind of way."

"What kind of way is that?" Todd glared at him.

"In a story kind of way. This isn't a movie, you know. This is real life. And enough cops with weapons can take us."

"Yeah, man," Rick said. "I don't know what you think being a vamp is all about but, we're not gods."

"Close enough."

Todd saw Rick and Stephan exchange looks and he fumed. "We should have killed them all."

Rick held up his hands. "Whoah. I don't know what your problem is..."

"I'll tell you exactly what my problem is."

Todd walked to Rick, reached out and shoved him.

"Stop it," Elena said.

"He's a wuss," Todd said. "You're all nothing but wusses."

"At least we're not crazy." Stephan said.

"You calling me crazy?"

"That's enough," Ciara said. "No more fighting. Let's wait here for the others, if they're brave enough to show up after all this. We need to decide what we're going to do."

"The police are going to want to talk to us." Stephan said. "All because of you and your father."

"So, what?" Rick said. "We had nothing to do with the meds."

"We knew about it."

"That's not illegal. They can't pin anything on us."

"Are you sure?" Elena said. "Can they match our teeth marks on the dead people or anything?"

"Don't be stupid," Todd said.

"Well, you don't know."

"They've already buried them all. We'd have heard something if they could match bite marks."

"Maybe," Rick said. "But that part is all your fault."

"Why? Because I actually went and did what you told people you were doing?"

"I never said I was murdering people, you freak."

Todd lurched forward and took Rick by the throat; he lifted him off his feet and shook him. "That's the last time any one of you calls me a name. You got that?"

"Sure, sure," Rick squealed.

Todd dropped him to the ground and looked around at the rest of them. They backed away, fangs bared.

"Ciara's right," Todd said. "We wait for the other ferals. Then we work on our stories in case the police question us. Until then, Rick, you and Stephan get the fire lit. Ciara, you come sit with me."

As they moved to obey him, Todd sucked in a long, slow, powerful breath.

CHAPTER TWENTY-SIX

Livia woke slowly and stretched. It felt so good to be at home in her own bed. She curled under the covers and closed her eyes again, smiling. When the screaming in her head returned she smacked her forehead several times.

"Go away," she said.

"If you insist," Cole said.

She sat upright.

"Cole," she said. "I didn't know you were here."

He was smiling down at her, a bouquet of yellow and pink flowers in his hands.

"Lay back down, or I'm leaving." He said.

She fluffed her pillows behind her and leaned in to them with a contented sigh. "I feel great, really. I don't need to stay in bed anymore. It's been two days."

"But you still hear the screams."

"That may never go away."

"Any recollection of what happened?"

After thinking for a moment, trying to force herself to remember what made the screaming start, she shook her head.

"Still nothing. My mom can't remember anything, either. But she thinks there were vampires. Rick and Stephan."

He set the flowers on her bedside table and she watched as he lifted the card on the bouquet her dad had sent her and read it.

It said, "To my little Cookie." Livia felt a warm glow at the thought of her father picking out flowers for her from jail.

"I know what happened to you," he said. "We zombies dug you up. You need to press charges against the vamps."

"If I can't remember anything, I don't think the police can help." She patted the side of the bed and he sat there. "Any news?"

"They're letting your dad go. I told them that he was the one who gave me the papers."

"And they believe you?"

"They have to believe me now, don't they?"

"Well, I'm glad he's coming home, but I want to know why he didn't give me the papers."

"No, it was ingenious. He knew I'd look into it. And he hoped I'd give them to Mr. Samuelson."

"Why didn't he just give them to Mr. Samuelson himself?"

"I don't think Samuelson would have fallen for it. Not at the time."

"Are you saying he needed a stupid zombie?"

"Hey," he poked her arm. "No. He needed a suspicious zombie."

"Maybe." She pouted.

"Who's Cookie?"

She looked to the vase of flowers by her bed again.

"I'm Cookie. It's my dad's name for me. I'm his little

Cookie Mist."

"CookieMist345?"

Her brows raised. "How did you know?"

"You IM'd me, remember?"

She chuckled. "I've never IM'd you. But I kept meaning to get your ID."

Cole looked back at the vase and the card.

"Of course," he said.

"What?"

"It was your dad, using your computer. He was trying to get me to look at those papers." Cole sighed and smacked his head. "He even told me to find a former Welsh employee. He must have thought I already knew about Samuelson."

"You didn't?"

"Not until Mr. Lute told me. Your dad sure picked a stupid zombie to ask for help."

She reached out and put her hand on his arm. "I think he picked a zombie genius."

"Cole," her mom's voice sang from downstairs. "Can I get you anything? I know zombies don't eat. Do you want to smell something?"

"I'm fine, Mrs. Duvessa," he called. "Livia's awake again. You want to come up?"

"No, no. You two enjoy your together time."

"What did you do to my mom?" Livia chuckled.

"Nothing, I swear. Except, save her life, I guess."

"I think she actually likes zombies now."

"I have to tell you something."

"Sounds ominous."

Cole smiled and reached out to caress one of the curls on her shoulder. "You have a vocabulary unlike any vamp I've ever known."

"Rick told me you only loved me for my brains."

He lowered his eyes to the bed.

"Are you blushing?"

He shook his head.

"Well, go on," she prodded. "What do you need to say?"

"The police are still searching for Slade and his ferals. We think we know where they are."

"So tell the police."

He looked up at her and she saw determination in his gray face.

"Oh, no," she said. "You're not going after them."

"Brock and I know a path that approaches the Welsh woods from the back," he said. "We can find them. And we'll bring them in."

"The woods? Where they found Tina and her friends dead?"

Cole nodded.

"Please don't go."

She reached for his arm again and squeezed it, but she had little strength to even attempt to make him stay. His hand covered hers; he pulled it from his arm and pressed it to his cold lips, sending shivers down her arm.

"We'll go up Bent Creek Road, away from the mansion. No one will know we're there. It'll be okay."

"That doesn't make it okay. That makes it worse."

"We'll be okay," he insisted. "We're taking Trevor."

Z

Cole drove up Bent Creek Road with the headlights off and parked by the boulders he and Brock climbed when they were kids. Brock, Alan, and Trevor waited for him to lead them.

"We walk from here," Cole said. "Don't make noise."

They closed their car doors with quiet clicks and walked into the muffled night. The woods were dark and a light snowfall hovered around them as they moved between the trees. Their boots crunched on the needle-covered ground. After a mile, Cole held up his hand; they stopped, and listened. He heard them in the distance and nodded to the others. They moved forward until they saw the light of the vamps' fire through the pines.

In a small clearing, Slade, Todd, Elena, Ciara, and Stephan Hack huddled in a group near the fire arguing.

"No more waiting," Todd was saying.

"We should have brought more zombies," Alan whispered.

"Who's left?" Brock said. "Bill's mom wouldn't let him come out."

"We wouldn't want Bill, anyway," Trevor said. "Even on his meds he's unreliable."

"Come on, let's just do it," Cole said and they emerged from the woods, startling the vamps.

In a ripple, the vamps turned and posed, fingers spread like claws, fangs bared. The zombies stood watching them for a few seconds until Brock could no longer hold his laughter.

"What are you going to do?" He said. "Suck the air out of us? You may as well bite teddy bears."

"Okay," Alan said. "It sounds like you just called us teddy bears."

"Yeah, not so cool," Trevor said. "And I'm not a zombie, if you recall."

"Sorry dude," Brock said.

"What are you doing here?" Slade moved forward.

"We came to take you in." Cole said.

He let out an exaggerated laugh. "You? Take *us* in?"

"That's right."

"What for?" Todd said, tossing a stick into the fire.

"Yeah, we didn't do anything but whack the heads off some zombies. That's no crime." Elena said.

"True," Cole said. "But we'll let the police decide if

you had anything more to do with the outbreaks than being related to the mayor."

Slade hissed. "My dad's innocent. You'll see."

"And there's the matter of your feral activity," Alan said.

"You don't have any proof of that," Elena said with a smile.

"Maybe." Cole said.

"So why are you here?" Slade said.

"We told you," Alan said. "The police are looking for you, and we're taking you in."

The vamps behind Slade turned to each other and whispered.

"You're not taking us anywhere," Todd said coming forward to stand beside Slade.

"We're taking you," Cole said. "If we have to pull you apart trying."

"You're not full zombies, you don't have the strength." Todd said.

"Try us."

Cole reached out to grab Slade, but Slade stepped back and swung around to take Cole's arm. He pulled his elbow around Cole's neck.

"Let him go," Brock said.

The vamps were at them a second later. Cole elbowed Slade in the chest, forcing him to loosen his grip. He turned and punched Slade in the face. Slade staggered backward and put a finger to his mouth; he glared at Cole.

"You're a dead man," Slade said.

"Tell me something I don't know."

Slade rolled his eyes. "You know what I mean. I'm going to kill you right here, right now, and nobody will give a damn because you're a zombie."

"I'm already dead."

"You know what I mean."

"So, where's your hatchet?"

Slade growled and lunged at him, forcing him to the ground. His slender white hands found their way to his neck and squeezed.

"For a skinny vamp, you're pretty strong," Cole wheezed.

He reached up and put his thumbs in Slade's eye sockets.

"Aaah," Slade screamed and rolled off him.

Cole jumped onto Slade's back and pushed his face into the forest floor. He looked up to see his friends fighting the other vamps and decided they hadn't thought the plan through very well.

"You know," he said. "For zombies, we're not always so smart."

"Oh, yeah," Brock said, sitting on top of Todd, his hands easily thwarting Todd's attempt to land a punch in his chest. "Now you decide?"

"I'm just saying."

"We could tie them up, if we had rope," Trevor said. He had Elena Worthington by the waist, holding her off the ground, and Ciara Wister by the hair, trying to drag her over to Cole.

"They're strong," Alan said. "For being so scrawny."

Stephan stood behind Alan, pulling Alan's left arm back in a hammerlock, his other arm wrapped around Alan's neck.

"What now?" Alan said.

Cole laughed. "Let's drag these to the car and Stephan will follow along beating up on Alan. Once we get these guys into the trunk, we can all get Stephan."

"We can hear you, you know," Ciara said; she twisted and turned against Trevor's grasp on her hair.

"What makes you think I'll follow you guys?" Stephan said. "Maybe I'll just kill Alan."

"Not funny, Stephan," Alan said.

"Is so funny," Trevor said. "Just try to kill him. You'll see."

"Not funny, Trevor," Alan said.

"Come on, Alan, you're a zombie," Trevor said. "Push the little vamp off you and take him down."

Alan seethed and looked up and across the small clearing at Cole. Cole nodded and Alan flung his shoulder down, unwinding his arm as he turned on Stephan belting him with his fists. Suddenly, Cole felt a force against his chest as he was thrown backward off Slade. Slade scrambled to his feet and lurched at him. Cole heard the girls shrieking and Trevor's muffled groans while he fought off Slade as best he could.

"Dang it, hold still you little—" Brock yelled.

Before he knew it, Cole was on the ground with Slade's bony elbow sunk hard between his shoulder blades.

"Uh, huh," Slade said "See how you like it in the dirt."

Cole looked up to find the other zombies pinned to the ground.

"Great." He said. "So we'll just take turns like this. Just try to move toward the car a little more each time and eventually we'll get the vamps pinned in the trunk."

"Are you out of your mind?" Brock said. "The car's miles away."

"One point two miles."

"Oh, so it's technically only one mile, is that what you're saying?" Alan said, struggling under Stephan's weight.

"Are they all going to fit in the trunk?" Trevor said.

Shadowy figures moved into the clearing and Cole's head jerked this way and that. Vampires. Cloaked. Hooded. Ferals? Dozens in black, their faces hidden,

294

crowded into the clearing.

"Oh, shit," Brock said.

"This is just great," Trevor said, his voice muffled by the ground in his mouth. "We're hacked. We're totally hacked. And I'm not even a zombie."

"Get up boys," one of the vampires said with a husky feminine purr. She walked toward Cole.

"Who the hell are you?" Slade said.

Cole heard fear in Slade's voice and took the opportunity to turn under him, grab his head, twist, and throw the slimy little vamp off him. He stood and grabbed Slade before he could get off the ground. Pulling Slade to his feet, he wrapped his elbow around his neck.

"That's enough," the lady vamp said.

She slid the hood from her head and Cole recognized her from school.

"Wanda?" Todd said.

Wanda smiled and purred.

"How does she do that?" Cole whispered in Slade's ear.

"Do what?"

"Purr like that? Can all vamps do that?"

"Sure. It's just like your growling. Cooler though."

"Yeah, well, according to you everything vamps do is cooler than anything zombies do."

"Exactamundo."

"Did you just say...?"

"Leave them to us, boys. We'll handle it from here."

"Who are all these other vamps?" Slade said.

"I buried you in the back yard," Todd whined. "You're dead."

"I was always dead, little brother. And now I'm your worst nightmare."

Cole groaned. "Do you guys have to talk like you're in a movie all the time?"

"Let him go." Wanda said.

"No."

"We'll take care of it," she said, smiling deeper.

"What does that mean, exactly?"

Wanda turned to the others, raised her right hand, letting the cloak fall away from her pale arm, and snapped her fingers. Several hooded vamps walked forward and revealed themselves.

"Holy crap," Todd said. "Tina?"

Tina West, her sister, and her sister's friend, along with Cole's neighbors, the Epperson's, and what looked like a male nurse in a dirtied uniform, eyed the vamps maliciously.

"Show them," Wanda said.

The new vamps hissed, pulled at their cloaks and let them fall to the ground. Instead of pale, lithe vampires, they were thick and muscular. Even old Mrs. Epperson's wrinkles were replaced with taut, toned skin brimming with a pale gray tinge, unaffected by the cold.

"Gray?" Cole said. "Are they zombies?"

"We don't know what they are," Wanda said.

The new vamps growled and bared their fangs.

"Zombie vampires?"

"The point is, they're not dead. So, you really have no reason to take these vamps to the police."

"But they were declared dead. They were buried."

"And they dug themselves up."

"They're zombies," Alan said.

"We're still taking them in," Cole said. "They're wanted for questioning."

"Fine." Wanda's brows rose and she lowered her chin condescendingly. "We'll drop them off at the station when we're finished with them. But you will leave them to us."

"What if we say no?" Brock said.

Wanda chuckled. "Look, you can't beat all of us. So just let the ferals go and I promise you, we'll take care of it."

Cole looked around at the hooded vamps; there were dozens of them and who knew how many more were hiding in the woods. Wanda was right. They had no choice. They'd be lucky if they got out of the woods alive.

"All right," he said and shoved Slade away from him. "What are you going to do with them?"

Wanda laughed. "Just get out of here. You don't want to be around for this."

Cole nodded to his friends. The hooded vamps forced Elena, Ciara, and Stephan to let them go and they all walked quickly into the woods.

CHAPTER TWENTY-SEVEN

The lunch room at Darkspur Night High School was still abuzz with stories of zombies run amok, hacking off heads, and vamps being torn apart. The Welsh Corporation controversy, and Mayor Slade's disappearance from police custody and, consequently, from the country, were less appealing. They were still teens, Cole supposed, and couldn't be bothered with the important stuff.

"Well, are you going to write it?" Brock said, dropping into the seat across from Cole in the zombie corner of the lunch room.

"Write what?"

"The history," Brock said. "The whole shebang. How it started, what the vamps did, the zombie apocalypse. You know."

Cole shrugged. "Maybe I will; some day."

"Make me cool, okay?" Alan said. "I want to be a vampire slayer."

"It won't be fiction. It's history."

"You can embellish a little."

"Hey zombies," Trevor said. He sat down with his tray and looked sadly at his meatloaf.

"Still not hungry?" Cole said.

Trevor shook his head. "I miss Rachel and Kyle."

"We all do." Cole flinched at the thought of Rachel's head falling with a thud to the carpet in his mother's bedroom.

"Ah, well," Trevor said, stabbing a piece of meatloaf with his spork. "Here's to their memory. They were good zombies."

"Whoah," Stu said. "Look who approaches."

Livia and Darlene had come through the line with their blood boxes and sauntered seductively toward the zombie tables. The lunch room hushed somewhat and heads turned to stare.

"Mind if we join you?" Livia said.

Cole stood and pulled out the chair next to him, offering it to Livia. Darlene timidly sat next to Brock and smiled coyly at him.

"Kyle would really be pissed off that he missed this." Trevor said.

"Missed what?" Stu said.

"This inter-undead love thing."

"I don't know what you're talking about," Brock said.

Cole watched him try to look everywhere in the cafeteria except at Darlene's ashen face. He leaned to Livia and whispered in her ear.

"He's got it real bad."

"Zombies are cool," Trevor said. "And Kyle's not here to see it. How about you, Alan. You okay with it?"

Alan nodded absent-mindedly, staring across the lunchroom at a small group of vamp girls. "I think I'll get used to it."

Several more vamps entered the lunch room and looked toward the vamp tables in the opposite corner.

300

Again, a brief hush fell on the crowd as they watched the vamps move to tables with regulars or magick. Cole turned to look at Slade, Ciara, Stephan, and Todd, huddled at the big, empty table from which they used to wreak their havoc. They fumed, arms folded across their chests, eyes cast to the table, and the word "feral" carved in deep red gashes on each of their cheeks.

"Looks like the vampire reign is over, finally." Cole said.

"And the zombie revolution has begun, I suppose?" Livia said, smiling at him, sipping at her blood pack.

A deep, resonating growl echoed in the room and Cole leaned forward to look past Livia at Trevor.

"You okay, man? Something wrong with the meat-loaf?"

Trevor's hairy arms, reaching across the table in front of him, trembled, and his fingers spread wide, grasping at the air.

"Oh, man," Trevor moaned. "I don't feel so good."

In one leap, he left the table and was ten feet toward the door. In another two, he was through the cafeteria door and gone.

"I told you he was a werewolf," Brock said.

The bell rang and they all got up to leave, casting pitying glances at Slade and his ferals. Livia was right; the zombie revolution was at hand. And that meant big changes for Darkspur Night High. Cole figured he may have to hang around a few more years, just to make sure the vamps didn't get any crazy ideas.

Once out in the main hallway crowded with students, Cole took Livia's hand and turned her to him. He smiled down at her thin, pale face, and ran his fingers along her cheek.

"Well, at least Slade was smart about one thing."

"What's that?" She said.

"I do love your brains."

He pulled her into his arms and kissed her. Things had definitely changed in Darkspur.

"Mr. Bertrand," Principal Lute's voice sounded far away. "Mr. Bertrand, kindly take your zombie lips off the vampire and get to class."

BOOKS BY Dianna Dann Narciso

Mainstream/Literary Fiction by Dianna Dann
Camelia
Always Magnolia
Bury Me

Romantic Comedy by Dianna Dann
Bookish Meets Boy

Fantasy by Dana Trantham
Children of Path: The Kell Stone Prophecy Book One
The Wretched: The Kell Stone Prophecy Book Two
Mark of the Faire: The Kell Stone Prophecy Book Three
The Kell Stone Prophecy: Complete Trilogy

Story Runners
Shards of Kholkari (2018)

Paranormal Humor by D.D. Charles
Zombie Revolution

Children's Fiction by Dana Trantham
Wayward Cat Finds a Home
Zombie Cats

For more, visit
waywardcatpublishing.com

www.ingramcontent.com/pod-product-compliance
Lightning Source LLC
Chambersburg PA
CBHW021946170626
46808CB00001B/39